My Mary

A Story of one Barnardo Home Child

DAWN BEECROFT
TEETZEL

Black Rose Writing | Texas

The author grants the final approval for this literary material.

First printing

ISBN: 978-1-68513-372-6
PUBLISHED BY BLACK ROSE WRITING
www.blackrosewriting.com

Printed in the United States of America
Suggested Retail Price (SRP) $21.95

My Mary is printed in Minion Pro

*As a planet-friendly publisher, Black Rose Writing does its best to eliminate unnecessary waste to reduce paper usage and energy costs, while never compromising the reading experience. As a result, the final word count vs. page count may not meet common expectations.

Praise for Dawn Beecroft Teetzel's

My Mary

Ripped from a family she loves, forcibly transported to a new country, and treated like an indentured servant, Mary struggles to overcome the childhood trauma that robs her of her self-worth and the electric shock treatments that rob her of her memories. Ultimately, it is Mary's inner strength and the love of the one man who believes in her that enables her to live the life she had so long been denied. Beautifully written and psychologically astute, *My Mary* is a novel that will stay with you long after you've read the last page.

–Natalie Zellat Dyen, author of *Finding Her Voice*

What makes someone worthy of a good life? In this personal epic of a novel, *My Mary* explores this theme beautifully. With honest looks into depression, isolation, aging, the story follows the titular Mary as she deals with her traumas. More than that though, Dawn Beecroft Teetzel's superb writing will make sure *My Mary* sticks with you long after you've finished reading.

–Ryan Calorel, author of *The Vain Curse*

For Mary
And her Family

Acknowledgements

This work would not have been possible without the love, support, and input from Mary's family—my family through marriage.

I owe a huge debt to my critique partner, Natalie Cross, and to my toughest beta reader, Sarah VanGoethem. Your encouragement and insightfulness was invaluable.

To Colleen Glassford, a family member, who assisted me in so many ways. Your support was priceless.

And my heartfelt thanks to my many readers:

Kate Boak, Yvonne Woods, Kim Kelly, Renee Cronley, and Suzanne Seifert Groves. Your thorough critique and comments were greatly appreciated.

My Mary

Chapter 1

January, 1945

Something has got to give.

It's another blustery morning; the sun obscured by leaden clouds and falling snow. At the enamel sink, I sigh as I pump water into a large kettle and carry it to the cookstove; this morning being no different from any other. It seems the only difference between one morning and the next is the change in weather.

The entry door creaks open on its rusty hinges, and Charles, my husband, materializes in a flurry of frosty air. Like a dog shedding water, he shakes the snow from his wool cap and shoulders, and stamps his rubber-clad feet. Stepping into the kitchen, he lifts the pail of still-warm milk and basket of brown eggs onto the kitchen counter. His hands are red with cold.

I feel his eyes on me as I chuck two split maple logs into the stove. My unkempt auburn hair falls into my eyes. I brush it aside.

He clears his throat. "I think I'll head on down the road and visit the Shermans this morning." His words are apprehensive, more a question than a statement.

I straighten my back and mumble, "In this snow?"

"Oh, this is nothing more than a little squall—it won't last." He pulls his wool gloves from his pockets and wriggles his hands into them. "Care to come along?"

I stare at my soiled print apron and threadbare housedress and shake my head.

"You'll be okay while I'm gone?"

I narrow my eyes. "And just what do you mean by that?"

He looks away, perplexed. "Nothing. I was only asking." He opens the back door. "I'll be home for lunch." The whirling whiteness devours his dark silhouette.

The worn soles of my shoes drag across the linoleum. Carrying the plates to the counter, I scrape the remains of burnt crusts and overcooked eggs into the dog dish. I scan the room, overwhelmed by the many chores awaiting me. "Listen to your body," Mrs. Little used to say. "It'll tell you what it needs."

I find myself back in the bedroom, where I slip, fully dressed, beneath the covers of the unmade bed.

"Mary?"

I bolt upright and slip into my shoes. Charles is standing in the archway between the kitchen and the parlour. His eyes roam over my rumpled clothing, tousled hair, and creased face. "Are you alright?"

"I'm fine," I lie. My head jerks toward the mantle clock as it strikes the hour—twelve noon. "I guess I must've fallen asleep."

"I'll say you did. Are you sure you're okay?"

"Stop asking me that! I just said I was, didn't I?"

His jaw drops, and he lowers his eyes—I had hurt him with my curt words. He turns his back on me, and after hanging his coat on the hook in the entry, he removes the kettle, long since boiled dry, and carries it to the sink.

I clear the remaining breakfast dishes. Once again, I feel him watching me as I gather the mugs and silverware. My cheeks grow hot with shame. *Why am I so tetchy with him?* Charles is such a good, kind man. He deserves so much more than I ever give. "Why don't you sit and read your paper for a few minutes? I'll have lunch ready in no time."

Our paths meet in the centre of the kitchen floor. He gently grazes his fingertips across my cheek.

His forgiving nature moves me. Brushing a tear away, I prepare our simple lunch and carry mugs, a teapot, and sandwiches to the table. He folds the newspaper and lays it on the table.

As I sit, I read the bold print headline: World War II Top Ace Major Greg (Pappy) Boyington shot down over Pacific Ocean.

My hands tremble. *Oh my God, will this war never end?*

Charles' words break into my thoughts. "Oh, by the way, Jean sends her regards. It surprised her you didn't come along with me." He pours the tea. "She says she misses you and will drop in on you tomorrow."

I don't answer; my attention being held by a small white envelope lying in the centre of the table.

Charles watches me while sipping his tea, his blue eyes twinkling over the steaming mug. He lifts the letter with his free hand, a smile playing at the corner of his lips. "Look what I found tucked away inside the folded newspaper. It's a letter for a Mrs. Mary Thistle," he teases, "and you'll never guess, but it's come all the way from England."

My heart flutters as I reach for the envelope; it's been so long since I've had any news from my foster family. I slide my finger under the seal, unfold the single sheet of paper, and skim the text. "Oh, no," I gasp.

"What is it?"

I choke on my words. "It's from my foster sister, Dorothy. It's Papa. He had a heart attack last month."

The playful smile slips from his face. He stretches his arm across the table and cups my hands in his. "Ah, Mary. I'm so sorry. Will he be alright?"

I shake my head and close my eyes, fighting back tears. For over thirty years, I've grieved the loss of my foster family, but I've always hoped that someday I might see them again. I can see Papa like it was yesterday, the day they took me away. His arm was wrapped around Mama Annie, her face hidden in the crook of his neck. He smiled at me, but it wasn't a cheerful smile—it was a be-brave smile, a keep-your-chin-up kind of smile, and tears glistened in his eyes. He hugged and kissed me goodbye, and whispered in my ear, "Be brave, my Mary, and if you can't be brave, pretend."

How I loved that man. I open my eyes. "The war's not over yet. They should have come here when I asked." My words sound harsh.

Charles rubs his thumb across my knuckles. "It was a nice offer you made. But they wouldn't leave their farm and come here, no more than we would if the tables were turned."

I look down at my plate. "At least they would have been safe. Away from the war."

"True. But you couldn't have prevented his heart attack."

I huff and say, "How do you know?"

Charles opens his mouth, then quickly closes it again. After a moment, he says, "Mary, we need to talk."

I raise my tired eyes and study him. A few more grey hairs dust his temples, the wrinkles intensifying around his eyes. "Go ahead," I say. "Talk."

He hesitates a moment and slowly begins. "Okay, I've been worried about you, and now I'm afraid this bad news is only going to make things worse." Charles is a quiet man, never has a lot to say, but now he's started, the words tumble from his mouth. "You must agree your melancholia is getting worse every day. You never smile anymore—you're either sad or you're angry. Mostly angry, it seems."

My gut simmers with rage. It must be nice to be him—the eldest and only son, raised by parents who loved and valued him, adored by his younger sisters. His temperament is calm, stable, and strong. He's always in control of his feelings, his attitude and his outlook. How could he possibly understand? I glare at him. "I can't help it. This isn't the first time."

"C'mon Mary. Don't be angry with me. I understand you can't control it, and I know this isn't the first time. But you have to agree this is the worst."

I look away; I hate that he's right.

"It hurts me to see you like this. I feel like you're pulling away from me." He pauses. "Mary, you need help."

I raise an eyebrow. "What kind of help?"

"What do you say we have Dr. McDermot stop by? Maybe he'll have some ideas how to get you some help or, at the very least, he could give you a script for some medication. A little something to get you over this slump—get you through the winter. You always perk up in the spring."

Tears threaten again as self-pity washes over me. I ignore it by biting off a corner of my sandwich. It lodges at the lump in my throat and I choke. I grab my mug and gulp. The scalding tea burns as it pushes the food ahead of it. I cough, and a tear courses down my cheek.

"Ah, Mary. Things will get better."

How many times have I heard that line? He always says that—but they never do. And yet he stays so damned optimistic.

My cheeks burn again. *Why am I so angry with him? When did I become so mean-hearted?* I turn and stare out the window, fearful he will see the wretched woman I've become.

Charles was right about the weather, too. The snowstorm is over; the sun glistening on the newly formed drifts.

We finish our lunch in silence.

He dons his coat and boots and escapes outdoors. If I was a good farmwife, I'd ask him what he is working at this afternoon—but I don't. Perhaps I'd even check up on him later—but I won't.

I tidy the kitchen. My uneaten sandwich slides off the plate into the dog dish. Ruby will eat well tonight. I wash the dishes while my eyes travel over my dated, cramped kitchen. I think of all the kitchens I'd worked in over the years—to the spacious, modern kitchen where Jean would have served Charles tea this morning. Bob and Jean Sherman's large, two-story farmhouse, the next one down the road, sits proudly on a rise of land. Unlike ours, it exudes pride of ownership. Jean is my best friend, and yet I'm often ashamed when she comes to visit. She's kind-hearted, always assuring me a lovely house doesn't make a home.

That's easy for her to say when she has it all.

Some eighteen years ago, before our wedding, Charles had vowed to build me a new home. That never happened. I shouldn't blame him for that; it's not like he could have prevented the Depression, or the war. He keeps telling me we should thank our lucky stars we live on a farm; we're far better off than most. I suppose we are, but, by golly, they've been hard times.

That's Charles, though, always looking on the bright side.

I yawn, snatch the newspaper and drag myself to the parlour sofa. If only I could sleep, a deep, undisturbed sleep, maybe then I wouldn't be so tired all the time. I open the paper and read until the print fades before my eyes.

The sound of whimpering startles me. It's me—I've been dreaming. I'm eleven years old, standing on the deck of a steamer, watching my home country slowly fade into the early morning mist.

And then it comes back to me, like a blow to the chest. Papa is gone.

A pony neighs. I rouse myself from the sofa and gather the fallen newspaper puddled on the floor. Winny, our large Welsh pony, draws the cutter past the house, her heavy footfalls clomping in the new-fallen snow. Ernest and Tommy are home from school. I brush the tears from my face and race to my bedroom. Briefly glancing in the bureau's mirror, I see a work-worn woman with cavernous eyes, slack, sallow skin, and dirty disheveled hair. I quickly brush my hair into a bun, secure it with a few pins at my nape, and look away.

In the kitchen, I don a clean apron and begin supper preparations. Several moments later, they, along with their father, burst through the entry, their man-size bodies and boisterous voices filling the small room.

The boys set their tin lunch boxes on the counter, their schoolbooks on the table. Tommy, recently turned fifteen, hurries over to where I'm peeling potatoes and buzzes my cheek. Charles smiles at me, obviously pleased to see me up and doing something—anything. Tommy slips his hand into the crockery cookie jar. He pulls it out, empty.

"Sorry, sweetie," I mumble.

Ernest roughly tousles Tommy's light brown hair. "Sweetie—Ma still calls you sweetie." He pokes his brother's soft belly. "You know, it wouldn't hurt you to go a few days without cookies."

Yes, I still call him that. Sweetie was Mama Annie's pet name for all her children and, believe me, I'm going to use it as long as I can.

Ernest's tall frame towers over his father. "Did you fix the chicken coop roof today, Dad?"

"I did, this afternoon. Took me a bit to clear the snow off first, though."

"You should've waited until the weekend. I could have helped you with it."

"I can't leave everything for the weekend." Charles drags a chair out from the table. "I visited with Bob this morning. You know that heifer he's been worried about?"

The boys nod.

"Well, it looks like she's gonna calve early. Like any day. Be a shame, too, in this cold weather."

Tommy opens a book. "How'd that happen?"

Ernest slaps him on the shoulder. "C'mon Tom. Haven't you figured that out yet?"

Tommy blushes. "Idiot. You know what I mean."

Charles eyes his eldest, with the stern 'lighten up on your brother' look. He turns to Tommy. "I guess the bull broke out of his pen and got in with the heifers late last spring."

The ground beef sizzles as I break it apart with a wooden spoon. It's becoming extremely close in this room, thick with the aromas of meat cooking, male bodies, and damp woolen clothes. Their voices diminish to a faint buzzing in my ears.

"Hey Ma, I see you got a letter in the mail today." I turn to see Tommy holding the envelope. Almost a man now, he prefers to be called Tom, but I still call him Tommy. He'll always be my baby, that one. With the scare he gave us several years ago and the diagnosis of a heart condition, I suppose I've coddled him a bit too much. He's smaller, softer and sweeter than Ernest, who, at almost seventeen, has become his father's right-hand man.

I take the envelope, slip it in the pocket of my apron, and return to the stove.

Charles clears his throat. "Your mother received word today that her foster father in England has passed."

An awkward silence replaces their light-hearted talk. Finally, Ernest says, "I'm sorry for your loss, Ma."

Anger flares in me again. I want to scream, *"Really? That's all you can muster—I'm sorry for your loss?"* But I don't. Instead, I keep my face hidden and bite my bottom lip—it seems I only have harsh words for everyone today. Besides, it's not their fault; I've hardly ever spoken of Papa, let alone my childhood. To my boys, I have no history, no life before marriage. Papa means nothing to them.

Supper's ready, a simple meal of ground beef gravy over mashed potatoes. The men converse in subdued voices. Charles attempts to draw me into the conversation, but I have no interest.

Finally, it's chore time. They brave the cold, clearly relieved to escape the house, and me.

I do a shoddy job tidying the kitchen and retire to my bed. And as I lay alone and miserable in the silence of my room, I consider how much happier this house would be without me.

An hour later, they return, the hum of their activities wafting into the bedroom. I picture Ernest straining the milk. The stainless pail pings on the edge of the enamel sink. Tommy feeds the dog. "Wow, Ruby old girl, look at the feast you're getting tonight!" He playfully roughs up her neck fur. "Dad, it's freezing in the entry. Can Ruby sleep inside tonight?"

Charles' voice is low. I can't hear his response.

Eventually, his silhouette darkens the bedroom doorway as he draws it closed. In the parlour, they speak in hushed voices, but I catch a few words. Tomorrow morning, Ernest is to drop in to the doctor's office on his way to school and request a home visit as soon as possible.

Why would Charles put the weight of this errand on Ernest's shoulders?

Then I realize he does not trust me to be left alone.

Mid-morning of the following day, Charles escorts Dr. McDermot into our bedroom, his black medical bag and little brown bottle of tablets in hand. The doctor poses questions, which I'm slow to answer. He briefly examines me: his cold stethoscope pressed against my heart and lungs, his bony fingers squeezing my wrist as he measures my pulse. He witnesses me swallow the offered pill. They leave the room, closing the door behind them.

And that was that. I'm left wondering how a few moments with Dr. McDermot could make an ounce of difference because, believe me, I'm far beyond that.

As I slip into a blissful, dreamless sleep, I hear their muted voices conversing in the kitchen.

An icy draft keens through a crevice in the window frame, its high-pitched shriek awakening me. The mantel clock chimes once. I stretch my cramped legs. It's been over eighteen hours since I retired, evidenced by the odour of stale urine wafting up from the pot under the bed. I need to use the privy and empty my chamber pot. Turning back the bedclothes, I pull myself into a sitting position. Leaning my head against the headboard, I close my eyes and wait for the room to stop spinning.

At the back door, I draw my woolen coat over my nightgown and slip my bare feet into my wellies. *Wellies? Now, where did that come from?* I shake my cotton-filled head. I haven't thought of them as wellies in years. In Canada, they're just rubber boots. Stepping outside, I brace myself as I plow through the deep drifts. The raw, biting wind burns my face and clumps of snow tumble inside my boots. It's so cold, my nostrils stick together when I inhale. Inside the privy, I quickly do my business and step back outside. The farmstead is quiet. Charles has been called away to the Sherman farm. I vaguely remember him checking on me and saying something about Bob needing help with the heifer. He wouldn't be long, he promised. Ernest and Tommy are in school. I catch a flash of rust colour in my peripheral vision. Ruby, our old collie, is struggling through the snow drifts out by the barn. The wind whips my loose hair across my face, my sight obscured by the tangled curls. I brush them away, my eyes searching for her, but she's no longer there—she must have returned to the shelter and warmth of the barn. Grasping the collar of my coat, I clasp it around my neck, and head for the house.

Inside, the kitchen is in total disarray: the sink filled with dirty dishes, cold, congealed bacon fat coating the bottom of the cast iron frying pan. The red-checkered tablecloth is littered with crumbs, the tea towel hanging on the rack is dingy. I look away—the boys will look after it when they get home. They're practically grown men now, very capable around the farm. Plus, I've taught them how to be self-sufficient in the house, experienced enough to cook a simple meal, do the laundry, darn a sock. If I've done one thing well in my whole life, I have helped raise two good young men.

I pour myself a glass of water and swallow another pill.

The bedsprings rasp as I roll over, my back toward the door, face toward the window. My uneaten lunch sits on my bedside table beside a small vase of greenhouse flowers, Jean's signature arrangement of white hydrangeas, pale pink roses, and ferns. I look away; they give me no joy. I draw my knees to my chest and gaze out to the orchard and fields—a bleak, black and white landscape, the relentless wind driving the dry, crystalized snow across the hard packed drifts. So cold, so lifeless.

I hate winter. In this tiny frame house, not much more than a shack, the two woodstoves must be continually fed to keep the cold at bay. I think back to the warm, stately brick homes I served in as a maid. How I longed for a home like that of my own. No matter how much I clean or how hard I try to make this house pretty, without money, it doesn't happen. Sometimes, though, when the wind is not howling and the ill-fitting windows are not rattling, it has felt like a home. There have been moments when my breath catches at the sight of sunlight spilling over a vase of lilac blossoms, or when the lace curtains on the west window of the parlour waltz a delicate rhythm on a light breeze. In those moments, I have found beauty.

But that's certainly not today—not in this icy wasteland of winter.

My memories haunt me, snaking their way into my consciousness where I replay them, over and over, like a movie motion picture. *Why do I do it?* It will only lead me further down this dark path. It's like this bad habit I have of picking at my cuticles until they bleed—I don't know why I do that either.

And, I wonder, could there be anything worse than this feeling of not being able to control my mind?

Is there possibly anything worse than this feeling of helplessness and hopelessness?

Could there be anything, anything at all, more self-destructive than melancholia?

My eyes grow heavy—the sweet oblivion awaits. I hear a dog's whimper and scratching at the entry door as I drift off.

Chapter 2

The door slams.

Heavy footsteps clomp across the floors. I throw the quilt aside and scramble up in the bed. The light coming through the window is dim—it must be late afternoon.

My sons stand in the bedroom doorway. Snow is melting, puddling around their rubber boots on the hardwood plank flooring. I blink several times. Tommy's face is distorted in a controlled anguish. "Ma, how long have you been in bed? Didn't you hear Ruby?"

My head is heavy. My mind claws up through the fog as I make sense of his words. Grinding my palms into my eyes, I mumble, "I don't know. I took a pill."

Ernest glares at me. "Are you saying you didn't hear her at the door? How's that even possible; it's obvious she was scratching a long time?" His voice is contemptuous, his eyes accusatory.

My heart sinks as I recall the last sound I heard. "No, I didn't," I lie. I rake my hand through my unruly hair. "Is she alright?"

Tommy's arms stiffen, his hands curling into fists. "No, she's not alright. She's dead." His face crumples. Turning his back on me, he storms out of the house.

My gaze moves to Ernest, my firstborn. I seek compassion, redemption, but his eyes are ice cold.

He opens his mouth as if to speak, then clamps it shut. He turns to leave, but stops. I sense he's wrestling with himself. He draws his broad shoulders back, and turning, he stares at me. Finally he speaks. "What's wrong with you? Why can't you deal with things like everyone else?"

I look into his steel-grey eyes. Words come to me, but I don't speak them aloud. How can I explain to him what I don't even understand myself? Where would I start?

He shrugs. "For crying out loud, Ma, just get out of the damned bed and pull yourself together."

I watch his tall, strong frame trudge away from me. And, in that moment, I feel my spirit fracture.

My body curls fetal into the bed. The house is cold; the fires have burned low.

I've hated how, all my life, my tears have laid in wait. I have always struggled to hold them back, but now I no longer care. They stream, unheeded, onto my pillow. My blurred sight returns to the frozen world beyond the window glass. I envision the frosty air slipping over the windowsill, dripping down the wall, and spilling across the floor. I yank at the quilt hanging over the side of the bed, but it's too late—delicate crystals form on the patchwork top. My skin crawls as gooseflesh forms. I feel the frost seep into my flesh, course through my veins, and settle in my heart.

Perhaps if I lay here still, I could slowly, painlessly, freeze to death.

Just like Ruby.

The mattress sinks as Charles lowers himself on it and lays a hand on my shoulder. Heat radiates through my flannel nightgown. "My goodness, you're so cold," he says as he pulls the quilt up, tucking it in around me. He slips a dirty, tangled curl behind my ear.

I shake my head—an act to make him stop.

"Mary, the boys told me what happened earlier—when they got home and found Ruby." His voice is gentle. "I'm sorry if they made you feel Ruby's death was your fault. They told me how you took a pill and slept all afternoon. So, of course, you wouldn't have heard her."

I roll over. "But it was my fault," I say, clearing my throat. "I lied to the boys. Before I fell asleep, I heard her whine and scratch at the door. I just couldn't be bothered to get up and let her in." Heat creeps up my neck. *Why do I still lie?* I hate myself for it. I would never tolerate it in my boys. When they were young, I threatened them with, "If I catch you lying one more time, I'll wash your mouth out with soap?" What a hypocrite I am.

Charles' shoulders slump. "Ah, Mary. She could have gone back to the barn."

"And what good would that have done?" I ask, my voice raised. "She needed help. Maybe she was sick. When I went to the privy, I saw her struggling through the snow out by the barn, making her way to the house, but I left her out there on this bitter day to die alone."

Charles rakes his hand through his hair. "Well, you didn't know that then. She doesn't normally come in the house during the day. She was old. I'm sure it was just her time." He thinks for a second and then, halfheartedly adds, "Besides, I've always heard dogs go off to die alone."

"Not Ruby. She wouldn't do that. Those boys were her world. She would have wanted to be in the house, to be near them when they got home. Don't you remember the time she snuck in from the entry and delivered her pups in their bedroom while they slept?" I shake my head. "Ruby never would have wanted to die alone."

"Regardless, Mary, it wasn't your fault."

I sigh. Why can't he just admit it? Why does he always have to be so damn optimistic and forgiving? I'm exhausted with dancing around this conversation. Charles will defend me, as he always does, but no amount of reasoning will make me see it in any other light. Maybe it was Ruby's time, but I could have let her in the warm house and comforted her. That is something I would have normally done. *When did I become so heartless?* I hate who I've become. I roll over, turning my back on him.

He rises. "I'll bring supper when it's ready."

"Don't bother. Just turn off the light so I can go back to sleep. Please."

I hear his footfalls retreat. A soft stream of light spills through the door, left slightly ajar, along with the muted voices and smells from the kitchen. Shouldn't I feel guilty? The kitchen is my domain. My men are doing my chores—tasks I have neglected over the past two days. Yet, I feel no remorse. I feel nothing. I've become strangely detached.

I'm in a daze, a grey zone between the worlds.

Eventually the house quietens. The back door opens and closes several times as they take turns going to the privy. The mantel clock chimes ten and the parlour lamp is switched off. I lie with my back to the door, feigning sleep.

Charles undresses. He lays his clothing neatly over the chair before turning back the covers. It's not a large bed—I feel the warmth of his body as he slips between the sheets, his breath in my hair. The weight of his elbow pushes down on the pillow as he raises himself and leans over me. He places a tender kiss on my cheekbone.

For a moment, my frozen heart melts.

Damn. He's so good, so kind. I consider turning over, facing him, talking to him, holding him. *But what will that change?*

I lie still.

It will change nothing.

I wake to the aroma of frying bacon. My sight clears. It rests on the faded, dirty wallpaper—a watercolour of wisteria, vines, and leaves on a cream background. It was so beautiful, once upon a time. In a fairy tale time.

Another day has begun.

The memories of the past two days slowly scramble up through my drugged, foggy brain.

Another day to get through.

Charles pushes the bedroom door open. His voice is hesitant. "Mary, are you awake? I've brought you some breakfast." I close my eyes and ignore him as he places a tray of food on the bedside table. I sense him standing over me, watching me before he leaves.

I don't want to get through another day.

I wait a reasonable time frame for Charles to occupy himself in the barn with his many chores before I rise.

The heartless wind whips my hair like a punishment. It tears at my worn and rumpled nightgown, threatening to pull it off my shoulders. With one hand, I grasp the neckline, the other tightly gripping the coiled length of rope. I glance behind me. My footprints are clearly visible in the knee-high snow—a telltale path leading from the house, across the lane to the workshop, and then through the backyard to the privy. Dry crystals swirl across the snow-packed ground, busily sculpting new drifts. Hopefully, within moments, my prints will disappear. I trudge beneath the sprawling butternut tree, its pale grey bark ghostly in the whirling snow, the low-hanging, leafless branches eerily moaning in the wind. I scrape a drift away from the privy door and drag it open. Stepping inside, the door slams against my shoulder. I gasp as pain radiates down through my arm into my numb fingers.

Wasting no time, I climb atop the privy seat. The three roof rafters are two to three feet above my head. I toss one end of the rope over the middle rafter. I'll secure it to a wall stud later. Stepping down from my perch, I sit on the privy seat. My numb hands shake as I study the rope. I've never done this before, but I know how to make a good slip knot. I form a large loop.

The faces of Charles and my boys float before me. "Don't think about them," I murmur. "They're better off without you." Thoughts of my death and whether or not there is a place for me in heaven niggle at my mind. If I go through with this, my Bible says there is not. So, I fight them off and focus on the physical task—like I do when I pluck a chicken, or any other distasteful job required of me on the farm.

On the third attempt, I have successfully fashioned a decent noose. I slip it over my head and give the long end a solid yank. The rope glides easily inside the knot and tightens around my throat. I inhale deeply and climb up onto the seat.

The door swings open, the snow gusting and swirling around Charles' stocky body. The same shock, which must surely be on my face, is reflected in his.

Grabbing one of my hands, he yanks me down and pushes me onto the seat. With the other, he pulls the rope off the rafter and throws the loose end on the floor. I lean away from him, but he kneels in front of me, grips my shoulders, and draws me into his arms. His chest shudders.

My arms hang stiff at my sides; I have nothing left to offer. I focus on the fine flakes of snow clinging to his coat and hat. He smells of the barn.

After what seems to be a very long time, he slowly draws away from me. He holds my face between his hands, a gesture of love, but mostly to hold my attention. "So, it's come to this, has it?"

I avert my gaze, but his hands tighten on my cheeks. "Look at me. Talk to me." He tips my face up, forcing my eyes level with his.

I gaze past him—I'm a coward—I can't look in the depths of those brilliant blue eyes and witness the pain I'm causing. My voice sounds cold and distant. "Yes."

"But why? I know things aren't good right now, but how could you think of doing this?" He stands and yanks off his gloves. His rough, calloused hands reach behind me and loosen the knot. He slips it over my head and drops it on the floor. Removing his coat, he wraps it around my shoulders. "Mary, talk to me." Once again, he grasps my shoulders.

I remain still, silent, my eyes on the floor.

"Mary!"

I flinch; at this proximity, his voice is deafening. He tightens his hands on my shoulders and without warning; he gives me a good, hard shake.

Charles is not one to raise his voice. His actions rattle me. I blurt, "It's just so hard. I can't do this anymore." I stumble on my words, but somehow, I continue. "You know as well as I do, you and the boys would be better off without me."

He sucks in a breath. "Oh, Mary. Is that what you think?"

I don't answer, nor do I look at him. I continue to stare at the floor. How can he possibly understand how I feel when I don't understand it myself? All I know is I've always been ashamed of who I was—an unwanted bastard, a Barnardo Home Child. And now I'm ashamed of who I've become—an envious, bitter woman, a burden to him and my boys.

He takes his time. He's choosing his words carefully. "So, this is the plan, my Mary," he says matter-of-factly.

What's left of my cold, hard-shelled bit of a heart, melts. I love it when he calls me 'my Mary.' It's the one thing that makes me feel like I am home, like I really belong to someone. I remember my Mama and Papa—not my real parents, of course, but my foster parents—referring to me as 'our Mary' and how wonderful it made me feel. Charles never knew about that and then one day, out of the blue, he called 'my Mary.' That day, I knew I would love him until the day I die.

He continues. "It's time you knew. Dr. McDermot is arranging treatment for you at the hospital in St. Tomas."

I recall my brief consultation with the doctor and hearing their hushed voices in the kitchen afterward. I wrench myself away from Charles; he can't possibly think I will agree to this arrangement.

"No, no, hear me out." His words rush on. "He says they're making excellent progress in the treatment of melancholia."

My body registers the numbing cold. "No, you can't ask me to go there. I won't go there!" I'm shaking my head and trembling from head to toe. The thought of a mental asylum fills me with dread; I've heard the horror stories.

"I'm not asking you, I'm telling you. And they're not like they used to be. For goodness' sake, this is the 1940s—they're so much more advanced now. Besides, I don't see we have a choice."

My head is still shaking with a will of its own. "No, please, Charles, don't make me go there."

"Mary, it's for the best. I can't have you here, wondering every time I leave you alone if you're going to—" His voice breaks.

My mind scrambles for a reason, any reason, I shouldn't go. "We don't have that kind of money. How will we ever afford it?"

"Don't you worry about that—we'll make do." He holds my face again and gazes deeply into my eyes. "Now, I want you to listen carefully."

I nod. His hands are icy on my cheeks.

"Even though you've told me very little, I've picked up enough to know your past wasn't good. And with all we've gone through over the past two decades, it's taken its toll on you. It has on everyone, but I know it hits you harder than most. I understand you've had more than your share of heartache in your lifetime."

His words sound rehearsed. I picture him in the barn, practising his speech on the cows as he milked. Likely, his plan was to have this talk with me later today when he had the boys for backup. However, seeing my tracks going from the house to the workshop and then to the privy changed everything.

He slides his hands down to my shoulders, pulling me close. His clean-shaven face brushes my cheek as he speaks softly into my hair. "I can tell this has been building in you for some time now. And then you've had the added shock of your Papa and Ruby dying." He takes a deep breath and swallows. "And the more you draw away from me and the boys, the less time we spend with you, and the more alone you feel. It's a vicious cycle. You probably feel that the boys are avoiding you now, but that's because your state of mind scares them. They don't know how to act around you and frankly, I don't either. And, yes, you've had a hard time dealing with things. I don't know, maybe that's your way—to draw away from us." He shrugs. "But what I do know is we want you to get better. They want their mother back and I want my Mary."

He pulls away from me and tips my face up once again to look at him. "So, I think I understand . . . if only a little."

I study his face—his expressions changing by the second as new thoughts apparently race through his mind.

His chin quivers and his voice breaks. "But what you don't understand is the one most important thing: if you think we would be better off without you, you are wrong." His watery eyes search mine.

My resolve crumbles. Tears bubble up, like water in a kettle on the verge of boiling. My vision blurs and I close my eyes. His thumb slides across my cheekbone, wiping away the tears before they freeze. I snake my arms around his neck and bury my face in his flannel shirt.

He draws me to my feet, and sheltering me against the cruel wind, he escorts me to the house.

Chapter 3

The train heaves forward with jerks and clanks. I scrape a peephole of frost from the window, where I see Charles, dragging his feet through the snow toward the waiting pony and cutter. He looks dog-tired, like he does at the end of a long hot day following Daisy, our workhorse, as she drags the moldboard plough through the heavy clay. And now, with the Model T stored in the barn over winter, he'll have a cold five-mile ride back to the farm. The train chugs away and Charles diminishes before my eyes.

I exhale, relieved to be away from his watchful, sorrowful eyes.

Dr. McDermot's nurse is accompanying me to the hospital. She watches me like a hawk, no doubt with strict orders to keep me within sight at all times. That's unnecessary; I've not had any more suicidal thoughts and I most certainly wouldn't try anything on a moving train. My body shudders at the mere thought of it.

"Mary, are you cold?"

She's the one who looks cold with her limpid blue eyes and alabaster skin. Nurse Pritchard, always so very prim, dressed in her crisp, starched white uniform and cap, stockings, and shoes. I'm sure today feels like a holiday, a pleasant break from another routine day in Dr. McDermot's stuffy little practice in Eastgate.

My mind returns to Charles, heading home alone. He says he will visit if he can find the time and money. I doubt he will, but we'll see. I glance sideways at the nurse—she's still watching me. Unbuttoning my coat, I remove my gloves, and stow them in my handbag.

"Are you too warm, Mary?"

I sigh; it appears I've traded Charles's watchful eye for Nurse Pritchard's.

As the air warms, my peephole enlarges. We're heading east toward St. Tomas Psychiatric Hospital, where I'll be spending the next few months.

Now, that gives me something else to mull over. How was a stay of three months determined? Will I be well by then? Or, maybe after three months in a mental asylum, I'll be as crazy as the other patients there.

I clutch my hands to still their shaking.

Nurse Pritchard lays her hand on mine. "You're frightened, aren't you?"

I nod.

"Yes, I'm sure you are. I know I'd be. But trust me, it'll be okay. Three months isn't very long. It'll be over before you know it."

Is my face so readable? I'm full of questions. Charles had no answers—perhaps Nurse Pritchard has. They spill from my lips. "How was it determined my stay would be three months? Do you know anything about the treatments? Or what the hospital is like?"

Nurse Pritchard takes a moment to form her answers. She reaches into her handbag, draws out a little tin of peppermints, and offers me one.

"Thank you." I pop it in my mouth.

She helps herself to one. "Hmm . . . about the three months. I really don't know, but this is what I do know: a doctor will be assigned to your care and it will be up to him to decide when you're well enough to go home. Perhaps three months is a typical time frame to treat most patients with melancholia."

I nod.

"And I don't know what treatments you'll receive . . . that'll be up to the doctor, too. There are new treatments, though, that have proven to be very successful, like hydrotherapy and electroconvulsive."

I work the peppermint into my cheek. "Charles tells me psychiatric hospitals are not at all what they used to be and I've nothing to fear. But I can't help wondering what's in store for me. Both those treatments sound scary enough, but I remember hearing something about the latest new treatment, a lobotomy. They wouldn't do that to me, would they?"

She gasps. "Oh no, surely not that. Not in your case, Mary." She pats my hand. "Charles is right. The hospitals are nothing like they used to be. I've heard St. Tomas is very nice. It's fairly new, one of the most advanced in the country."

"Yes, I've heard that too." I relax. On the window glass, a reflection of myself phantoms over the moving, winter landscape. I study this middle-aged woman. She's barely recognizable—an aged, exhausted version of myself. Her thick, curly, shoulder-length auburn hair, streaked with a few greys, hangs limp and dirty, her brown wool tam cocked off to one side. Her skeletal face is ashen, with dark circles under her deep-set hazel eyes. I'm not used to her being thin; her strong, sturdy bones should have some flesh on them. I close my eyes and recline my head against the leather seat. I don't want to look at her anymore.

"You're tired, aren't you?"

I am tired. I'm physically tired, and I'm tired of being watched, but I say nothing. My body relaxes into the seat and I rest my head against the cool window. I force my eyelids open, only to have them lock with the stranger's in the glass. *Who is she?* I think of all I've been in my life, the roles I have played which have brought me to this place. I've been an orphan, a daughter, a Barnardo Home Child, a servant to others, a wife and a mother. Again, I study this woman. I peer deeply into her weary eyes, searching for the fresh, young face—the girl she once was.

That little girl is in there somewhere. To find her, I simply must remember.

December, 1908

The raw December wind whips around the corner of the school and the cold from the stone steps seeps through my coat and garments. With mittened hands, I tug on my woolen cap, drawing it down over my ears.

"Race you home!" Eight-year-old Dorothy smacks the back of my head while rushing past me, out the school gate, and down the lane. She can always outrun me; she's two years older.

"Wait up!" I grab my books and dinner pail and race down the steps, my short legs pumping. I pass through the gates and turn a bend in the lane. My chin quivers; Dorothy is nowhere in sight.

"Boo!" she yells, jumping out from behind a large elm tree.

I flinch.

"Ha-ha, scared you, didn't I?"

"No," I lie. Relief floods over me, though tears sting my eyes.

Dorothy laughs and rubs my woolen cap with her free hand. "Don't cry, you silly goose. I wouldn't leave you here alone. You know very well that Mama would skin me alive if I ever came home without you."

I swallow. My grin stretches wide as I peer up at her. She's not my real sister, I know this, but she's the best sister a girl could have. I shift my books into my left arm, grab her free hand, and hold tight. We leave the lane and walk along the village of Stretham's quiet back streets. First Wood Lane, then we turn right on Top Street, then left on High Street, and follow that route along to the Cambridge country road, a two-mile walk to our farm. If I had to, I could make it on my own, but I'd rather not; it'd be such a long, lonely walk by myself. The wind picks up as we leave town, the raw, damp air cutting through my woolen coat and mittens. I'm chilled to the bone by the time we scurry up our lane, through the gate in the dry stone wall, and up the steps to the back door.

We bustle into the warmth of the scullery, engulfed in the aroma of freshly baked bread. Mama wipes her dripping hands on her apron. "Good, my girls are home." Mama's tall and lean, with shiny dark brown hair drawn into a bun at her nape. She leans over and smacks mushy kisses on our cheeks. “Get out of your coats and boots, girls, and come along into the snug. A parcel came today for our Mary.”

My eyes grow big. “A parcel? For me?”

“Yes, for you.” She winks, her lovely brown eyes sparkling. “But perhaps you’d rather save it for Christmas?”

“Christmas is still three weeks away! I can’t wait that long.” I set my books and dinner pail on the table and unbutton my coat.

Mama laughs, a sound like tinkling bells. “No, I didn’t think you could.” She hugs me tight and then strolls ahead into the snug and sits on the sofa. Beside her is a large, long box, wrapped in crinkled brown paper and tied with string.

She pats the cushion beside her. “Come, sit here.” I wiggle up onto it, tight against her. She hands me the parcel while Dorothy squeezes in beside me.

My hands tremble as I untie the string and unwrap the paper. “Is it from my real mama?”

“I don’t know, sweetie. We can only presume it is.” She takes the string from me and wraps it around one hand, tying it together in a neat bundle. Smoothing out the wrinkles in the brown paper wrapping, she refolds it neatly in her lap.

I open the box. Inside is a beautiful porcelain baby doll wearing a white eyelet nightgown. Her cheeks are rosy and auburn curls peek from under a white bonnet. My breath whistles as I inhale.

Mama reaches over and touches the baby’s pink cheek. “Oh my, isn’t she beautiful? She looks just like you did when you were a baby.”

“She does? I was that pretty?”

“Of course you were, you silly girl, and you still are. What are you going to name your new baby?”

I carefully lift her from the box and look into her face. “Hmm, I can’t name her after my real mama ‘cause I don’t know her name, so I’m gonna name her after you. I’m gonna call her Annie. Do you think that’s a good name?”

Mama wraps her arm around my shoulders and squeezes.

"Or you could name her Dorothy." Dorothy giggles. "I'm just teasing—Annie's the perfect name for her." She holds out her arms. "May I hold her?"

I pass her to Dorothy.

Dorothy gently turns her over in her arms, admiring her tiny porcelain hands and feet. "She's so lifelike. She almost looks like a real baby."

I gaze up at Mama. "Was there a return address on the parcel this time?"

"No, there wasn't a name or address. You know, sweetie, it's like I've told you before—your mother's not to have any correspondence or contact with you. Those were the terms she agreed to when you became a Barnardo child."

I frown. "I only wanted to thank her for all the beautiful presents."

"You're such a thoughtful girl. But that's not possible and your mama knows that. She's not expecting any thanks from you."

I feel my face crumple. *Why am I such a cry-baby?* Dorothy is never sad—she never cries unless she gets hurt. I don't want Mama to see; I don't want her to think I'm not pleased with my new baby doll, so I turn my head toward Dorothy and reach for Annie's tiny hand.

"However, this is what I believe about your mama—"

This is the first time I've been offered information about my birth mother. I try not to pester Mama about her; she's told me plenty of times the information is confidential. I didn't know what confidential meant until Mama explained it means the information is private, like it's locked in a safe, and Mr. Barnardo is the only person with the combination.

But sometimes, when I'm alone, I fancy my real mama is a beautiful lady with long black hair and skin the colour of cream. I imagine her floating through a glorious garden, filled with the scent of flowers and birdsong. But a tall stone wall encloses this garden with no gate to the outside world. My mama clutches a bouquet of lilac blossoms at her breast and her bright blue eyes, the colour of the sea, never twinkle, nor do her lovely red lips smile. She's always sad; she misses me.

I stop my daydreaming and raise my face. "Yes?"

Mama's not looking at me. She's gazing out the window—the winter sun boring down on the horizon, blazing golden red behind the gnarled old apple trees of the orchard. With a far-off look in her eyes, she says, "I believe your mother is the daughter of a well-to-do couple. She's honourable and kind, and likely became pregnant with you out of wedlock, which is not at all acceptable in the upper class." Mama Annie looks at me and tips my chin up with her fingertips. "And, I'm sure, given the choice, she would never have given you up. I believe she loves you, misses you, and thinks of you every single day." She pauses for a moment. "I'm sure that's why she sends you these lovely gifts."

I was right—my real mama is just as I imagined her to be. I rub my palms over my eyes and nod my head in agreement.

Chapter 4

We've arrived.

The steel rims screech, bringing the train to a halt. I drag my thoughts from my memories and brace myself for what lies ahead.

Nurse Pritchard holds my valise in one hand. Her other hand clasps my elbow. The massive building looms: an impenetrable fortress, the huge sand-coloured limestone blocks stacked one atop the other. Two round windows, one on either side of the columned entrance, glare down at me as we climb the wide steps.

The grip on my elbow tightens. I drag my sight from the all-seeing windows. Nurse Pritchard offers me an encouraging smile. She opens the heavy oak door, we cross the threshold, and proceed through a large open reception room to the office.

In no time at all, we're through the admissions process and it's time for her to leave so she can catch the last train back to Ridgeland. She clasps my trembling hands. "Trust me, Mary, it'll be alright. You'll be home again before you know it."

As much as I resented her company earlier, now I hate to see her leave. Her cornflower coat and starched white cap float away from me. She's gone—my last link to home.

In stark contrast, Nurse Ryckman, the nurse now accompanying me, is the opposite of Nurse Pritchard. She's younger than I, a sturdy woman of above-average height, dark hair sternly pulled back under her white cap, deep-set eyes recessed under dark bushy brows, a large, bulbous nose, and mouth. I will not allow myself to judge her on first impressions—I dislike it when people do that—however, she does seem rather brusque.

"Come along," she snaps. She scoops my valise like it weighs no more than a feather pillow. I follow, but I'd much rather be following the meek Nurse Pritchard.

Nurse Ryckman sets a brisk pace, her white leather shoes slapping on the tiled floor. We pass through a set of double swinging doors and leave the lobby. My nose crinkles at the powerful smell of disinfectant. We tread down a long corridor, the east wing of the main hospital building. My breath quickens; she's now several feet ahead of me.

Nurse Pritchard was correct—my surroundings are quite nice. The building is modern, with polished tile floors and freshly painted walls in shades of cream, blues, and greens. It looks shiny, clean and efficient, but as nice in appearance as this building may seem, it's not a home and it will take some getting used to. Nurse Ryckman slows her pace as we approach an open door. "This area is the women's common facilities. The door to the toilets and the shower rooms are to remain open at all times."

Imagine that, I muse, indoor plumbing.

Nurse Ryckman marches down the hall. "And here are the women's showers." I peer inside the open door. It's a long room with wooden stalls along both sides and one window at the far end. "You're one of the lucky ones," she says as she moves along. "Your room is next—close to all the facilities."

We pass through the open door. It's a fairly large room, painted a soft tan, with four identical single white metal beds. Beside each bed is a dresser and a small wardrobe closet. While Nurse Ryckman places my valise on the bed closest to the door, I walk over to the large window. I'm surprised to be looking at snow-covered farmland.

Nurse Ryckman gives me a sideways glance. "Those fields you're seeing there are on hospital grounds. Come spring, the patients and staff will plant and tend large vegetable plots, enough to feed the entire hospital for most of the year." She takes a deep breath. "Studies have proven it's beneficial for patients, those who are able, to be busy working with their hands, you know, doing something constructive."

I nod. Of course, that makes sense. I always feel better when I'm busy with my hands. Just the thought of knitting calms me, the way the wool slides over the needles. Or quilting—I love seeing the piece I'm working on coming to life in my hands.

Thin grey lines obstruct my vision. I step back and focus on the window rather than the scenery. Ah, yes. My first impression was right—this building is an impenetrable fortress—there's wire mesh inside the glass. Although I'm still wearing my coat, I shiver.

Nurse Ryckman extends her hand to me, palm up, fingers wiggling. "If you're planning on staying for any length of time, you may as well take off your coat and boots. I'll take your handbag too."

"My handbag?"

"Yes, I need to go through your things. Can't have you smuggling in any drugs or weapons."

My mouth drops open. "I have nothing of the sort with me."

"I'll be the judge of that. Hand your things over."

I remove my coat and boots. She checks the pockets before storing them in the closet. While she efficiently unpacks my few belongings, I sit on the side of the firm, single bed.

"You're right; no contraband at all. Usually, women come with at least a razor, you know, for shaving legs and underarms."

I blush. "I forgot to pack it."

"Just as well; I would have confiscated it anyhow." She sets my empty valise on the floor in the closet. "You sure didn't bring much with you."

I didn't have much to bring, and this was the best I had. I feel her eyes travel over my tangled, dirty hair and rumpled clothing. She tsks to herself, "I suppose it's too late in the day now . . . we'll let the morning nurse have a go at that."

I believe I shall find it hard to warm up to this woman. Heat rises in my cheeks and I hang my head. It's not in my nature to be slack about my personal hygiene, but I'll admit, I've been neglectful these past few weeks. Even when I'm well, it's exhausting to bathe in the winter. I'm sure she has no idea the effort it takes to bathe in a home without indoor plumbing: pumping water from the kitchen sink, heating it, and filling the washtub. Smoothing the wrinkles in my dress, I clasp my hands in my lap to still their trembling. I turn my face and catch her scrutinizing me.

Her voice softens. "Your name is Mary, right?"

I nod.

"Okay, Mary, I'm guessing you're exhausted after your travel today. What do you say we get you tucked into bed?" She doesn't wait for a reply. She walks over to the dresser beside my bed and draws out my flannelette nightgown and slippers, hands them to me and continues, "I know it's early, barely supper time yet, but I'll head to the kitchen and fetch you a nice cup of tea and a sandwich. After that, you can get a good, long night's sleep. Come morning, we'll get you acquainted with the hospital and the other patients, including the women sharing this room with you. There's plenty of time for all that, but, right now, you need to rest." She draws the long white curtains around the bed.

Her voice filters through the curtain. "I'll be back in a few moments." I hear her heavy footfalls march away.

Nurse Ryckman's unexpected display of sympathy brings tears to my eyes. I've never been one to handle sympathy well; when it's shown, any strength I have melts away. The room falls silent. I'm alone and unsupervised for the first time in several days. I thought I'd wanted that, but I don't, and, oh my goodness, I feel so out of place. My breath catches in a sob, and I clamp my hand over my mouth. I haven't felt this way since Charles and I were married.

Now is not the time to be crying. Nurse Ryckman will be back in a few moments. I suspect she won't approve of me leaving the room, but I really must use the facilities before retiring. I proceed down the hall to the toilet and enter the first stall. There's no lock on the inside, so I move on to the next. It's the same.

As I sit on the toilet, I hear heavy footsteps approach. Grabbing the bottom of the stall door, I hold it closed. A set of feet, clad in rough leather loafers, passes and enters the stall beside me.

A woman's rough voice growls. "What d'ya think you're doin?"

I stop my pee, mid-stream, and hold my breath.

"I'm not doing anything," another voice barks.

"Stupid bitch!" the first voice squawks.

Only one pair of feet passed, yet both voices came from the same stall. I straighten my clothing and race from the room. I should have flushed, I should have washed my hands—things I'm not used to doing in an outdoor privy—but I did neither. Changing into my nightgown, I scurry beneath the covers.

Nurse Ryckman returns, carrying the promised tray. "Here we are." She offers me a small glass of water. "Take this pill. You should have just enough time to eat your sandwich and drink your tea before it kicks in." She holds a small tablet between her large fingers.

"What is it?"

"A sleeping pill . . . a sedative. It'll help you get through your first night here."

I hesitate.

She holds it before my lips. "C'mon now. Open," she orders.

I obey. She lays the bitter pill on my tongue. I swallow.

Another memory surfaces. Mama Annie is spooning cod liver oil into my mouth. Oh, how I hated it: the fishy flavour, the oil slick on my tongue, but then, as soon as I swallowed it, she would pop a tasty barley sugar drop between my lips.

It's a shame Nurse Ryckman doesn't have a barley sugar drop on that tray. She sets the tray on my lap, marches across the room, and drags over a straight-back wooden chair. Reaching into a pocket of her uniform, she draws out a small book. "I'll wait here until you're finished," she states as she flips open the book.

I nibble at the cheese sandwich and pour myself a cup of tea from the pot. It's black, not the way I usually take it, but I don't complain. I prefer my tea laced with real cream and sugar, if we have sugar on hand. Sometimes we didn't, but I won't dwell on those thoughts right now. And tea from a small metal pot never tastes as good as tea from a big crockery pot, like the one I have at the farm, or the one Mama Annie had. My, that was some pot—I've never seen another like it since I came to Canada.

June, 1910

Mama's clear voice flies up the staircase. "Hurry, girls!" She's referring to Dorothy and me, the dawdlers. I share a bedroom with her and baby sister, Evelyn, under the eastern gable of the farmhouse. It has steep, sloping walls and a long, deep-set window. Kathleen, the eldest girl at thirteen years of age, has a small room of her own at the top of the stairs. It's tiny, what was called the box room, but she prefers it over sharing a room with us. The boys, all three of them, share the other big room at the west end of the cottage. Mama and Papa's bedroom is downstairs, off the main reception room.

I quickly lace up my ankle-high boots. "Coming, Mama." I love Sundays; it gives me occasion to wear my special dresses and ribbons. I receive regular clothing parcels from the Barnardo Home, but they're all so sensible, nothing pretty like my real mama sends me. I glance in the small mirror one more time and admire myself. Sitting in front of me and also reflected in the glass is Dorothy. She runs the brush through her long brunette hair, pulls back the sides and ties them off with a large blue ribbon. She smiles at herself, clearly pleased with the effect.

I nudge her shoulder. "C'mon, time to go."

We race down the stairs, through the kitchen and out the back door.

Papa stands at the back of the wagon. He's a large man, with black hair, a full beard, and dark blue, flashing eyes. When he sees us coming, he winks. "Ah, here they come. You can always count on those two to keep us waiting."

I hasten toward him. "Sorry, Papa."

He chuckles as he scoops me up in his powerful arms and swings me over the back, with Dorothy right behind me. We settle ourselves beside the other children on the plank seats. There's Henry, Albert, Kathleen, Dorothy and Evelyn. And then there's me and the latest addition to the family, Stanley. He's another Barnardo child, only seven years old. My goodness, he was a sorry sight when he arrived on our doorstep. It broke my heart; he was so raggedy, dirty, and skinny. Having come directly off the streets, it took him a while to settle. Not me; I came to live with them when I was a wee baby, nine years ago. Sometimes, I'm in awe of how much love Mama and Papa have in their hearts—enough for their own five children, and plenty left over for Stanley and me.

Papa helps Mama before stepping up beside her. He plants his feet firmly on the toe-board, grabs the reins, and clicks his tongue twice.

"Step up, girl!" Nancy, his favourite horse, a beautiful sorrel Haflinger, obeys, and the wagon creaks forward. It's such a beautiful day for a ride beneath the cloudless blue sky. The roadside and pastures are abloom with early summer flowers, the lovely purple lousewort and the dainty white mouse-ear. I adore flowers and Mama Annie is teaching me all their pretty names. "Dorothy," I shout, "look at all the daisies!" She and I love to gather daisies. We sit in the shade of the apple trees and make chains, then we pile them on our heads and drape them around our necks until our faces are barely visible.

Dorothy giggles. "It looks like it's daisy-chain time again."

Papa is very strict about attending church. Although it isn't my favourite part of the day, I enjoy singing the hymns. Mama says I have a lovely singing voice.

We scramble out of the wagon while Papa helps Mama alight, and then we follow her down the graveled walkway, amongst the weathered, lichen-covered gravestones, while Papa drives the horse and wagon to the parking area.

It's cool inside the old stone church, and the doors and windows are propped open to allow the warmer air in. The sun glints through the stained-glass windows and, drifting in on the gentle breeze are the bird songs of the Woodlark and the Mistle Thrush.

After what seems an especially long time, the service and visiting is done.

There is no work on Sunday, according to Papa, except the essentials: feeding the livestock, milking the cows, collecting the eggs, and preparing the meals. It's still a lot, but it's much less than what we accomplish the other six days of the week.

Sunday dinners are special too, not only because of the food, but because Papa always treats us with a story. He sits at the head of the table, Mama at the end, and all the children crowd along the sides. Today's dinner is roast chicken with all the trimmings, which we eat after a solemn prayer of thanksgiving. When we finish the main course, I help Evelyn and Dorothy clear away the dishes while Mama makes tea in the huge, brown crockery pot and Kathleen cuts the treacle tart. Once we're seated, Papa raises his hand for silence. He begins, "So, you've all heard about those new-fangled automobiles."

Henry, the oldest, picks up his fork. "Of course we have."

Papa looks down the table at each of us. We nod in agreement. "Okay," he says, "I heard a tale the other day involving a couple of those automobiles not too far from here." He glances at us one more time to see if we're all paying attention. "Well, it just so happened there was an Englishman and an Irishman driving toward each other only a few nights ago on that dark, twisty road . . . you know the one, east of Stretham. You can almost picture it, can't you . . . ink-black dark with ground fog rising all ribbon-like across the road?"

His eyes glitter as they rest on Evelyn. Hers are as big as saucers and her mouth hangs open.

"So, they were both driving way too fast as they approached that sharp bend. And when they meet, well, blimey, don't they collide! There was an enormous bang, steam's rolling off the engines, and glass shattering everywhere!"

I lean forward in my chair. Evelyn, sitting beside me, inhales sharply.

Papa has our undivided attention and continues, "To the amazement of them both, they're unscathed, with nary a scratch on their bodies. Sadly, though, both their cars are destroyed."

"Whew," says Evelyn as she exhales.

Papa winks at her. "Now, in celebration of their good fortune, they both agreed to put aside their mutual dislike from that moment on, which is a wonder because you all know as well as I do that the English and Irish have never got along. They still don't get along to this day, and probably never will. Anyway, I won't get into all that right now. At this point, the Englishman went to the boot of his automobile and fetched out a twelve-year-old bottle of whisky. Ya know, he's English, so he's bound to be a polite gentleman. He uncorked the bottle and offered it, first-off, to the Irishman as anyone with fine manners would do. The Irishman raised the bottle and exclaimed, 'May the Irish and the English live together forever in peace and harmony.' The Irishman then tipped the bottle to his lips, gulped half of it down, and handed it back to the Englishman. The Englishman corked the bottle again and replied, 'No thanks, I'll wait for the police to come along.'" Papa leans back in his chair, a huge grin plastered on his face.

"Oh, Albert!" Mama throws up her hands, laughing. "And on a Sunday, too."

Papa gazes around the table at the laughing brood of young ones and grins at Mama. At six years old, Evelyn is too young to understand the yarn, but she puts on a good show by laughing the hardest. What a comical girl she is.

"Mary."

I hear a voice in the distance. Someone's calling my name. *Is it you, Mama Annie?*

"Mary!"

No, it's not her; the voice is too harsh. *Whoever you are, go away—I don't want to leave this dream.*

She's shaking my shoulders. "C'mon. Time to wake up."

I feel as if I am coming back from a great distance. I drag my eyes open and blink several times. My vision is blurry.

"Well, it's about time." An unfamiliar nurse stands over me. "I'm Nurse Martin. How are you this morning?"

"It's hard to tell," I say, clearing my throat, "you just woke me." I shake my foggy head. My, that was some pill. "Where am I?" I run my thick tongue over my parched lips. The inside of my mouth is gritty, like it's coated with sand.

"My goodness, have you forgotten so soon? You're in the St. Tomas Psychiatric Hospital."

I groan as reality hits me.

"It's seven o'clock now, time to be up and doing. You've got a busy day ahead of you. Here are your slippers and wrap. Put them on and we'll head on down to the showers, shall we?" Last evening, I had thought Nurse Ryckman was a wee bit brusque—it appears Nurse Martin has her trumped. She glides about the room, drawing open the window drapes and the curtains from around my roommates' beds.

It's obvious there'll be no lying around in bed for me anymore. My three roommates stir. I clasp the neck of my nightgown; I can't fathom having spent a night in a drug-induced sleep with three total strangers.

"Get a move on now, Mary." I suppose I have no choice but to do as I am told—I rise and follow my guardian to the showers. Ten minutes later, we return. The other women are moving about, dressing, making their beds, brushing their hair.

"Ladies, I'd like you to meet your new roommate, Mary Thistle," Nurse Martin announces. "Mary, this is Florence, Margaret, and Helen." She gestures toward each of the women as she speaks their names. Florence offers me a sad smile, Margaret nods, and Helen stands mute, staring at me.

"Nice to meet you," I mumble before returning to the privacy of my curtained area. The room and my body are warm, yet the hairs on my arms and neck bristle. I shake off the feeling and dress in one of my two everyday shirtwaist woolen dresses, stockings, and brown leather pumps. I drag my large tooth comb through my wet, tangled hair, which is dampening my neckline and shoulders. It's far too long—I should have had it cut months ago.

Nurse Martin abruptly opens my curtain. "Come along now, Mary. Breakfast is being served."

At a brisk pace, I follow her down the long corridor. Through open doors, I glimpse into the other rooms. Most are empty; likely the patients have gone to the dining room for breakfast. Others are not. Some patients are yet in bed, sleeping or staring at the ceiling. Others are sitting in chairs, staring at nothing. They don't take any notice as we walk past their doors.

I pause at an open door. It's a private room, sparsely furnished. Unlike the embedded wire mesh of my room's window, there are metal bars on the outside of this window. A nurse is doing something at the bedside table, her back facing me. In the room's corner, belted into a wheelchair, is a shell of a woman. Her head dangles forward on a long thin neck, her face shrouded by ragged hair. Dressed in nothing more than a thin cotton gown, her gaunt wrists, and ankles struggle against the binding. The nurse moves toward her, a syringe in her hand. The woman raises her head. Her bleak eyes find mine. Her lips move, forming the silent words, "Help me."

I gasp.

When Nurse Martin notices I'm no longer keeping pace with her, she stops, and marches back to me. Her eyes follow mine. "It's for her own protection," she says as she grips my upper arm.

I shudder with an unspeakable dread. *If I don't improve, might that poor soul possibly be me?*

Chapter 5

It's mid-morning. The doctor stands between a massive cherry desk and a bookcase filled with medical journals. He extends a hand toward the two comfortable chairs before his desk. "Mrs. Thistle, please have a seat."

Nurse Martin, hand still on my elbow, leads me to one chair. My body tingles with an annoying, quivering sensation. I withdraw into myself, crossing my ankles as I sit.

"Nurse Martin, you may leave now."

The leather chair creaks as the doctor sits. "Mrs. Thistle, my name is Dr. Clark, one of the hospital's psychiatrists, and I will be in charge of your care while you're here with us. Now, the information provided to me indicates you are suffering from severe melancholia. Do you agree with Dr. McDermot's diagnosis?"

I gaze past him and stare at the bookcase. "Perhaps," I mumble.

"Perhaps? Do you disagree with his diagnosis?"

I squirm in my chair. "Um, no."

"So, you *do* agree?"

I take several quick breaths. "Yes."

"Your file also states you've attempted suicide. Is that information correct?"

I lower my head in shame. I feel the weight of Dr. Clark's eyes on me, scrutinizing me, analyzing me as if I'm under a microscope. Wrapping my arms tightly across my abdomen, I make myself as small as possible.

Finally, he speaks. His voice has lost all trace of professional inflection. "Mrs. Thistle, there's no need for you to feel shame. I'm here to help you, not judge you."

I slowly raise my eyes and take a good look at him. He appears to be about my age, fortyish, dark hair, greying at the temples, black-rimmed glasses. Not an unattractive man by any standard. His face is kind. He's tall, slightly stout, dressed in a fine navy pin-stripe suit, starched white linen shirt, and bow tie. I suppose there's no lack of money in his household; he obviously enjoys many good meals. My gaze wanders about his elaborate office, and finally rests on the view from a large window overlooking the park-like hospital grounds. Against a brilliant blue sky, a soft blanket of fresh snow swathes the trees.

"Let's start, shall we?" He taps the pen on a sheet of lined paper. Beside it is a manila folder with my name printed on it in bold script. "I see your Christian name is Mary. May I call you that or do you prefer Mrs. Thistle?"

"Mary is fine."

"Splendid. I'll be asking you questions and I'd like for you to give me frank, honest answers. To enable me to address the underlying cause of your melancholia, I must uncover the circumstances that brought you to this point in your life. And to do so, I need to get to know you. It's all very simple . . . Mary, are you following me?"

My eyes flick back to the doctor. I'm afraid he lost me at 'honest.' Surely Dr. McDermot's notes didn't include the little white lies I tell? No, of course not; that line is likely something Dr. Clark says to everyone. I continue to look him in the eye.

"Okay, moving along. Why don't you tell me about yourself?"

"Where would you like me to start?"

"At the beginning, of course."

"That's a long way back."

"Not so long ago," he says, smiling. "I see your birth year is 1902. I don't tell everyone, but for your information, mine is 1905. Now, you really don't want to insult me too badly, do you?"

I'm well aware of his intentions—he's trying to make me comfortable in his presence—and it's working. I settle into the back of the chair.

He flips open the folder and removes the top sheet of paper. "Here, let me get you started," he says. "This paper says a Mary Clifton was born on February 19th, 1902, in Leeds, England."

"That far back?" I rub my fingertips across my forehead.

"Yes, that far back. Now it's your turn to elaborate on the story."

He stares at me, waiting for me to speak. I take a deep breath. If he wants my story, well, then I'll give it to him. "Yes, I was born on that very day and in that very place. My mother's name was Annie Louisa Clifton, and my father's name was Frank Black, although I did not know of them until I was thirteen years old."

"Why was that?"

"Because, shortly after I was born, I was taken away from my mother and put into the care of the Barnardo Home. I became an orphan."

He nods his head. "I see. Please go on."

"At three months of age, Barnardo's placed me in a foster home in Stretham, England. My foster parents' names were Albert Charles White and Annie-Maria White. Now, don't you think it's rather ironic my biological father's surname was Black and my foster parents' surname was White and both my biological and adoptive mothers have the same first name?" I don't wait for a response, but quickly carry on. "I always have. Anyway, my foster parents had five children of their own, four when I came to live with them, and one was born after I arrived. Later on, they also took in two more Barnardo boys, first Stanley, and then Fred." I stop for a quick breath.

Dr. Clark is taking notes. He glances up at me. "And what was your life like while you were living with this foster family?"

I smile. "It was wonderful. I have so many fond childhood memories of my time with them. You see, they treated me like I was one of their own." My heart aches with longing even now, as I recall my early life with them.

Dr. Clark leans forward and rests his elbows on the desk. "Go on."

"When I was eleven years old, I was taken from them and placed in the Girls Village Home in Ilford to complete my schooling and training as a domestic worker."

"How did you feel about that?" Dr. Clark rests his face on his left hand and rubs his index finger across his lips.

What a silly question. Can't he imagine how I felt? I blink a few times, and say, "I didn't mind the school, but I was very upset to leave my home and family."

"Why?"

I bristle; I wonder if he even thinks about the logic of his questions. "I would think it should be quite obvious. How would you have felt had someone plucked you from your family at that age?" I gasp and lower my head. "I'm sorry; that was impertinent of me to say that."

"No, it's alright. That's a natural response. Go ahead, though, and try to explain how you *felt.*"

Oh, I get it. Now I understand why he asks those questions. I've never once tried to put those feelings into words. "I suppose that was the first time in my life when I felt," I shrug, "like I was nothing more than a possession. It seemed as if it was of no consequence to take me away from my family at that early age."

"Did it seem that way to your foster family? How did they react?"

I look out the window and allow the memory of that day to wash over me.

August, 1913

It's a sultry, lazy, August day with a view as pretty as a postcard. The cattle doze beneath the sprawling oak, their ears, and tales flicking.

Even the flies have retreated to the shade. The heat rises off the pasture in shimmering waves.

Dorothy, Evelyn, and I toil leisurely in the garden patch. I wipe the sweat from my brow with my apron. The crops are ripening in the fields, and the garden is abundant with vegetables—it's a daily chore to pick and tote them to the house for Mama and Kathleen to process. Every day, they pack more and more jars with pickles, tomatoes, beans, and relishes. We younger girls had best not complain, though; it takes Mama and Kathleen far longer to process the vegetables than it does for us to pick them. Today, we have orders to pick two bushel baskets of tomatoes, one peck of green peppers and pull another quart of onions.

Squatted in the tomato patch, I turn my head as Nancy's clomping steps approach. She nickers at us. Henry, riding on her back, has returned from town. He dismounts and leads Nancy into the barn to remove her tack and put her to pasture. A few moments later, he strolls to the house, an envelope clasped in his hand. I grasp another ripe tomato, twist it gently to break it off the vine, and lower it into my apron.

Dorothy stands and straightens her back. "Bring your tomatoes over here, girls, and let's see how many we've got."

Evelyn and I rise, and holding our aprons by the corners, we step between the plants. Two bushel baskets sit on the grass at the edge of the garden plot. We crouch beside them and roll the tomatoes into the baskets.

"Good. They're full," Dorothy says. She and I each grasp a handle of one of the bushel baskets while Evelyn takes hold of the smaller basket of green peppers. Struggling with the weight of our burdens, we head to the cottage. While walking past the kitchen window, I sense we are being watched. I look up.

Mama stands at the window. Her eyes are sad and her pretty mouth, usually wearing a serene smile, is drawn down at the corners. Even with the extreme heat of the day, the hair on my scalp prickles. She holds the door open as we amble through, burdened by the weight of the baskets.

Mama's lips tremble and her voice falters. "Henry, please take your sisters out to the garden and help them carry in the other baskets, but leave them outside the door. I'd like a few moments alone to speak with our Mary."

"Yes, Mama. Come along, girls." His large boy hands rest on their shoulders as he ushers them out the door. They look back, their faces a mixture of apprehension and curiosity.

Mama pulls out two chairs from the table and sits. She pats the seat of the other. "Come sit with me, sweetie." She reaches for the open letter on the table. I recognize the stationery—it's from the Barnardo Home.

My feet freeze to the floor. I hold my breath as a tremor ripples through me. I don't want to know what's written on that paper.

Mama comes to me and kneels so her eyes are level with mine. Her large, worn hands take mine in hers. She presses them to her lips.

I don't need to be told what's in the letter. My time with this family is coming to a close. Mama pulls me into her arms as a sob escapes my lips.

My chin trembles as I recall that day. It was so long ago and yet it's still so fresh. Will I ever recall them without pain?

"Mary?" Dr. Clark's voice calls me out of my reverie.

I draw my gaze from the window. "I'm sorry. What was the question?"

"How did your family react to the news? How did they feel about you leaving?"

My mind wanders again to the actual day I was taken away. I quickly summarize it. "The day they came for me, my Mama cried. My Papa held her. There was nothing they could do."

"How did the other children in the home react?"

"They weren't there. It was mid-morning on a school day. I think it was planned that way so there would be less fuss. You know, when I think back on it, it always put me to mind of what a kind father would do with a beloved pet that was dying. He would put it out of its misery while the child was not home. There'd be no need for a child to hold on to a memory like that."

"Hmm, that's an interesting thought." Dr. Clark scribbles some words down on the paper before continuing. "Were you aware your time with your foster family was to be ended at that age, or did it come as a surprise?"

"It wasn't something we talked about often, mostly because it always made everyone feel sad. To answer your question, though, yes, I was aware it would happen someday. . . but not so soon. I thought I would have more time with them."

"Okay, so getting back to the school. Tell me about that. What was it like?"

"Actually, I enjoyed my schooling and the lessons in knitting, lace-making, baking and all those other things reminded me of being with Mama Annie, and so it wasn't as bad as I had imagined it might be. My family wasn't far away, and I hoped they might come and visit. I even imagined that, when I finished the ten-week training course, I would find a placement close to them in Stretham." I pause and sigh. "But those dreams didn't last."

"Why was that?"

I look down at my hands as I am buffeted by another memory.

September, 1913

Lessons are finished. My classmates and I are about to leave the schoolroom when our teacher, Miss Stevenson, announces several students are to remain after class. I am one of those students.

When the classroom has quieted, she rises from her desk. "I have been asked to pass on some very exciting information to you girls. You have been chosen, along with many other young girls, to immigrate to Canada."

An intake of breath is indescribable. It feels like there isn't enough air—it's all been sucked from the room. A second later, many of the girls start chattering amongst themselves. Miss Stevenson calls out, "Girls, Girls! Quiet down, please."

The room falls silent. She continues, "Now girls, I'm sure you have some knowledge of the current situation in England. There's little chance of employment for you or the thousands of other Barnardo Home children. Canada is a young country, full of promise and opportunities for girls such as yourselves. You will board the next ship, leaving London, England for Ontario, Canada."

Once again, I'm immobilized. *Did I hear that right?* There's an ocean between England and Canada. *How will I ever be with my family again?*

Charlotte, a fourteen-year-old, boldly asks, "Miss Stevenson, when will we be leaving?"

"Very soon. The ship sails on September 25th."

I gasp. That's only two days from now.

"If any of you would like to write to your friends or families before you leave, now is the time to do it. You'll find stationery and envelopes on my desk. Please help yourselves." She sits behind her desk once again. Without looking up, she says, "You are free to leave now."

Somehow, I will my legs to function. I follow the other girls toward Miss Stevenson's desk and take one sheet of Barnardo Home stationery and one envelope.

Dazed, I stumble from the room. Thousands of children over the past few decades had immigrated to Canada and Australia to serve as farmhands or domestic workers, but from what I understood, the age requirement was fourteen years old. How am I, an eleven-year-old, included on this list? I look at my newfound friends walking beside me. They all wear the same dazed look.

Emma, a girl slightly younger than myself, weaves through the crowd toward me. She's such a sweet little thing, always singing or humming. Most times, it's the same song—a lovely old Irish ballad. My concern for myself dissipates. Emma's smaller and thinner than I. She looks fragile, her eyes haunted. She carries no paper or envelopes. *Does she have no one to write to?* I grasp her empty hand.

In silence, we move down the hall to our bedroom, a long room housing twenty small beds and dressers. When we come to hers, she drops my hand, lies on her bed, and buries her face in her pillow. I sit on the side of her cot and awkwardly lay my hand on her back. She rolls over and gulps back tears. “Mary, will you stay with me?”

“Sure. I’ll stay here with you as long as you like.”

“No, I don’t mean here. I mean, when we get to Canada. I don’t know anyone there. Will you be my friend and stay with me?”

“Yes. Of course, I will. I don’t know anyone there either. Let’s make a pact right now—we’ll stay together and take care of each other.”

Emma rubs her palms across her tear-stained cheeks and gives me a weak smile. She nods. “Okay. It won’t seem so bad if I know I’ll always have you.”

I move along to my bed. Sitting on the side, I pull out the top drawer of my small dresser and remove the letter which arrived yesterday from Mama. Carefully, I open the envelope again and draw out the single sheet of paper. I unfold it. Inside is a small black-and-white photograph, the edges slightly tattered, the image grainy. It’s of my family, all together. Seated in straight-back chairs in front of the cottage are Papa and Mama Annie. The older children stand behind them, the younger ones sitting on the ground at their feet. I remember the day well. Mama’s nephew had been visiting from London. He had recently purchased the latest camera invention, a Raisecamera, and had taken several photographs that weekend. We were so excited to receive copies in the mail the following month. I clasp the photograph to my heart.

I lay it beside me on the bed and remove a pencil and my Bible from the drawer. Placing the paper on the hard cover of the book, I begin my farewell letter to my family.

“Mary, you seem to have left me again.”

The colour rises to my cheeks. “I’m sorry, Dr. Clark. I’m not prepared for these questions.”

“That’s okay, take your time. You’ll improve with time. So, what were the ten weeks like at the girls’ school?”

"I didn't stay the full ten weeks. On September 25th, I boarded the SS Corinthian with well over a hundred other girls, and a few chaperones, and we set sail for Canada."

Dr. Clark's eyebrows raise as he peers at me over his spectacles. "And once again, you were how old?"

"I was eleven years old."

"I see," he says as he continues writing. "And what happened after that?"

"As frightened as I was, I have to admit it was rather exciting, at least once I got past the seasickness. We all had our small wooden trunks, built by Barnardo boys, and filled with all our worldly possessions, which, trust me, wasn't much. It rather felt like we were on a vacation—a real adventure. The voyage lasted ten days. We travelled up the St. Lawrence Seaway to Quebec. It was strange, being in a different country with people who spoke an unfamiliar language. Some of the older girls tried to fool us into believing we had only crossed the English Channel and were in France."

Dr. Clark chuckles. "And from there, where did you go?"

"The next day, they split us into smaller groups. You can't imagine how it feels to wake up in the morning with no idea of where you're going. Along with a chaperone, some of us boarded a train, the Grand Trunk Railroad, dubbed 'The Barnardo Special', and headed for Peterborough. When we arrived, we were taken to Hazelbrae, another of the Barnardo Homes."

He glances up from his notes. "Continue."

I sigh. "I recall disembarking the train. The station was at the bottom of a hill . . . I believe it was called Conger's Hill. We walked up the hill toward a stately brick manor. I remember thinking it was so beautiful, and it was—at least the exterior and the large reception room inside the front door. But that's where the beauty ended. Thank heavens, I wasn't there long, although I heard some girls were. It seemed if a girl wasn't strong and healthy, nobody wanted her; you see, we were expected to work. Sadly, I heard some never left . . . if you know what I mean."

My mind wanders back to that awful place. Poor little Emma. I wasn't able to keep my promise. She stood all alone as I followed my new master and mistress out through the front doors. I turned and called out to her, "I'll write to you, Emma. We'll stay in touch." A few weeks after I had settled into my home, I asked my mistress for paper and envelopes so I could write Mama Annie and Emma and give them my new address. Mama Annie wrote back, but I never heard from Emma. I always wondered what happened to her. *Was she one who never left?* I choke on my words. "I don't want to think about that place; it was nothing more than a clearing house."

Dr. Clark is busy scribbling more notes on the paper. His writing looks like hen scratch. Eventually, his eyes leave the page. "Mary, it appears you have quite a story to tell, but our time is up and this is a good place to conclude our session today. I'll meet with you again Thursday, two days from now, where we'll pick up where we left off. In the meantime, you'll be weaned off the pills Dr. McDermott prescribed and start on a different one next week. You're dismissed now. You'll find Nurse Martin waiting outside in the hallway."

A blush rises to my cheeks. "Thank you." Closing the door behind me, I exhale. I'm embarrassed and emotionally exhausted. In the future, I should form my thoughts ahead of time so my mind won't drift off again. Plus, I can decide what I want to share with the doctor and what I'd rather not.

Nurse Martin escorts me to the dining room, a large, bright room filled with long tables. Dozens of women are finding seats. "It's time you became better acquainted with your roommates," she says while manoeuvring through the bobbing throng. She scans the room. "Oh, there they are," she says, pointing. We move toward them.

"Mary, once again, this is Florence, Margaret and Helen." She seats me beside Helen, with Florence and Margaret across the table from us. I look sideways at Helen, a wiry, young woman with thin blond hair secured by a rubber band. She leans away from me, rocking in her chair. She appears anxious. I believe she may have some serious mental issues. I glance across the table. Margaret, a stout woman of about sixty years of age, boldly ogles me. Her mouth hangs open. I look away; she scares me. Florence appears to be fortyish and, for lack of any other word, she is simply lovely: tall, willowy, fine-featured with brunette hair styled into a chignon at her nape. She comes across as a very well-mannered, proper lady. It puzzles me why someone like her would be here.

I reprimand myself for making such swift, unfounded judgments. Did I not tell myself yesterday I dislike it when others do that? *Who am I to judge any of these women?* Walking away, Nurse Martin turns to me. "Oh, I almost forgot. Helen is deaf."

The lunch is served, consisting of platters of sandwiches, pickles, tea, and coffee. My thoughts must be very morbid right now; it brings to mind a funeral luncheon. I'm sipping my tea when Margaret bluntly asks, "So, Mary, where are you from?" My arm jerks, and tea sloshes over the side of the mug. I recognize the voice—it's one of the two I heard in the toilet yesterday.

Sopping up the spill with my napkin, I reply, "A farm outside Eastgate."

"Eastgate? Where's that?" Biting off a large mouthful of sandwich, she chews with her mouth open. Her stained brown teeth are visible as her tongue rolls the food around in her mouth.

"About halfway between here and Chester." The sandwiches are disappearing quickly, so I choose a salmon salad and take a bite.

"A farmwife, are ya?" Soggy bread crumbs and egg salad fall from her mouth onto the blouse stretched across her large, sagging breasts.

I'm repulsed. My stomach churns as I swallow. I nod and reach for my teacup with one quaking hand.

"Why are you here?"

Florence turns in her chair. "Margaret!" Her voice, even raised, is genteel. She lowers it and continues, barely above a whisper, "That's not an appropriate question. I know you're new here, but still you should know it's none of your business." She looks across the table at me and adds, "If Mary wants to talk to us about her personal life, she's more than welcome to, but it's not your place to pry."

"Blah, blah, blah." Margaret takes another bite.

I feel a kinship with Florence and offer her a nod of appreciation. She tips her head, ever so slightly, and raises her teacup.

Perhaps, someday, I will want to talk about my personal life with someone other than Dr. Clark, and if I do, I suspect it will be Florence who will lend me her ear.

Chapter 6

The library's bank of windows overlooks the expansive front gardens of the hospital. A funnel of snow pirouettes around the corner of the limestone wall. The swirling powdered mass loses momentum and sifts to the ground, like flour onto a bread board. Off in the distance, the tall spruce trees sway in the relentless wind.

In a private corner of the room sits an empty wingback chair—a quiet retreat to reflect for an hour or so. My mind is restless, fretting over Charles and my boys. *Are they well? Are they overwhelmed with the extra work?* This winter has been nothing but one snowstorm after another. *Is it keeping my boys from attending school?*

It's cool beside the windows, and I tug my brown wool cardigan across my chest. I've only been here two days, but it seems much longer. My next appointment with Dr. Clark is tomorrow morning, where I'm expected to continue my story.

Our conversation ended with my arrival at Hazelbrae. Where to from there? I rest my head against the chair's cushioned wing, close my eyes and let my mind go back—not to the happy time of my childhood in England, but to the time I'd rather forget—those years that lie between my life with my foster family and my life with Charles.

My first placement was so short and inconsequential, it's difficult to even recall. I'll begin with my second placement. The Metcalfes.

September, 1914

The mantel clock on the fireplace chimes once, indicating the half hour. It's already two-thirty and we're expecting Miss Silas, a Barnardo inspector, at three. I met her once at my first placement, but today will be my first interview with her. I'm anxious; I can't put my finger on it but there's something about the woman that unnerves me. The day I met her she seemed haughty, insincere, and judgmental. I suppose that's not *something*—that's a lot of things. Hopefully, she's not like that today. I rub the polishing rag over the parlour table one last time, replace the doily, and ever so carefully set the crystal vase of flowers in the centre. I give the room one more overall inspection. Yes, everything is in order. At twelve years old, I'm quite proud of my accomplishments over the past year. Mrs. Metcalfe, although stern, has been most thorough in my proper housemaid training.

Back in the scullery, off the kitchen, I place the kettle on the stove, and arrange the sugar biscuits I baked earlier this morning on a serving plate. The rear staircase door is open. The muffled voices of my mistress and her children tumble down the steps. I climb that dark, narrow, staircase and enter my bedroom, a stark, small storage room at the rear of the house. Removing my apron and brown work dress, I hang them on the hook behind my door and don my one and only good dress, my Sunday dress, a serviceable blue print. I've grown out of all the dresses I brought with me—the pretty ones my real mama gave me. Mrs. Metcalfe took them and hung them in her daughter, Clarice's closet. I hear the noisy chatter of the children and their mother as they descend the wide, open staircase at the front of the house. My gut curdles with resentment.

Standing before the mirror, I pluck the hairpins from the bun at my nape and vigorously rake the brush through my long curls. I pull the sides up, secure them with a scrap of ribbon, and descend the back staircase.

Mrs. Metcalfe and her five children, ages two through ten, are in the kitchen, the children seated around the table, enjoying biscuits.

"All's ready, Mary?" Mrs. Metcalfe asks as she pours glasses of milk.

"As far as I can see, ma'am."

Without looking at me, she says, "You did a fine job in the parlour, and the children all agree the biscuits are wonderful." She places the tumblers on a tray and carries it to the table. "Now, hurry and finish up, children. Miss Silas will be here within moments." She directs her gaze at her eldest. "Clarice, after Miss Silas has arrived, I want you to bring the children in for a quick visit, and then you may take them out to play in the garden. Is that understood?"

"Yes, Mama."

Mrs. Metcalfe moves around the table, placing the drinks in front of the children. "And Clarice, make sure you keep them occupied and quiet."

Clarice rolls her eyes behind her mother's back. "Yes, Mama."

What a naughty girl she is! I bite my bottom lip and turn my face to hide my suppressed smile. Clarice might be mischievous, but I still like her. At times, she reminds me of Dorothy. And it's not her fault she now has my pretty dresses—she didn't take them from me—her mama did.

Earlier this morning, I thought about what I would discuss with Miss Silas. I attend school, for which I'm thankful. It's not very pleasant, though, as it seems my classmates don't care to be associated with me, and, because of this, I don't have friends. That saddens me. But none of that will matter to Miss Silas—she's only concerned about my treatment in this household. The work is hard; the days are long, and caring for the children can be trying, but it's not so very different from my life in England.

The difference is, this family doesn't love me. I am their servant.

Rapping at the front door. I smooth the front of my dress and scurry through the kitchen and down the hall. "Won't you come in, Miss Silas?" I say, holding the door open. I step aside as she whisks past me.

She's exactly as I remember: tall and wire-thin, wearing a starched white shirtwaist, navy skirt and jacket. Her dark hair, peppered with a few greys, is drawn into a stern knot at the back of her head. Dark shadows and small wrinkles encircle her eyes. She wears a forced smile. "Thank you, Mary. Is Mrs. Metcalfe at home?" Even as she speaks, the smile remains on her lips.

"Yes, she's in the parlour. Won't you come this way?" I specify the room with a sweep of my arm. Miss Silas walks ahead of me.

Mrs. Metcalfe rises from her seated position on the settee. "How nice to see you again, Miss Silas." I wonder why my mistress would have sat, knowing she would have to rise again within a moment. I suspect it was only for show. "Please have a seat here beside me." Mrs. Metcalfe lowers herself onto the edge of the sofa and crosses her ankles. Miss Silas joins her at the other end, duplicating her posture.

On cue, Clarice enters the room, her four small siblings in tow. Mrs. Metcalfe beams as she introduces her children. I stand at the edge of the room while Miss Silas asks a few questions of the children. After a few moments of conversation, Mrs. Metcalfe motions to Clarice to take the children outside. As they leave, I ask, "Will you be taking tea now, ma'am?"

"Yes, Mary, that would be lovely," she says, dismissing me. I follow the children to the kitchen. They dash out the back door into the garden. Once again, I'm gripped with jealousy as I watch them race to the rope swing and wooden teeter-totters under the maple tree. I hear one child ask Clarice if they can play the Ear Soup game, the one where Clarice pretends to be a witch and chases the children, screaming, "If I catch you, I'm going to cut off your ears and make soup!" I shudder; it's such a perverse game, but apparently the children love it. I suppose it is thrilling in a deliciously, wicked way. Clarice replies, "No, Mama says we must play quietly."

Good girl, Clarice.

Only two years older than her, I would rather be playing Ear Soup with the children than serving tea to the ladies. I wish I were Clarice.

No, that's not true. I wish I were Dorothy . . . with Mama Annie as my real mama.

I blink several times, forcing back tears, and enter the scullery. Mama Annie is not my mother. I have no mother, and apparently, I am no longer considered a child, nor will I ever be again. It's high time I stopped acting like one. It's high time I stop being such a cry-baby.

The water boils. Over the whistle of the kettle, I hear the low murmured voices of my mistress and Miss Silas. I carefully prepare their tea. Everything must be perfect; Mrs. Metcalfe or Miss Silas must not find fault with me today. I arrange the dishes, cutlery, and napkins on a serving tray and, using my backside, I push open the swinging door.

"That is unfortunate," Miss Silas says. "Yes, of course. I'll explain it to her." The ladies raise their eyes and the conversation trails off as I appear in the doorway. I sense I am intruding on a private conversation, and I stand still, uncertain whether to enter.

Mrs. Metcalfe inclines her head. "Mary, come in and set the tea service on the table right here." Her fingers rest on the low table in front of her. After I place it on the table she says, "You may take a seat over there." She points to a chair near Miss Silas.

Miss Silas studies me. "Mrs. Metcalfe was telling me how far you've come this past year. She says you're doing very well in school and, for such a young girl, you've become quite accomplished in your housemaid duties. She also says you're good with the children and you're even being of help in the kitchen."

My shoulders soften; this interview is going very well. I had been informed at Hazelbrae what to expect at the interviews. First, Miss Silas will speak in private with my mistress and then I will have a few moments alone with her, enabling me an opportunity to express my concerns.

Mrs. Metcalfe pours the tea. "Cream and sugar?"

Miss Silas shakes her head, smiling all the while. "Just black. Thank you."

Returning to the earlier conversation, Mrs. Metcalfe adds, "All that's true. As a matter of fact, Mary baked these biscuits this morning. Would you care to try one?"

Miss Silas nods. "Yes, of course."

I wonder if that smile ever leaves her face.

She nibbles a corner of the biscuit and remarks, "They're lovely. Simply melt in your mouth. Well done, Mary!"

The exchange is pleasant, but brief between my mistress and Miss Silas. I find it odd the conversation is about the five children playing outdoors rather than me, but I suppose Mrs. Metcalfe had time to discuss me while I was out of earshot. Finally, Miss Silas steers the conversation in my direction and addresses my schooling. I sit and politely listen. She expresses the importance of applying myself to my studies, as it will be my last year of formal training. If, at the age of twenty-one, I wish to further my education, I may do so at my own expense. Until that time, any education or training I receive will be from my place of service.

My heart sinks. Even though I have no friends, I like school. The notion of working all day, every day, is dreadful. I doubt Clarice will be expected to end her studies in another two years and join the workforce.

"Mrs. Metcalfe, I'd like a few moments alone with Mary now, if you don't mind."

Mrs. Metcalfe's tea cup clinks as it contacts the saucer. "Yes, of course." She walks to the kitchen, pulling the door closed behind her.

A chill settles over the room.

Miss Silas pats the horsehair cushion of the settee. "Mary, come and sit beside me." Her smile has grown wider. It's deceptively kind looking—it confuses me.

An uneasy feeling creeps over me as I cross the room and sit on the edge of the sofa. My hands are trembling, so I tuck them under my knees.

Miss Silas gazes at me. "Mary, I have something I must tell you." She forces the corners of her mouth into a frown. "Mrs. Metcalfe has informed me her family will be relocating to the northwest in the next few months and they will no longer require your services. I'm afraid we will have to find a new station for you."

I'm stunned and awash with emotion as her words sink in. Miss Silas smiles again as she breaks the unpleasant silence. "Mary, have you nothing to say?"

I find my voice. *Yes, I have something to say.* "W-why can't I move with Mrs. Metcalfe? She will still need me wherever she goes, won't she?"

Miss Silas shakes her head and sighs. "Not necessarily. Sometimes a family's circumstances change and placements become temporary." She picks at an invisible piece of lint on the sofa and flicks it to the floor. Her annoying smile grows wider.

"Miss Silas, this is the second time I've been moved," I plea. "It's not fair. I've worked really hard for Mrs. Metcalfe." My palms are sweaty. I yank them out from under my knees and wipe them on my dress.

She takes another sip of tea without looking at me.

Heat rises to my face and I stand. I have plenty to say. "So, what you're saying is I can be shuffled around any time someone fancies a change in their life."

"Mary, that's impertinent of you," she scolds. "Of course not . . . that's not what's happening here. The Metcalfes have simply had a major life change and you've been caught in the middle, that's all." She helps herself to another biscuit.

My entire world has, once again, been jerked out from under me, and all she does is munch on her biscuit and drink her tea with that mock grimace still pasted on her face.

What is wrong with her?

My cheeks burn.

I hate her. I hate being a servant and I hate living in Canada.

I want to go home.

I stamp my foot. I will get her attention and she will listen to me. "It's not fair, I tell you! I hate it here. Send me back to England. Maybe there's some way my foster family can take me back. I want to go home."

"Oh my goodness, Mary, now you're being ridiculous. Obviously, that's not possible. By now, I'm sure your foster family has taken in another home child to replace you. You *do* know we paid them to keep you, don't you?" She doesn't wait for an answer. "It's high time you faced facts. You're a Barnardo child and you're of working age. It's really a shame your foster family didn't make that crystal clear instead of spoiling you and treating you like one of their own." She shakes her head and stares at the wall beyond me.

I turn my face and follow her line of vision. A tiny spider crawls up the white wall. In that moment, I feel less significant than the spider.

I watch it while she speaks. "I positively hate it when foster families do that; it only makes my job that much harder. You children should be raised with a firm hand, taught to work hard at an early age, not coddled and pampered. If foster families would only realize the harm they're doing." The volume in her voice increases substantially. "Mary, I'm speaking to you!"

My head snaps back.

She lowers her voice, just a tad. "Face it. You can't go back. There's nothing there for you. Why do you suppose England's unloading all their orphans into the colonies? Because there's no work. You should consider yourself fortunate. If you hadn't been taken in by Mr. Barnardo and placed into foster care, you would surely have been in a workhouse years ago—that is, if you'd survived infancy." She takes a measured breath and another bite of biscuit.

My gut burns with anger. *Why would I not have survived infancy?* Workhouses are places for the very poor, the destitute. My mother was neither of those things, and even though she hadn't been able to keep me, she knew I was cared for and loved. She would never have allowed me to go to a workhouse. "You're lying! I would not be in a workhouse. My birth mother cared about me!" I grab the front of my skirt and knead it between my hands. "And why are you still smiling?"

Miss Silas springs to her feet. "You saucy little brat!" She spits the words as she hovers over me. The smile has finally crawled from her face and bright red blotches emerge on her cheeks. She narrows her eyes at me and hisses, "You need to learn to hold your tongue and know your place. For your information, you are not a member of this family or any other with whom you'll ever be assigned. You are nothing more than an indentured servant, do you hear me? Have you any idea how much better off you are living here, considering your birth circumstances?"

She's angry, but so am I. I stand my ground, my face inches from hers. "What about my birth circumstances? How would you know anything about it?"

Miss Silas scoffs, a crumb of biscuit crusted to her lip. "As if you do."

There's no holding me back now—the words fly from my mouth. "I do know. My foster mama told me."

She narrows her eyes. "And just what did she tell you?"

I draw my shoulders back. "She said my mother was the daughter of a wealthy couple and because she got pregnant out of wedlock, her family forced her to give me up. I came from a good home and I know my mother loved me. She would not have allowed me to go to a workhouse!"

She huffs. "Really? Is that so? I have no idea where your foster mother got that information, but it's not the truth. She lied to you." Miss Silas' anger has vaporized, like steam rising from her cup, and that smile has slithered back on her face. She pats the seat beside her again and sternly says, "Sit down, Mary."

I'm beginning to hate that gesture—the patting of a seat—lately it only foretells bad tidings. An intense chill settles in my chest and creeps down my appendages, making my hair bristle. Apprehensively, I take a step toward her and lower myself on to the edge of the sofa.

She retrieves her leather satchel off the floor, unbuckles the clasp, and pulls out a manila folder. Opening it, she leafs through a few pages, draws out one, and shoves it toward me. "Read this."

I hesitate a second before extending my arm. I'm trembling as I take it. The paper shivers in my hands.

MARY CLIFTON
Admitted–May 28, 1902
Age–3 months

When the mother was about twelve years old, the grandfather being at the time in a hospital, she was committed, for wandering, to an Industrial School at the instance of the School Board authorities and was transferred from London to Thorp Arch, near Leeds. She had always been very deficient mentally and never got beyond the 1st standard.

At the age of 16, the mother, being very mentally deficient, was placed in service with a Mrs. . . . . At Whynn's Farm. While there, the mother was seduced by a fellow servant, a youth of twenty. When her condition was discovered, he denied responsibility and absconded. The mother was removed to a Rescue Home where her child was born. It was proposed to send her to a penitentiary for a couple of years, and afterwards if possible, to secure her permanent work in the laundry, where she would remain under supervision. Were she to be sent out again in the ordinary way, it would be almost certain that the same misfortune would occur again.

A tear splatters on the paper. I watch as it obliterates a few words from the page, along with my illusory life.

"B-but, she sent me beautiful clothes and gifts."

Miss Silas snatches the paper from my hands. "I don't know who sent you those things, but it certainly wasn't your birth mother." She smiles, and this time it's genuine; she appears to be very pleased with herself. "So, you see, you truly are far better off here with us. And don't worry, Mary, we'll find you a new placement. There doesn't appear to be any lack of work for you Barnardo children," she says as she pats my knee. "Now, go tell your mistress I'm ready to leave."

I wipe the tears from my cheeks. I sense a change come over me. Stumbling to the kitchen, I realize I have learned three things today: my birth mother is not who I believed her to be, there is no one in this vast country who loves me and, most importantly, I am disposable.

"Mary." A voice barely above a whisper speaks my name.

I open my eyes. Florence is standing before me. "I'm sorry to wake you, dear, but it's suppertime."

I brush a tear from the corner of my eye. "Oh, you didn't wake me." I push myself out of the comfortable chair. "I was deep in thought . . . reminiscing."

Florence lays a hand on my arm. "Are you alright?"

"Yes, I'm fine." I nod. "I suppose some of my memories leave me feeling rather melancholy."

"Yes, I get that way when I'm reminiscing, too. If you'd like, we can go in to supper together."

"I'd like that. How did you know where to find me?"

She raises an eyebrow and whispers, "I pulled the chair into this corner a while ago. It is a nice little spot, isn't it?"

"That it is. Perhaps we should pull another over," I say as we stroll together to the dining room.

Chapter 7

I wake with a start, clinging to the wispy fragments of a dream, my heart hammering in my chest. Instinctively, I reach for the robe at the foot of my bed, and shove my arms into the sleeves as my feet hit the floor. With one shaking finger, I part the curtain hanging around my bed, just enough to peek through a slight gap. Heavy drapes are drawn across the window. It takes a moment before my sight adjusts to the inky room.

Florence's bed is beside mine. She sleeps with her curtain drawn, as does Helen, whose bed is across from Florence's. I notice Margaret's curtain isn't closed—her shadowed hulk is visible beneath her covers. My heart races. *Breathe*, I remind myself, *slow and deep*. I listen. Florence snores softly behind her curtain. A repetitive faint knocking, squeaking, and low humming is coming from Helen's. Those faint sounds would not have dragged me from my drug-induced sleep. The mattress squeals against the metal frame as I sit on the edge of my bed.

"I said, be QUIET!" Margaret snarls. I gasp and hold my breath. The constant noise continues.

"Damn you, Helen! Lie down and go to sleep!" Margaret grunts as she throws back her covers and hauls her enormous bulk off the bed. She flings open Helen's curtain.

Helen huddles at the head of her bed, her arms wrapped around her folded legs. Her body is as thin as a thread. She wears a short gown that covers her torso. At the sight of Margaret, she shrieks. It's the first sound, other than the continual humming, I've heard her make.

"Listen, I've had just about enough of your stupid rocking and humming. Now lie down, shut up, and go to sleep!" Grabbing Helen by the ankles, she drags her down the bed.

Helen's short gown bunches up under her bottom. She's frantically screaming and flailing her arms and legs.

In an altered voice, Margaret growls, "You stupid bitch!" The hairs on my neck prickle; that's the second voice I heard in the lavatory three days ago. There was only one woman. Margaret.

"I swear I'll shut you up, if it's the last thing I do." Margaret grabs a handful of Helen's lank hair, twisting it around her wrist. With the other, she clasps a pillow over Helen's face, muffling her screams.

My mind and body finally connect. I can't stand here and watch this abuse happen. Taking a deep breath, I fling open my curtain and run toward them. "Stop!" I shout. "Oh my God, Margaret. STOP!"

Our bedroom door flies open and light from the hallway floods in, along with a nurse and an orderly. I stumble out of the orderly's way as he pushes past me. Standing behind Margaret, he grips her by her arms while the nurse wrestles the pillow from her hand and throws it off the bed. She attempts to pry Margaret's fingers from Helen's hair. In the semi-light, I see Helen's contorted face—her bulging eyes, her mouth open in a silent scream.

The orderly now has Margaret clutched in a bear hug, her arms pinned at her sides. He pushes her, still in his grasp, forward into the hall. Dangling from Margaret's fist is a clump of long blond hair.

Helen lies fetal, her knees pulled to her chest, her body violently rocking back and forth. Her screams fill the air, and no amount of reassurance from the nurse will calm her. The nurse glances at me. "She needs a sedative. I'll be back in a few minutes." I'm still standing in the centre of the room, tears streaming down my face. Staggering to my bed, I sit on the edge, and cover my ears with my hands.

The nurse returns. A quick jab to the arm and, after a few seconds, Helen's body relaxes. The nurse gently pulls the covers over Helen's thin frame, tucking them snugly around her shoulders.

She turns to me. "Now, what about you? Are you okay?"

I nod.

"Margaret didn't touch you?"

"No." My voice sounds choked and strange in my ears. "I'm okay, just scared, that's all. Nurse, what will happen to Margaret?"

"Obviously, she's a danger to others, so she'll be assigned to a different ward, where she'll be monitored closely. She's only been here for about a week now. You're new too, aren't you?"

"Yes. I only arrived a few days ago."

"I thought so. What's your name?"

"Mary. Mary Thistle."

"Nice to meet you, Mary. I'm Nurse Johnson. Mostly I work night shifts, so you shouldn't see me very often."

I attempt a smile. Nurse Johnson seems very kind. I wish she worked day shifts and Nurse Ryckman worked nights.

"I should get back to my station now. Are you quite sure you're alright?"

I nod.

She turns toward the door.

I look over at Florence's drawn curtains. "Nurse Johnson?"

She halts. "Yes?"

"How could Florence have slept through all this commotion?"

She smiles as she walks back to me. "Florence has been here, on and off for some time now, and she's shared this room with Helen for several weeks. I suspect she wears earplugs to block out the humming and rocking sounds. You know, that might not be a bad idea for you either."

"Oh, okay. Thank you." I stand and remove my robe. My hands are still shaking.

Nurse Johnson lays a hand on my arm. "Mary, you've nothing to be afraid of now. With Margaret gone, you're in a good room. Both Florence and Helen are gentle souls."

She pulls the door closed behind her. Drawing the covers over my shoulders, I breathe a sigh of relief. I'm not sorry, not one little bit, that Margaret will sleep elsewhere. I hope it's far away from me, in another wing, preferably behind a locked door.

I wonder what happened to Margaret to shape her into the person she is today. A seed of pity grows in my heart for her as I think about what she may have endured as a child. Certainly, my childhood and adolescent experiences played their part in shaping me into who I am today.

And as I drift off to sleep, a new question forms in my mind: *Is it possible to fully recover from childhood trauma? Will I ever move on?*

The next morning, I'm back in Dr. Clark's office.

"Mary, you look tired. Are you not sleeping well?"

I'd ask him the same question, but that would be inappropriate. There are dark shadows around his eyes. Good Lord, it must be a burden listening to everyone's sad stories. "I normally do, with the drugs. But that wasn't the case last night."

His chair creaks as he leans forward. "Why is that?"

"A disturbance in our room woke me. I was awake for some time after that."

"Oh, that's not good. I trust it was resolved." He doesn't look to me for a response; obviously uninterested in details. Opening the manila folder in front of him, he shuffles through a few pages. "So, let's see where we're at," he says, scanning his notes. "We left off with your stay at Hazelbrae. Shall we carry on from there?"

I nod. "Certainly. I've organized my thoughts. I didn't want another repeat of my first session."

"Good for you." He smiles warmly. "Go right ahead then."

I take a deep breath and relate my placement with the Metcalfes, before the interview with Miss Silas.

"Were you happy with them?"

"No. I wouldn't say I was happy—that would definitely be stretching the truth, for sure—but I was content."

"And how long were you with them?"

"Oh, about a year." After that, I told him about my conversation with Miss Silas, when we were left alone—how she relayed the news of my upcoming relocation and the truth about my birth parents. "That was my second shock of the day."

"Why was that a shock?"

I comb my hand through my hair. Even though I had rehearsed this part, my composure weakens. "Because it wasn't what my foster mother had led me to believe."

He sits for a moment, deep in thought. "And why would your foster mother have lied to you? Is lying something she did often?"

"Oh, no. Mama Annie would never lie. She had no more knowledge of my birth circumstances than I did. After Miss Silas told me the truth, I understood why Mama Annie did it. She made up a story about my birth mother and gave me beautiful gifts, supposedly from her, so I would think I came from a wealthy, respectable family. You see, she wanted me to believe my birth mother loved me; she didn't want me to feel like a cast-off and ashamed of my lowly beginnings."

"Ah, I see. Your foster mother sounds like a remarkably kind woman."

"She is. I'm amazed when I think of all the lovely things she gave me. She never took credit or expected any thanks for them. And she must have purchased those gifts with the pay she received from Barnardo. I doubt she kept much for herself."

"That is commendable. And how did leaving the Metcalfe farm make you feel?"

My, how I hate how his questions always circle back to 'how did that make me feel?' "I was heartbroken, for even though I wasn't treated as one of the family, they were kind to me, and I felt safe. I worked hard and expected to be with them for a long time." I shrug my shoulders. "So, when they wouldn't take me with them, I felt I was nothing more than a possession, an old article of clothing, easily discarded and replaced. I felt betrayed and lied to. Actually, I was feeling like I didn't belong anywhere, that I wasn't good enough to be loved."

I exhale as I feel a shift deep inside, like I've shaved a layer of callus off my heart. I've never been so honest and open about my feelings with anyone, not even Charles.

Dr. Clark studies me and rubs his fingers over his chin. "Hmm," he says. "Mary, I'd like you to consider something."

I lean forward in my chair.

"Is it possible you felt that way because you didn't have anyone in your life who loved you or cared about you?" He pauses for a moment. "What are your feelings on that?"

Tears burn my eyes, and I blink them away. His words cut deep—it hurt to hear them—but he's right, though; I felt that way because I had no one who loved me. I nod.

"You never felt that way with your foster family, did you?"

A sob rises in my throat and I clamp my mouth shut.

Dr. Clark stares at me, waiting for an answer.

I take a moment and calm myself. "No."

"Of course you didn't; they loved you. Mary, it wasn't you. You were always good enough to be loved." He pauses for another moment, allowing time for his words to sink in, and in a soft voice, he says, "So, from there, Mary, where did you go?"

I'm unable to answer; I'm still stuck on the words, 'You were always good enough to be loved.' *Was I?* Without thinking, I say, "But they discarded me."

His brows furrow. "Who?"

"My foster family."

He inclines his head. "Did they have a choice?"

I pause for a moment, deep in thought. The Barnardo Foundation's transactions were done legally. When my birth mother gave me away, she signed papers. When my foster family took me in, they signed papers. Those papers would have specified payments, supplies and dates. If they'd had a choice, if I'd been allowed to stay with them until I was grown, would my foster parents have allowed them to take me away?

I doubt it, and answer, "No. They didn't."

Dr. Clark taps the end of his pen on the paper. "They loved you, but they had no choice. Life circumstances change and, often, there's nothing a person can do to alter it, regardless of how hard they try. So, once again, where did you go from there?"

"My next placement was with the Nelson family. They lived on a farm near Alton. I had only been with them eight months when Mrs. Nelson told me they were moving. Mr. Nelson's father had recently passed, and he had inherited his family farm."

Dr. Clark stares at me over his spectacles.

We've moved along at a faster pace than I imagined. I need time to think; I hadn't gone this far with my thoughts yesterday.

A moment later, the soft tap of his pen gains my attention. "They, on the other hand, took me with them." I am now anticipating the doctor's questions—I know he not only wants my story, but he wants to know my feelings. Rather than wait for him to ask, I volunteer, "It thrilled me they kept me on and, when the time came, I moved with them. I felt fortunate to still be a housemaid; the war had started the previous year and there weren't enough men or boys left behind. Many Barnardo girls were forced to take their places in the barns and fields. Believe me, field work is much harder than housework and I wanted no part of that. Mr. Nelson had a farmhand, Jerry, who slept in the bunkhouse. He was a pleasant, older gentleman and I spent quite a bit of time with him over meals in the kitchen. My, but that man could talk. Sometimes when he would get going, I couldn't help but wonder how much glue it would take to keep his mouth shut."

Dr. Clark chuckles.

Heat rises to my face. Good Lord, I've given my mouth free range. I imagine he's thinking the same thing about me right now.

He smiles warmly. "It appears you've a knack for story-telling, Mary. Please, go on."

Imagine that. Me, a story-teller. A hint of a smile plays on my lips, the first genuine joy I've felt in a long time. "The years slowly crept by, with my daily routine being much the same, day after day and year after year. I no longer attended school, devoting all my time to cleaning, childcare, food preparation, and some light yard work. The Nelsons had six children, ranging in ages from three to twelve, so there was always lots to do around that household. When I was fourteen years old, World War One finally ended and Mr. Nelson hired a new farmhand, Sam. He was twenty years old, fresh home from service. I liked him immediately. No, that's not quite true; I had a crush on him." I blush, immediately wishing I could retract my last sentence. *Why am I so comfortable talking to this man, disclosing my deepest secrets?* I've told no one about Sam. Not one soul.

We're moving on quickly to the years in my life where I've kept secrets. I should be careful what I say.

"Anyway, Sam was always teasing the children and playfully flirting with me. He was handsome and cut quite a figure, even in his overalls. On Saturday evenings he would clean up, and off to town he'd go, carousing with his friends. Once in a while, I'd overhear him bragging to Jerry about some girl or woman he'd met. And even though he'd come in late, usually sauced, the Nelsons liked and depended on him. Sometimes they even left Sam and me in charge of the farm and children when they had social engagements to attend. They felt we were trustworthy and, together, quite capable of handling any situation."

Dr. Clark fishes his pocket watch from his breast pocket. "Excuse me, Mary, our time is up." He slips the loose papers into the folder.

I clamp my mouth shut; I was on a roll with so much more to say, but I suppose it can wait until next time. Besides, I need time to think about what I want to tell him and what I want to keep private.

Dr. Clark stares at the folder in his hands. "I'll see you again Monday afternoon."

Assuming my session is complete, I stand.

He clears his throat. "Before you go, though, there's one more thing. A new treatment has recently become available to us. You may have heard of it—electroconvulsive treatment?"

My heart plunges. With shaking hands, I grasp my chair.

Dr. Clark hesitates as he registers my reaction. "Mary, I understand you're feeling very apprehensive right now, but, with the treatments, I believe we'll see a marked improvement in your well-being within a very short period." He steeples his fingers and looks at me. "I'll be scheduling your treatments to commence soon."

I bite my bottom lip. *How many treatments? How long?*

Obviously, my face is readable. "It all depends on the patient, but eight weeks of treatments seems to be the average."

So, that's how the three-month stay was determined. A week to settle in, eight weeks of treatments, and a few more thrown in for good measure. I take a few deep breaths. Maybe it won't be as bad as I imagine. I find my voice. It sounds feeble to my ears. "Will you be there? Will you be performing the procedure?"

"No, I'm sorry, Mary. I won't be present. A trained doctor and nurse will be with you during the administration of the treatments."

My legs turn to jelly and I collapse into the chair.

Chapter 8

My roommates and I sit at our usual table in the dining hall. I relax as I glance at Margaret's vacant chair; the tension that reigned over this table and bedroom left with her. I turn to Florence. She's studying her plate of food. "Florence, can I ask you something?"

"*May* I ask?"

My hand flies to my mouth. I'm humiliated by her reprimand; it's been years since my betters have criticized me.

She looks at me, puzzled. It's obvious from her face she meant nothing by it. Besides, I need to stop thinking of her or anyone else as my betters—they're simply people who have finer lifestyles and more advantages. Raised as a lady, Florence thinks and speaks proper English. It comes naturally to her, as does correcting someone's grammar. It certainly did with Mrs. Little, my last placement while I was still in the care of the Barnardo Home. Now, what made me think of Mrs. Little? There must be something about Florence that brings her to mind although, other than being well-to-do ladies, I can't think of any similarities between the two.

I still don't know much about Florence or Helen and I'm thinking I'd like that to change.

Florence watches me, patiently waiting for me to continue.

I take a deep breath. "Dr. Clark told me I will start electroconvulsive treatments soon. I was wondering if you've experienced them yourself or if you knew of others who had?"

"Yes, I have."

"You've had them yourself?"

She nods.

I lean across the table. "What was it like?"

Florence lays her fork down and reaches across the table, taking my hand in hers.

Her display of empathy surprises me.

"You mean, what *is* it like?"

I cock my head. "Oh, you're still taking them."

She nods again. "Trust me, you'll be alright. It's really not all that bad. The first time is the worst."

"Do you find they've helped?"

"I believe so."

"How long have you been taking them?"

"Oh, I suppose it's been a few months now," she says, releasing my hand.

I furrow my brows. "A few months? I thought they only lasted eight weeks?"

She looks away. Apparently, this conversation is beginning to upset her. Avoiding eye contact, she continues, "For some. Not for others." She's quiet for a moment and then adds, "Mary, some people are here indefinitely."

Silence hangs between us. Eventually I say, "I'm so sorry, Florence. Please excuse my ignorance. It's just you seem so well."

She sighs. "I'm glad to hear that. I'm hoping my family will feel the same way and allow me to go home, to my own home, soon."

Allow you? I recall Nurse Johnson's conversation with me last night. She told me Florence had been here, on and off, for some time. So, this isn't her first time. My heart breaks for this gentle woman.

"I hope so, too," is all I offer. We eat the rest of our dinner in silence while, between mouthfuls, Helen rocks, and hums her forlorn tune. I know it from somewhere, but where? Or, perhaps I'm so focused on my memories right now, everything seems vaguely familiar or connected. Like Florence and Mrs. Little—really, they're not at all alike.

Still, I wish I could place that tune.

The following morning, Nurse Ryckman wakes me by shaking my shoulder. "No need to get dressed. Put your robe and slippers on and come with me," she whispers. There's scarcely a hint of daylight, the sky a predawn grey.

My stomach muscles clench; something doesn't feel right. "Where are we going?"

"Have you forgotten? You're to start electroconvulsive treatments."

"No one told me they were to start today," I say, rubbing my forehead. "It's so early."

"It's done on an empty stomach before breakfast. Hurry up now. Get a move on."

No wonder I never knew Florence was taking the treatments—I slept through them. We slip from the darkened room into the bright hallway. I trail her as she strides a few paces ahead of me. She stops at the bathroom.

"Go do your business; we don't want you making a mess on the table. But be quick, you hear me?"

I waste no time. We proceed down the silent corridor, through a heavy door, and into a chilly stairwell. As we descend, my body starts to shake. I find it difficult to keep pace with her.

She's standing at the bottom of the stairs. "Any time now, Mary." She taps her foot impatiently, the soft thud echoing in the hushed staircase. She opens another door and I pass through ahead of her.

We're in the basement. It's all white tile and bright lights. Down a long hall, we come to a door, above which hangs a sign: ELECTROTHERAPY. Inside the room is sparse and cold. White lights glare above a high, narrow cot. Four straps hang from it. That bed must be what she referred to as 'the table.' Besides the cot, there is a wheelchair and a closet.

Nurse Ryckman marches over to the table. From underneath, she pulls out a small stool. She pats the thin mattress.

My eyes grow huge; *Good Lord, it's the dreaded pat.*

"Okay, climb up and lie down."

I gasp in quick, shallow breaths and my entire body shakes uncontrollably as I hoist myself onto the cot. I'm terrified and confused. I keep recalling Florence's kind words, 'The first is the worst.' If she's lived through these treatments, surely they can't be all that bad. Of course, it might not seem so terrifying if Nurse Ryckman weren't in such a rush, or if she could show one ounce of compassion—but I suppose that would be asking too much of her.

Last night, for the first time in a long while, I had put my hair in pin curls, an attempt to style my naturally curly hair which has grown far too long. How silly of me. Nurse Ryckman's hands are in my hair, yanking them all out. Never would I have made the effort if I'd known what was in store for me this morning.

I flinch as the door swings open. A booming voice echoes off the walls. "Are we ready, Nurse Ryckman?"

"Almost, doctor." She tugs on another hairpin.

"Almost? What's the holdup?"

"It's Mrs. Thistle's first treatment. She's a bit nervous about the procedure, so I've been taking a little extra time with her."

You liar, I think. *If you're running late, it's your own damned fault.*

She yanks out the last hairpin and, as she rakes her hands through my curls, her ring catches.

I wince and massage my scalp.

She offers no apology but pulls the hairs free from her ring. They float to the pristine white tile. "Now, place your arms by your side and lie still."

The doctor and nurse reach for the straps and pass them across my body. His hand brushes my breasts as he tightens the strap. I snicker nervously and think, *If you're going to be this familiar with me, Doctor, you might have introduced yourself first.*

"What's so funny?" Nurse Ryckman asks as she opens a jar of vile smelling grease and rubs it into my temples.

Hysteria grips me. I'm either going to start laughing or crying, I don't know which. I shake my head and bite my lip—I don't want to do either.

She steps away, standing a few feet behind me, beyond my vision. I fixate on the doctor's every move. He's a tall, middle-aged man, lean and balding. His face is stern with hard, chiseled features, beady eyes and a prominent hooked nose. He moves over to the closet, unlocks it, pulls out a wheeled cart, and rolls it beside Nurse Ryckman. On top is a black box with dials and wires. I press my head into the thin mattress, tilt my head back and watch as he fits two metal plates on my greased temples. He buckles them in place with a strap. They crush into my flesh like a vise.

Nurse Ryckman steps beside me and grasps my chin, forcing my head down and my mouth open. She shoves something in my mouth. It feels like a cloth-covered wire. Between the stench of the grease and the cotton in my mouth, I gag. Her voice is stern and impatient. "You stop that right now," she says. "Now, bite down hard."

The doctor and Nurse Ryckman back away from the cot. He flips a switch. The air crackles with a dazzling brightness. With each blaze, an immense shock courses through my body, causing me to rise against the restraining straps and then drop, deadweight, onto the bed. I hear an absurd snorting sound—I believe it's coming from me.

My body shatters into a million bits.

The light has vanished. I am in a blackness, darker than any moonless, starless night. And in that darkness, I am cleansed.

When I first open my eyes, I do not know who I am, nor where I am, and I'm seated in the wheelchair with no memory of getting there. Slowly, it all comes back. The doctor is gone and Nurse Ryckman is tidying the room. She lays the hairpins in my palm and I gaze at my open hand before slowly making a fist. Fascinated, I watch my fingers curl, encasing the pins in my palm. I rotate my hand and admire the tiny veins, a network of miraculous vessels carrying blood to the tips of my fingers.

A tear drops to my wrist and trickles onto my robe.

I scarcely register as she wheels me to the elevator and back up to the main floor. She pushes my bedroom door open with her backside, as a young orderly saunters past. He stares at me, a knowing smirk on his face, and then he dips his head, and runs his tongue over his lower lip. I gasp. *Good Lord, it's Sam.* I squeeze my eyes shut—I must be hallucinating—Sam is not a young man anymore, no more than I am a young woman. Nurse Ryckman pulls the wheelchair into the room and roughly puts me to bed. Without a word, she leaves.

I lie still, listening to the sounds of the room: the occasional click of the hot water running through the iron coils of the heating system, Florence's purring snores, and Helen's rocking. *Does that poor girl ever sleep?* I can't sleep. My mind is a whirlwind, struggling to understand what happened to me. How long was I unconscious? Even though it felt like I was in that velvety darkness for a long time, I know I wasn't.

It's early dawn. Thin sunlight trickles through the partially opened window curtain. I shudder, recalling the initial impact—the voltage—the brutality. Did Charles know what they were going to do to me? And if he did, how could he have possibly consented to it? I'm bewildered, torn between the violence of the treatment and the tranquility of the darkness. Another tear escapes the corner of my eye and spills onto the starched pillowcase. I raise my hand to wipe it away. It's still formed in a fist. Opening it, I regard the handful of hairpins.

But what I really notice is my hand is not trembling. I shake my head. I can't believe the change I'm feeling with only one treatment. Surely it won't last, or why would I require more?

"Okay, Mary," I whisper to myself. "You've work to do. You came here to get better and to do that, you're going to have to go through with these treatments."

Oh my, did I just say that aloud?

October, 1919

Five years of my youth have passed, working for Mrs. Nelson. I'm seventeen and Sam is twenty-three. Through the kitchen window, I watch his lithe frame spring off the wagon seat. He secures the horse's reins, saunters to the house, and slips through the back door. His gaze flashes around the room. "Where's everyone?" Sam's careful and cunning—he'll not be caught flirting with me. Mrs. Nelson has witnessed nothing, and yet I sense she knows how Sam and I feel about each other, and I fear she is growing displeased with me and my performance. But, in my defence, it's difficult to focus when my mind is always on Sam. I guess she's too old to remember what it's like to be in love.

Still, I must try harder. I dry my hands on a tea towel and nervously glance at the closed kitchen door. "They're upstairs. You off to town?"

Seizing my damp hand, he pulls me to him. He wraps his arms around me, his open mouth covering mine. It grazes across my cheek and I sigh as his tongue teases my earlobe. "Come to me tonight." His lips move down my neck, his breath warm and moist.

Shivers race over my skin. I lean against him, my legs incapable of holding my weight. "Where? When?" I murmur. My mouth hungrily searches for his.

His voice is throaty and his eyes smoulder. "Slip out to the bunkhouse after everyone's asleep. Jerry's away tonight—it'll just be us."

My body is willing, but my mind hesitates. The bunkhouse. Alone. I pull away. "No, I can't do that."

His tongue grazes his bottom lip. "Of course you can." He grins as his powerful arms encircle my waist. He backs me against the wall, leaving me no escape. I gasp as his hand creeps up over my ribs, cupping my breast. His thumb rubs circles around the nipple. My belly muscles clench as the nipple hardens under his touch. Every cell in my body tingles with excitement as his mouth, once again, finds mine.

Damn. My conscience makes another rude appearance. According to Miss Silas, this situation is exactly what happened to my mother. My inner voice screams for me to stop, but I'm helpless; my body seems to have a will of its own, so I silence the intrusive voice and melt into his arms. I will not listen to it—I love Sam and he loves me—I can tell by the way he looks at me, holds me, and kisses me. Sometimes, when Mr. and Mrs. Nelson leave Sam and me in charge, we pretend this is our farm and our family. Did he not comment, only last week, about what a fine wife I will make? I'm sure what he meant to say is 'what a fine wife I will make *for him.*'

He withdraws, leaving me breathless.

I grip the door handle for support. "Okay," I whisper. "I'll come."

"That's my girl." He flashes me a smile, and then he's gone, just like that.

He called me 'my girl.' I'm Sam's girl. I watch his tall, lean frame stroll away, a slight swagger to his step.

The door opens and Mrs. Nelson enters the kitchen. Her voice, normally soft, is raised. "Mary, have you not finished the lunch dishes yet?"

I flinch. Keeping my face turned to the window, I compose myself. I run the back of my hand across my swollen lips.

She moves toward me, her head inclined. "You're flushed. Are you not feeling well?"

I lower my face and return to the sink of dirty dishes. "I'm fine."

Mrs. Nelson stands at the window. My eyes follow hers. Sam, wearing a smug, satisfied smile, climbs onto the wagon. He takes his bottom lip into his mouth, and flicking the reins, he drives the horse and wagon out the lane.

The house is silent and ink-shadowed as I pad, shoeless, down the back staircase, and out into the moonlit yard. I drop my shoes and slip my feet into them. The autumn crescent moon hangs over the black silhouette of the large bank barn. It's a warm night and yet I shiver. I press my crossed arms to my chest; butterflies beat against my ribcage.

I've had hours now to think, flipping back and forth between following my desires and my conscience, and I have finally come to a solution. So, for the third time in the last three minutes, I remind myself why I'm here, outside, in the dark. Sam is waiting for me and he deserves an explanation. I'm going to the bunkhouse to talk to him—that's all—nothing more. I'll tell him Mrs. Nelson is becoming dissatisfied with me; I can't risk upsetting her. I'll tell him we can't allow this behaviour to go any further; I'm not that kind of girl. I'm saving myself for my husband and wedding night.

I pick my way over the yard and gently tap on the door. I listen. There's no sound. I rap again, a wee bit harder. Finally, I hear a groan, the squeaking of a bed frame, and heavy footsteps. Sam opens the door, rubbing his hands across his face. It's apparent he was asleep.

I step back, shocked. *Why was he was already sleeping? Was he only teasing me?*

Comprehension slowly registers on his face. His mouth breaks into that charming smile—the one I can't resist. He pulls me inside and kicks the door shut.

It thumps loudly, and I jump. His arms snake around my waist as he murmurs, "Ah, Mary, relax. You've nothing to fear." And then his mouth is on mine, and in one breath, we've picked up where we left off hours ago.

His experienced hands discard my cardigan. It drops to the floor while his fingers make quick work of the buttons of my blouse.

My conscience has lost its voice. I'm aware of one thing and one thing alone—my desire.

Sam tugs at the hem of my blouse, freeing it from the waist of my skirt. It slides off my arms and puddles on the floor. In the next motion, his fingers slip beneath the straps of my chemise. They slip off my shoulders. He trails his lips down my neck while he moves to the bed, drawing me along with him. The mattress squeaks as he sits. I moan as his hands and mouth fondle my breasts.

I am utterly lost to him. Lacing my fingers through his hair, I hang my head, my long curls tumbling across my face. I tremble as he cups and squeezes my breasts together and a whimper escapes my lips as his tongue circles around one nipple and latches on.

There's pounding on the door and a deep voice yells, "Sam, wake up!"

My head jerks, my eyes fly open. I'm motionless, shocked, like a cornered, frightened animal.

More pounding. "Sam, wake up! Didn't you hear that bang? There's someone out here."

I spin around and scramble across the floor as the door swings open. The moonlight spills around Mr. Nelson's silhouette, illumining me.

"Holy Christ," he says.

I pull my chemise up over my bare breasts and snatch up my blouse and cardigan. Standing upright, I glance over at Sam. He's rubbing his eyes as if he's just waking.

Mr. Nelson stares at me, his mouth set in a harsh line. He growls, "Mary, you get to the house right now."

My cheeks burn with shame as I stumble through the yard to the house. The kitchen lights are on, Mrs. Nelson's anxious face framed in the door window, and as I come near, she pulls it open. I brush past her, and race to the staircase.

"Mary, you come right back here. I want to talk to you."

I ignore her and climb the stairs.

She shrieks, "Girl, don't you dare walk away from me when I'm speaking to you!"

Mary, you get to the house! Mary, you come right back here! Mary, do this! Mary do that! I cover my ears with my hands. Staggering up the stairs, I slam my bedroom door and curl into myself on my small bed. My heart hammers in my chest and my ears buzz. My mind runs wild, imagining the conversation between Mr. Nelson and Sam. Is Sam defending me? Is he telling Mr. Nelson he had planned the rendezvous? That he loves me and is going to marry me? Or is he actually pretending Mr. Nelson had woken him when he pounded on the door?

My heart hopes it was the first, but my instinct tells me it was the last.

Eventually, my heartbeat slows and the droning in my ears recedes. I hear the mantel clock in the parlour chime twelve times and Mr. Nelson's return.

His voice climbs the stairs. "Well, go upstairs and get her. Make her come down and explain her side of the story. I've heard Sam's and, to tell you the truth, I don't believe a word of it. Let's hear what Mary has to say. Surely we owe her that much."

Mrs. Nelson's voice is low, and I strain to catch her words. I pick up a few, "she's always distracted. She's careless and lazy."

"But Mary's been a good hard worker for us for over five years. And, yes, she's almost a woman, but she's also very naïve and impressionable. Except for going to church on Sundays and occasionally helping you with the shopping, she never leaves this farm."

Once again, I only catch a few of Mrs. Nelson's words. "Flirting . . . she's the one who starts . . ."

"No, that can't be true. You know how Sam is. I'll bet my bottom dollar he's been leading her on for a long time. And I don't believe one word of what he said—there's no way Mary snuck out there to be with him without an invitation and some damn good persuasion."

Mr. Nelson's not one to swear. He must be furious; this is the second time tonight.

Mrs. Nelson speaks again. This time I hear the word "promiscuous."

"Oh, c'mon. Mary's not promiscuous. She's not even eighteen years old and Sam's likely got her believing he loves her. And even though he did a good job of pretending, he sure as heck wasn't sleeping when I came upon them. I'm telling you, this is not all Mary's fault!"

My heart swells with gratitude toward him, and I breathe a sigh of relief. Mr. Nelson understands—he'll defend me even if Sam won't. Everything will be fine.

I slip out of bed and press my ear against the door. Mrs. Nelson's speaking. " . . . give us trouble. I can always get another girl. Someone younger. I don't want her around our daughters anymore." Her voice becomes stronger, more forceful. "What kind of example is she setting for our girls? Think about that for a minute."

"Ah, but Mary's always been such a good girl." Mr. Nelson's voice grows soft. He's caving.

"You can stop defending her right now; I've made up my mind. I'll get in touch with Miss Silas in the morning."

I back away from the door. *Oh my God, what have I done? Where will they send me now?*

I crawl back to my bed.

Every loss, every harsh word, and every heartbreaking memory of the past seven years surfaces. My body shakes uncontrollably. I draw my knees into my chest, and hugging myself, I weep.

Chapter 9

We're seated in our secluded corner of the library. Florence raises her eyes from the book lying in her lap and asks, "So Mary, tell me. How are your treatments coming along?"

I raise my hand to my temple and frown. One week has passed and I have now endured the second shock treatment.

She frowns. "Not so good, then," she says, sympathetically. "Trust me, they'll get easier."

She scolded Margaret for prying into my affairs, but since she started this conversation, I ask, "Have you been here long?"

She nods. "Yes. This isn't my first time. Actually, I've spent a good portion of the past two years inside this building."

"Oh," I say, feigning ignorance. Florence fascinates me. I'm lonely, and if I were to choose one person in this concrete fortress to be my friend, it would be her. Getting to know her would make my stay more tolerable and, I'll be honest, I'd love to know her story.

Luckily for me, I don't have to pry; she starts the following exchange. "What about you, Mary? Is this your first time?"

"It is." I hesitate, unsure whether I should ask, but, with years of practice listening to others and not talking about myself, curiosity gets the better of me. "I know this is none of my business, but you seem so well. Florence, why are you here?"

She looks me straight in the eye and replies, "You said that before—that I look well. It appears a nice hairdo and a little makeup can be very deceiving."

Florence is always the image of perfection, beautifully dressed and groomed. "That's very true."

"I could ask the same question of you, except, to be perfectly honest, you didn't look so well when you arrived." The suggestion of a smile plays on her lips.

Ah, she's avoiding the question; she doesn't want to talk about. I hold back; I'm not sure I'm ready to answer that question either.

As if sensing my reluctance, she leans forward in her chair. "The other day I overheard you telling Margaret that you live on a farm . . . you're a farmwife."

My shoulders relax. I can talk about this: our farm, Charles, my boys. "Yes, that's correct. Our farm lies west of Eastgate. It's been in my husband's family since it was Crown Land. It's not a large farm—about seventy acres, more or less. We raise beef, hogs, and chickens and have a few horses. Like most, we've struggled over the past several years and obviously, we're not well-to-do . . ." *Why did I say that?* "Anyway, Charles and I have been married eighteen years now and we have two teenage sons, Ernest, and Tommy." I've been rambling on about myself and finally remember my manners. I glance at her hand and notice a solitaire diamond and wedding band. "And what about you, Florence? Tell me about your home, your husband?"

"My home is in London, although I've seen little of it the past two years. My maid lives in the house and cares for it while I'm away."

Hmm, a fine home with a maid. Somehow, I'm not surprised. "And your husband?"

She glances away. "He died in the war. Two years ago."

My heart physically aches for her. "Oh, Florence. I'm so sorry." I pause. She's likely a little older than me—perhaps she has children. I hesitate to ask more questions, but I push on, "Children?"

Florence leans back in her chair and folds her arms across her midriff. I sense I have crossed the line. She turns her regal head and gazes out the window, a tear pooling in the corner of her right eye. "No, none that lived to take their first breath."

I'm thrown back some twenty-odd years. I remember dusting a reproduction print hanging in the upper hallway of Mrs. Little's fine home in Toronto. Picasso is the artist, the work entitled Woman with Crossed Arms. I always wondered why Mrs. Little would have chosen that painting, it being in stark contrast to the other lovely pieces adorning her walls: Monet in her bedroom, Constable in the parlour, and Renoir in the dining room. Ah, how Mrs. Little loved her fine art. I carefully studied this painting as I dusted the frame. I examined the woman's soft gown, her slender fingers, her drooped shoulders, and her sad, languid mouth. My eyes found hers. I absorbed her empty stare, one glistening tear about to fall from the corner of her right eye. Overwhelmed by a feeling of utter despair, I backed away from those eyes.

Hanging my head, I whisper. "I'm so sorry."

She startles me by saying, "Mary, you asked me why I was here."

Through my lashes, I watch her extend her arms and raise the cuffs of her blouse, exposing her wrists.

"This is why."

I cover my mouth, silencing my cry. Two scars are visible across each slender wrist, one slash is seasoned and white, the other an ugly red welt. I search for words. When they do finally come, my throat constricts and the words catch, "Oh, Florence, I apologize . . . I had no right to ask."

She draws her cuffs down, crosses her arms, and tucks them against her sides. Staring off into nothingness, her face softens and falls.

Through blurred vision, I regard her.

The woman sitting across from me is a living reproduction of Picasso's Woman with Crossed Arms. It's little wonder she wears the same look of despair. I'm drawn to her, but at the same time, I want to retreat. Is it in my best interest to get to know her, to spend time with her, to befriend her?

Florence raises her face and moistens her lips before speaking. "Mary, everyone is here for a reason."

We sit in silence. I feel the need to offer her something and, as I know she will never ask, I say, "Florence, we have something in common, although I have no visible scars to remind me. I was going to take my own life too, by hanging myself, and I might have been successful had it not been for Charles—he caught me in the act." I take another breath and shake my head. "Oh my. Now when I think of the appalling ugliness of it . . . what Charles would have faced when he found me. And of all the places to choose, I chose the outdoor privy."

Florence leans forward in her chair and peers into my eyes. Hers are full of understanding and compassion. "So, you have a good husband?"

"Yes. Charles is a wonderful man." I think for a moment and add, "I know he loves me and wants me to get better, but I still can't understand how he agreed to send me here, especially if he knew about the shock treatments."

"Did you give him a choice?"

Choices. Dr. Clark and I had spoken of choices a few days ago.

I hang my head again. "No, I suppose I didn't."

I sit quietly, thinking. It appears the only thing Florence and I have in common is our suicide attempts. We come from different worlds. I envision what I think her life might have been: she had a gentle upbringing in a nurturing home, her life spread out before her, full of promise. She married a good man but never felt the joy of bringing a child into this world; and now her husband is gone, leaving her alone. Her life may have started out idyllic, but it has deteriorated to this.

In contrast, my life has been anything but idyllic. However, I married a good man and have given birth to two healthy sons. I won't let myself think of the others; my heart is too full of empathy for Florence—I've travelled that same road far too many times myself.

In my mind, I exchange places with her. I imagine I am here without Charles and my sons waiting at home. *Would I want to get better?*

I think not.

Unlike the time I dusted the portrait, I will not back away. If Florence needs a friend, I will be that friend.

We've both said all we want. We raise our books and retreat into our own thoughts.

Dr. Clark refills his fountain pen and opens my folder. "So, tell me, Mary, you've had two treatments so far. Have you noticed any change?"

I ponder his question for a moment. "Well," I say, "my experience was dreadful, but then I think you know that much. It's a terrifying experience."

"Yes, so I've heard. It will get easier, I promise. But, you haven't answered my question—have you noticed any change?"

I suck in my lower lip and nod. "Yes, I feel there's been a slight improvement."

"Are you able to describe it?"

"I think so. Immediately after both treatments, I noticed my trembling had stopped. It came back after a bit, but it doesn't seem as bad. Also, I felt very calm afterward, but then that didn't last long either."

"It will. And those positive side effects will last longer with every treatment."

I glance at him and smile. "I'm looking forward to that." A giggle bubbles up inside me and slips through my lips. "Oh, no, I don't mean I'm looking forward to more treatments—can't say as I like them at all—but I'll gladly take the side effects."

The delightful sound I made surprises me. Other than the hysteria snicker before my first treatment, I cannot remember the last time I genuinely giggled.

"Wonderful, that's what I want to hear." He studies his notes. "Shall we continue? It appears we left off with the Nelson family. They had hired a new man, Sam. Would you like to carry on from there?"

So, I tell him of my growing affection for Sam, how I fell in love with him and believed he loved me too, until that fateful night. I don't go into detail about our stolen rendezvous in the bunkhouse—I've never talked about it with anyone, not even Charles. Actually, Sam's name has never come up in conversation. To this day, that event still leaves me feeling queasy.

"So, how did you become aware Sam didn't love you?"

I search for a way to express myself delicately. "Um. Let's just say he deceived me. He denied making advances toward me, even though he had been playing with my affections for well over a year. I believe he told Mr. Nelson I initiated the relationship."

He pushes his glasses up on his nose. "Hmm, not a gentleman, then?"

"No, not at all. He didn't love me. He was only looking for a romantic diversion on the farm and I fit the bill. I was just another girl who fell for his good looks and charm."

"I see."

I bet if I stall, he's going to say 'And, how did that make you feel?' I'll give him ten seconds . . .

"And how did that make you feel?"

A grin tugs at my mouth again, so I bite my bottom lip. A second later, the seriousness of his question strikes me like a slap to the face. *How did that make me feel?* The emotions of that night wash over me again. They're so painful and given the choice, I'd rather not experience them again.

"Mary, I've asked you a question. How did that make you feel?"

My, but he's persistent today. I huff. "Fine. If you must know, it made me feel like all the other times—I was of no value, disposable, easily replaced. The only difference between this time and the others is that I was starting to believe those things myself. Sam proved that to me. He spurned me. Rather than eating in the kitchen with us—and by us I mean Jerry, the old farmhand and me as we were not allowed to eat our meals with the family—Sam carried his plate out to the bunkhouse. Only Mr. Nelson and Jerry remained kind to me. They both knew how

Sam was, that he had led me on, but Sam was a hard worker and Mr. Nelson didn't want to let him go. So he stayed on, suffering no consequences for his actions and Mrs. Nelson's new housemaid, a young Barnardo girl, moved in the day I left."

The walls are coming down.

"And, as time carried on, I grew more ashamed of myself, an illegitimate bastard and a Barnardo Home Child." I take a deep breath and add, "It's hard to explain. Unless you're one yourself, you can't possibly understand the shame that comes with the term Home Child. We were outcasts and often treated that way."

Raising my eyes, I stare at him, all spiffy-polished in his three-piece suit, sitting in his comfortable leather chair at his cherry desk. I feel my anger roiling like ocean waves in a storm. I swallow it down. Dr. Clark has been nothing but kind and understanding—I have no reason to be angry with him. *Still, how could he know? How could he possibly understand?* I add, "I don't expect you to. No one understands."

He nods, but says nothing.

By the look on his face, I can tell he knows what I had been thinking. "I'm sorry," I mumble.

"What are you sorry for, Mary?"

I stare at him again. "I think you know."

"Yes, I believe I do. But I want you to say it."

I glance away. *Good Lord, it wasn't enough I apologized—now he wants me to explain.* I can't bring myself to tell him what I was thinking, what I felt. I blurt, "I'm sorry for all the other Home Children, the ones who were less fortunate than me."

Dr. Clark blinks twice. "Really? That's what you were thinking?"

"Yes." I hurry on, not giving him time to interrupt. "Over the years, I've met other Barnardo children and their stories aren't so different from mine, although many are far worse. Some children were abused, starved, and forced to live in barns, even in winter. Some were told so many times they were worthless liars, thieves, and beggars that some beat-down part of them eventually believed it. In my heart, I knew I wasn't a thief or a beggar, but what I had learned was I was nothing more than a servant, bought and paid for, traded off when I was no longer needed or wanted."

It feels good to say these words—I've been holding them in all my life. "There was no one left in my life I could trust. And honestly, at times, I didn't trust myself. If a situation called for it, it wasn't hard to tell a lie. I knew it was wrong, but if I thought a lie would save my skin, I didn't hesitate to use it." I sense another layer of leathery skin peeling from my heart.

Dr. Clark scribbles on the paper and raises his head. "Are you still deceitful?"

I didn't see that question coming. Blood rushes to my face. "Um. No."

"You're sure about that?"

"Maybe I am." I squirm. "Sometimes I am," I say, lowering my face. "It's a hard habit to break." I glance at him. "Mind you, I only tell little white lies."

He runs his index finger over his chin. "Such as?"

I advert my eyes. He knows—I told one a few moments ago, but there's no way I'm revisiting that. My thoughts wander. Before that, when did I lie? I'm at home and Ruby is whining and scratching at the back door. *Oh Good Lord, that was no little white lie, but I'm sure as heck not going to tell him about that one either.* I pick at my cuticle. "I can't think of an example right now."

"Okay then. From there, where did you go?"

I exhale, relieved to be moving on. "I left the Nelson Farm two weeks later. My next position was at the Ontario Ladies College in Whitby."

Dr. Clark makes note of this information on the paper and then lays down his pen. "It appears this is another excellent place to conclude our session for the day. Sometimes, listening to your story, I feel like I'm turning pages in a book and this is the fitting end of a chapter. Perhaps you should write a memoir. You've a way of telling a story, Mary, and you certainly have a story to tell."

Oh my, I can't see that happening; I've never even shared these memories with Charles. No, they're better left dead and buried.

"Shall we continue from here on Thursday?"

I nod and rise.

"Your next scheduled treatment is tomorrow. They'll be administered three times per week, on Mondays, Wednesdays and Fridays. I expect we'll see some very positive results soon." He closes my file. "That'll be all for today."

I head straight to the library. It's quiet there and I need to be alone. Entering, I notice Florence's and my favourite corner is empty.

"Well, that certainly didn't go the way I planned—letting my mouth run on like that." I'm talking to myself. Again. I glance around to see if anyone heard me, but I'm alone. *Good Lord, I can't let that become a habit.*

I relax into the chair, my thoughts drifting to the time after the Nelsons. This short period of my life is one I like to remember the least.

November, 1920

Two months ago, Miss Silas and I arrived at the Ontario Ladies' College in Whitby in a horse-drawn coach. We drove through the gates and up the long drive toward the massive, three-story mansion. My eyes grew wide; I had not seen a building of this proportion and grandeur since I arrived in Canada. The driver deposited me at the front door and unloaded my sorry, little trunk—it looked so out of place amongst such grand surroundings.

Miss Silas turned to the driver. "Please wait. I shouldn't be more than a few moments." The front door opened, and we were issued into a beautifully decorated reception room. A porter retrieved my trunk, and I watched as he whisked it away.

Time drags. The days and weeks pass, sluggishly becoming months.

My duty is to clean the students' rooms—the students being the daughters of the wealthy who attend this all-girl boarding school. Their ages range from ten to eighteen years. I'm slightly older than the eldest student.

In my mind, I've sorted them into three groups. The first group, the vast majority, is aloof. I am a subordinate and treated as such. To those, I am invisible. The second, the minority, is young and kind-hearted. They haven't grown callous . . . yet. And then there is the third, those who are haughty and mean-spirited. They treat me with contempt.

I detest them.

My tiny garret room is on the third floor and, typical of all grand houses, the servants' staircase, which runs from the kitchen to the servants' quarters, is narrow and dark. In contrast to my sparse, utilitarian room, the girls' rooms are beautiful. They've scattered their personal items about—porcelain dolls, tennis rackets, ice skates, lace doilies, and china tea services—items they have brought from home. I have nothing nice, other than my Annie doll and a few books. I long for pretty things of my own, but I've no money to buy them; my earnings are held in trust until I reach the age of twenty-one. Sometimes I dream of the lovely purchases I'll make when I receive those funds. Surely after ten years of service it will amount to quite a sum, plenty to purchase new dresses, shoes and coats. I allow my imagination to expand. Perhaps I'll even have enough funds to buy a hope chest for household items like china, silverware, and linens, items for the home I hope to have someday. I spend my solitary hours alone, dreaming about what my life might become, if I was happily married, caring for a home and a family of my own. I imagine a life like Mama Annie's.

But three long years loom ahead of me—an eternity—before any of those dreams can conceivably come true. And even after I've served those years, I will still need to support myself, and domestic work is all I know.

So, as I ever so carefully dust and sweep the young ladies' rooms, I wonder if I will ever have a home of my own, or will I be forever cleaning another woman's handsome home?

I collect the pail holding my cleaning supplies, the broom, and dustpan and leave Sylvie's room. She's a sweet young girl who reminds me of my foster sister, Evelyn, in England. Evelyn was only five years old when they took me away—I wonder if she even remembers me. I miss them all, and as much as we keep up correspondence, my heart is still so lonely for them that sometimes I cry into my pillow at night. In the entire world, they were the only people who loved me. I cling to those memories; some days they're the only thing that keeps me going.

I wish Sylvie and I could be friends, but I know the rules—there's to be no familiarity between staff and students. However, I've not made friends with any staff yet either; for some reason, of which I am not aware, they're either standoffish or they intimidate me.

It's a lonely life I live.

I close Sylvie's door and trudge down the hall to Martha's room. Martha—even her name leaves a sour taste in my mouth—belongs to the third group of girls. She's seventeen, haughty, and a goody-two-shoes who never misses an opportunity to make me feel inferior.

The door is slightly ajar. According to proper protocol, I am to knock on the door before entering and only clean the room if it is unoccupied. As I am about to knock, I hesitate, my hand hanging in mid-air. I hear soft voices and my name spoken. Standing perfectly still, I eavesdrop. I know it's wrong, but if they're talking about me, I have a right to know what they're saying.

"No, it's true," I hear Martha say. "That's why she was dismissed from her last station. Apparently, she was caught in the hired men's bunkhouse in the middle of the night, and from what I hear, she barely had a stitch on!"

I hear gasps. *How many girls are in there with her?* My knuckles whiten on the handle of the bucket. I picture them hanging on her every word, their little rodent faces all moon-eyed, anticipating the next titillating morsel.

Martha lowers her voice. “And,” she murmurs, “get this—the farmhand wasn’t even awake. Imagine the nerve! Mary was undressing, right down to her birthday suit, when her master found her.” Martha cackles. “It’s little wonder they sent her to work at an all-girls’ school.”

Another voice titters before adding, “I’ve heard Barnardo girls are *all* easy. They better keep a close eye on her or she’ll be slipping into the custodians’ quarters.”

Titters and whispers follow me as I back away from the door. I slink down the hall like some hollowed-out soul, deposit my cleaning supplies at the next door, and go in search of the Head Mistress. I don’t know how Martha heard this story—I assume Miss Silas passed it on to someone in the upper ranks and from there, it has trickled down to the students.

But this I *do* know—I can’t stay here any longer. I need to go far away, far enough my past can’t follow me.

For the first time in my life, I feel shame for simply being who I am.

Chapter 10

Three weeks have passed inside the walls of this asylum. At this time of year, as there is no gardening, the able-bodied are encouraged to help in other ways. My, but it feels good to be physically active again. I arrived here exhausted from the never-ending chores on the farm, but now the time drags. I've been assigned to work in the laundry with Florence and Helen two mornings each week. Helen is stationed at the washing machine, and Florence sits before a sewing machine, mending tears and sewing on patches.

They've given me the simple job of pressing. I've had lots of practice ironing over the years, but there's so much to press here: pillowcases, tea towels, nurses' uniforms, aprons, not to mention all the patients' clothing.

As I wait for the iron to heat, I slip my fingers inside an envelope and draw out a beautiful get-well card and a brief letter from Jean. I study the picture of the flowers on the card: white hydrangeas, pale pink roses and lacey ferns. Now, just where did she find a card with a picture of her signature flowers?

I open the letter and read:

Dear Mary,

I know you say I always have the right words, but for once in my life, I don't. I hope this card says all I cannot.

Bob and I are checking in on Charles and the boys. They're all doing remarkably well, but they miss you so. Please don't worry about them though—just concentrate on yourself—we'll make sure they're okay until you return home.

Please get better real soon. The South Centre Road is not the same without you.

Love Jean.

Oh, how I miss her. I smooth the letter, place it in the card, and tuck it inside my dress pocket to reread later.

I sprinkle a pillowcase with water droplets from a glass bottle, which reminds me of a huge salt shaker. I gaze across the laundry at Helen. This isn't the first time I've stared at her as she works. She's simply a wonder to watch as she drags the heavy sheets and towels from the soapy water of the washing machine and feeds them through the large wringer into the rinse tub. The timid soul upstairs, the one who hugs her folded legs to her chest as she rocks and hums, cannot be found in this capable young woman. Down here, in the bowels of this vast building, Helen is focused and competent.

Her back is to me, and as if she feels my eyes on her, she turns. My cheeks flush, but she doesn't seem troubled that I was staring at her. She inclines her head a wee bit and returns my intense gaze. Her mouth softens, the corners drawing up ever so slightly, and her eyes sparkle. My face breaks into a huge smile—she's warming up to me.

I lower my eyes and run the hot iron across the pillowcase. Ironing is a mundane job, taking little concentration, and giving me time to organize my thoughts. I've found it's good to talk to Dr. Clark; every time I share more of my story, my heart sheds another callus.

November 1920

I'm in the care and employ of Dr. and Mrs. Randall, a childless, middle-aged couple. Theirs is one of several Victorian grand homes sitting proudly on Ridgeland's treed Main Street. Since arriving in Canada, this is the first time I almost feel like I have a real family.

Almost.

It's been a long, tiring day, my mistress having entertained friends with a dinner party. I'm putting the last of the pots and pans away when Mrs. Randall enters the kitchen. She lays a hand on my arm. "Mary, are you okay? You seemed preoccupied when you were serving dinner."

I close the cupboard door. "I'm sorry, Mrs. Randall. I'll try harder next time."

"Oh, I'm not complaining. Your service was impeccable. I was only concerned; you didn't seem yourself."

I really could use a confidant, someone to talk to. I look into her kind face. "Mrs. Randall, could we talk?"

She pulls out a chair from the table and sits. "Of course. Come and sit, please."

I settle into a chair. "I suppose I was a little preoccupied this evening. You see, my thoughts have been with my foster mother."

She raises her eyebrows, concern written on her face. "Have you had news? Is something wrong?"

"Oh no," I quickly reply. "Everything's fine, as far as I know. It's just being here with you and Dr. Randall calls her to mind all the time. She was a parlourmaid, employed by a doctor in England too. Of course, that was before she married."

Mrs. Randall's face softens. "You must miss her very much."

"I do. But, other than the fact that I'm a Barnardo Home Child, it seems I'm following in her footsteps. I'm proud of that, really I am, and I'd like to think that someday I might marry a prosperous farmer, like she did, and live in a lovely farmhouse."

"Oh, that would be splendid, wouldn't it? I hope you do too, if that's what you want."

I stall for a moment. "Well, that's the trouble; I don't know what I want." I hesitate a moment. "Now, I wouldn't want you and Dr. Randall to think I'm not appreciative—you're so kind and generous, giving me evenings and Sunday afternoons off—I've never had free time to myself for as long as I can remember."

Mrs. Randall looks confused. "Everyone should have a little time to do as they please."

I've become sidetracked. Having time off is not the point I'm trying to make. "Yes, I suppose they should. But until now, I haven't. Anyway, what I'm trying to say is that, as thankful as I am, I'm growing tired of being a housemaid. But with no formal schooling and no other training, this is all I know. What if I never marry? Will I always be a housemaid?" My shoulders slump. "Sometimes I'm overcome thinking this is all my life will ever be."

Mrs. Randall is deep in thought. She's grown silent.

Oh, Good Lord, what have I done? She'll think I'm dissatisfied, and then she'll find some reason to send me away. My throat clenches and I swallow hard. "I'm sorry, Mrs. Randall, I shouldn't have bothered you with my concerns."

"Don't apologize, Mary. You've surprised me, that's all."

Suddenly I'm bone-tired. Wishing her a goodnight, I retire. I climb the only staircase in this home, the grand one off the front foyer, and walk down the hall, past the other four bedrooms. My room, beautifully decorated, is the nicest I've ever had. Its windows look out onto the ornate gardens behind the house.

A long hour passes. I'm sitting in the stuffed chair, an unread novel open on my lap, when I hear a timid knock on the door.

Dr. Randall stands in the hall, his arms laden with leather-bound books. "Mrs. Randall and I have been discussing your situation." He raises his eyebrows. "She says you're growing tired of being a housemaid?"

Why did I confide in her? I should have known better; she's not my friend, she's my employer. I glance around my pretty bedroom—I would surely hate to part with it.

"I'm sorry, Dr. Randall. I may have confused Mrs. Randall. I'm not dissatisfied here. I've never worked for anyone as good and kind as you and Mrs. Randall. I'll try harder. I'll work harder. I promise I won't disappoint you again."

"Mary, hold up. We're not disappointed with you. Actually, we're rather proud of you."

I'm confused.

Dr. Randall shifts the heavy load in his arms. "May I set these down?"

"Oh, I'm sorry. Of course." I move aside so he can enter the room. "What are they?"

He smiles. "Like I was trying to say, Mrs. Randall informed me you aspire to be something more than a maid. We wondered if you might be interested in training as a nurse."

"Me? A nurse?" My eyes grow huge. "I've never considered that option."

"Well, there's certainly no reason you couldn't, if it interests you. A nursing program is offered at St. Joseph's Hospital in Cheltenham."

I don't know what to say; my mind is all aflutter.

"Why don't I leave these journals here with you? Look through them and let me know what you think. If you decide nursing is something you'd like to pursue, I'll see it happens." He lays the books on my dressing table. "Have a good sleep, Mary. I'll see you in the morning."

"Good night, Dr. Randall, and thank you."

Somehow, I'm no longer weary. I open a journal and study it. And as I read, I feel a flicker of hope for my future.

Several months pass. I spend every free moment devouring the medical journals, except for Sundays, when I attend church services at the Presbyterian Church with the Randalls.

Sitting in the front pew of the choir loft, I study this morning's choir selection song, Whiter than Snow, which we are singing acappella. I sing alto. In my mind, I rehearse the chorus, *Oh, to live a life perfectly whole, my soul made perfect in love.* I adore this song; it epitomizes the struggles and goals in my life.

The organist softly plays as the congregation files through the front doors. I peek up from my hymn book, my gaze drawn to a man standing inside the door. I've never seen him before and, for the life of me, I have no idea why I'm attracted to him; he's nothing like Sam. Not overly tall or handsome—he's just an average guy, clean shaven, short cropped brown hair, a round face. Nevertheless, I can't take my eyes off him as he follows Dacre and Lotheria Thistle and slides into the pew beside them. He settles and looks up. My breath catches as our eyes meet. His are remarkable—the most brilliant blue I've ever seen.

I could lose myself in those eyes.

He nods, ever so slightly, a pleasing smile forming on his lips.

I blush. My gaze sinks back to the hymn book on my lap.

The following Sunday, he's standing behind me in the choir loft. At this proximity, I sense his very presence, his every move, his every breath. His silky tenor voice croons, occasionally lifting a curl on my neck. Delightful goosebumps form on my skin.

When the service is over, I feel a soft touch on my sleeve. I turn and gaze into those eyes. "Mary, may I walk you home?"

My heart flutters, hearing him speak my name. I nip at my bottom lip. After the way Sam treated me, I've not given another man a second look. But Charles Thistle doesn't strike me as being just another man. And he's not Sam, I remind myself. "I suppose," I say as we walk toward the waiting Randalls. "Dr. and Mrs. Randall, would it be alright if Charles walked me home?"

Mrs. Randall wears an all-knowing smile. Dr. Randall winks at me and says, "You take good care of her, Charles. She's very special to us." My heart swells and a blush creeps up my neck.

All the way home we talk, or more so I encourage him to talk. I'm a good listener as I'm not inclined to talk about myself. In total contrast to Sam, he's humble and soft-spoken. *Why*, I ask myself, *do I keep comparing him to that weasel?*

From then on, we spend time together each Sunday after church and Wednesday evenings after choir practice. Charles is eight years older than I, a veteran recently home from the war. He's ready to put all those memories behind him and live a quiet farm life.

June. The month named after Juno, the ancient Roman goddess of marriage, childbirth, and young people. The month of love. I think of Charles all the time.

It's Sunday and we are at the local diner. He's talking about his plans for the farm while we wait for our meals to arrive. His eyes twinkle over his tall glass of ginger ale.

"Someday, Mary, I hope to find a good woman, one who would make an excellent farmwife. And when I do, I intend to marry her, take her home with me, and raise a family of our own."

I suck in a breath. *Now, how do I respond to that? Is he referring to me?* I can't be sure, but why would he say that to me, with that twinkle in his eye, if he didn't mean me?

The waitress appears with our dinners. She places my meal before me: a pork chop, potatoes and carrots. Plain and simple. Why can't Charles be like that and speak plainly? For goodness sake, I can't read his mind and I hate when people talk in riddles.

He's waiting for me to say something. Perhaps I'll test him, make him explain himself. With downcast eyes, I say, "Well, I hope you find her."

I feel his eyes on me while the waitress serves him. I sense him withdraw. He's puzzled; I believe he took my words seriously. When she leaves, he's indifferent toward me—cool, reserved, and his eyes have lost their twinkle. I don't know what to do, how to go back to a few moments ago. For the very first time, I'm awkward around him. We dine in relative silence.

Later that night, in my room, I console myself by daydreaming about my future. I won't think about Charles tonight, I'll think about nursing. Nurses are not allowed to marry, so I will remain single, at least while I'm young. And then, who knows where it might lead. As a nurse, my options for marriage could be boundless. Perhaps I might even marry a doctor and have a fine home, the type of home I live in now, albeit as a maid.

Try as I might, my thoughts return to Charles' words at the diner. *Was he referring to me? Of course he was.* However, it seems he has little to offer. He aspires to be nothing more than a small-time farmer like his father, living a simple life, on their seventy-acre farm on the South Centre Road. The plan is for Charles to take over the farm within a few years, and chances are, if we marry, I would be living in that house, which, in my opinion, is not much more than a shack. Now, I have no doubt Charles would make an excellent husband and father, but the farmhouse is definitely not what dreams are made of. And why shouldn't I have a nice home of my own? I've been cleaning them for years.

My dream home would be Papa's and Mama Annie's—a spacious stone cottage—but there are none of those around here. Still, any of the farmhouses I've served in (the Metcalfe's or the Nelson's), or any of the other lovely farmhouses in this area would suit me just fine. One like Charles' closest neighbours, Bob and Jean Sherman—now their farm is one I would be proud to call home.

Sometimes, I ask myself why a nice house is so important to me. It's not that I have a high opinion of myself. No, that's the case at all. The answer is simple: I was born to impoverished parents, into a family who had nothing, and since they could not support me, they willingly gave me away like an unwanted puppy. Should I be blessed with children of my own someday, I want better for them. I want to provide for them, give them all the nice things I never had, and I want to raise them in a nice home.

Oh, what will I do?

Take a step back, I tell myself. Charles has only hinted—he's not asked. He's always been a perfect gentleman, has never even attempted a kiss. I've another year of servitude before I am free. One more year. I'll take my time and be his friend. I enjoy his company and value his friendship.

Yes, that is what I will do, I tell myself. *I will be his friend.*

December, 1921

Dr. and Mrs. Randall don't expect to be home until very late. They are attending a hospital Christmas benefit dinner and have generously given me permission to invite Charles for dinner at the house. Mrs. Randall says she trusts that I'll behave myself; I'm a good girl. But, the trouble is, I'm not sure I trust myself to be left alone with Charles. Lately, I find myself staring at his mouth and wondering what it would feel like to have those lips on mine, and I can never get enough of gazing into those brilliant blue eyes. I've lost myself in them several times, just as I had thought I would. Even when I'm not with him, I dream about those eyes and lips. My work has suffered, but Mrs. Randall gives me that wise old smile and says, "Try to focus, Mary."

That's easy for her to say.

I can't wait until I'm no longer considered a girl and done with the constant follow-up by the meddlesome Barnardo social workers. Even though not physically here, they've been by my side in everything I do. Every single time I've erred, they've been sure to find out. They're like a shadow I can't shed.

Dr. Randall assists his wife into her mink-trimmed velvet coat. "Mrs. Randall and I think, Mary, since it is Christmas, this evening should be special. Why don't you and Charles eat in the dining room?"

I shake my head. "Oh, I would have never considered that."

"Of course you wouldn't have, dear. But don't you think it'd be nice, once, to dine at that table, rather than serve at it?"

I consider their offer for a moment and then shake my head again. I don't want Charles to feel embarrassed; there's no dining room in his parents' house.

Mrs. Randall buttons her coat. "Mary, you're more than our housemaid; you're almost like a daughter to us. Please, pretend this home is yours tonight. Set the table as you would for us, use the good linen, china, and silverware, and enjoy your evening with Charles."

I nibble my bottom lip. How can I possibly say no?

Mrs. Randall clutches her handbag. "Mary, don't give it another thought. I insist." She pulls on her kid-leather gloves. "By the way, that dress looks stunning on you."

I smooth my hands over my new blue velvet dress and give her a quick hug. "Thank you, again," I whisper in her ear.

Dr. Randall is waiting patiently by the door. "Come along now, dear. The car is running."

I flutter about the dining room, doing a last go over. The house is, as always, spotless and as neat as a pin. It's six o'clock on the dot when Charles arrives. He's punctual, I'll give him that. My nerves are as jumpy as fleas. I press my hand against my abdomen and open the door. He stands on the front porch, a beautifully wrapped gift in his hand. "For you, Mary," he says as he steps inside. "Merry Christmas."

My goodness. Two gifts in one day. "Oh, you shouldn't have. I've nothing for you."

"I wasn't expecting anything." He eyes me, respectfully. "My, but don't you look especially lovely this evening. That's a new dress, isn't it?"

"Yes, it is. This morning Mrs. Randall surprised me with it. She thought I should have something new to wear tonight." My stomach begins to settle. "You look quite dashing yourself."

He shrugs the compliment off. "Can't hold a candle to you, though. I love how you've done your hair."

I finger a loose curl. "Do you? Because I've been thinking of getting it cut in the new fashion—you know those sleek little bobs most of the girls wear nowadays? What do you think? Should I do it?"

He furrows his brows. "Oh, they're nice for sure. But I like your hair long. I'd hate to see any of those pretty curls cut off."

He's just so sweet.

He follows me through the foyer to the dining room. I place the gift on the sideboard. "Why don't you sit here?" I ask as I pull out the chair at the head of the table. "If you don't mind, I thought we'd eat right away; dinner is ready now."

"No, of course not. That'll be fine. I'm used to eating promptly at six." His eyes travel back to the gift. "Well, aren't you going to open it?"

"Now?"

"Of course. I'm eager to see if you like it."

I sit while Charles stands beside me and hands me the gift. Carefully, I unwrap it. Inside the box is a white china vase, hand-painted with ribbons of flowers and yellow and blue horizontal stripes. My eyes sting with tears and I blink them away. This gift is my very first piece of china—something for a hope chest, if I had one.

Charles has been watching me. He sighs. "You don't like it."

I look up at him with glistening eyes. "Oh, but I do. I love it."

He looks confused, but grins. "I wasn't sure, but I'd hoped you would. Do you think we could eat now? I'm starved."

I laugh as I stand. "Of course."

"Can I give you a hand?"

"No, sit. I'll only be a minute."

I walk to the kitchen, but before entering, I turn and look at him. He sits at the table, and picking up one of three forks sitting on the left-hand side of his plate, he studies it along with the white linen, the fine china and the assortment of silverware.

In the kitchen, I remove the salad and mayonnaise from the icebox, and as I dress the greens, I ponder. Love comes with obligations. To be wholly loved, you must be worthy of that love and you must love back. I'm capable of loving Charles, but am I worthy of his love? He knows so little about me and, in my heart, I'm afraid he's in love with the person he believes I am. It's almost as if I showed up in Ridgeland, a girl with no past. If I tell him everything, will he still love the girl—the one *with* a past?

I don't want to think about it and ruin this lovely evening. I carry a tray laden with ham, scalloped potatoes, carrots, and a Waldorf salad to the dining room. Charles stands and pulls out a chair for me. I smooth my skirt and sit.

He watches as I take the napkin off my plate, open it and spread it over my lap. He does the same. His face is a mixture of confusion and amusement, his eyebrows drawn together as he picks up the tiny salad fork once again. His lips twitch.

I giggle; he thinks I'm putting on airs. This was not my idea—it was Dr. and Mrs. Randall's. Charles and I have an easy, relaxed relationship and I don't want that to change. I rise. "Enough of this malarkey," I say as I place the food back on the tray.

We're laughing as I remove the everyday dishes from the cupboard. A moment later, we're seated at the gingham-covered table enjoying our supper.

When we've finished our meal, Charles stands. He reaches for my plate. I start to rise, but he places his hands on my shoulders and eases me back into the chair. "No, you sit. It's time you let someone wait on you." He gathers the dishes and carries them to the porcelain sink. Glancing around the kitchen, he spots my apron hanging from the hook on the back of the door. He slips it over his head.

I giggle again; he looks so silly dressed in a ruffled apron. My breath catches and I cover my mouth with my hand. Lord, help me; he's so good and kind. I'm terrified; what I'm feeling for him at this moment goes far beyond friendship.

Now, how am I to stay Whiter than Snow?

Chapter 11

Six weeks in and, finally, news from Charles. Sitting on the side of my bed, I unfold the creased letter and reread it for the fifth time.

My dearest Mary:

Thank you for your letters. I'm sorry it's taken me so long to reply, but you know me, I've never been good at letter-writing.

I'm glad to hear you're getting better and I pray the improvement continues each day. Without you here, time drags. But we're getting along fine—I don't want you to worry. Just like before you left, the snow keeps coming, but on the whole, the boys have missed very few days of school. You'd be so proud of them, the way they're pitching in with all the extra chores. And you've done a good job with Ernest—he's a decent cook—but his cooking will never compare to yours. I miss your cooking. Actually, I miss everything about you. This house is not a home without you. The boys miss you too and we all want you back home—real soon.

I sense you're concerned about the hospital expenses. Mary, you know we've always got by. I want you to stop worrying and solely concentrate on getting better—that's the important thing. I assure you the doctor and hospital bills are all being covered by making a few extra sales from the barn.

Guess what? In two or three weeks' time (on a Saturday or Sunday so the boys will be home to look after things), I'm coming to see you. When I've made a definite plan, I'll write again and let you know when to expect me.

I have a silly request. I was wondering if you would fashion your lovely auburn hair in that style I love—you know, the one with those pretty little waves, and maybe wear a wee bit of that new red lipstick I bought you for Christmas? I know you're wondering why I would make such a request. Well, I'll tell you. Every day I picture you in my mind and, most times, the woman I see is the one I put on the train. I try not to remember you that way, but that is the Mary I see. I can tell by your letters you've improved so much since then. So, the next time I see you, I want to take a mental picture of your happy, pretty face to bring home with me.

I can't wait to see My Mary.

Love Charles.

I hold the letter to my chest. How could I have ever thought my life wasn't worth living when I have him to share it with me? Of course I can do that for him. The thought of all the extra responsibilities piled on him and my sons—things that, if I were at home, I would do myself—makes my heart heavy.

I straighten my shoulders. I'm halfway through. And soon enough, I'll be back home and I swear to the Almighty God I will make it up to them one hundred times.

Florence sits on the side of her bed, gazing out the window, a far-off look in her eyes. Complaining of an upset stomach, she declined joining Helen and me for lunch. I suspect that's not the case; the past two weeks she's been withdrawing. At first, I thought I had offended her, but I know it has nothing to do with me. When you've been in that place yourself, it's not hard to recognize the signs. I want to keep an eye on her, but, at the same time, I don't want her to feel I'm watching her. I remember how that feels, too.

Why isn't Florence's doctor concerned? I shrug my shoulders; I wouldn't be privy to that information. And who knows? Maybe I'm worrying unnecessarily. I hide a private smile as I run the brush through my curls. I can almost hear Charles' voice, 'Mary, stop worrying yourself to death. If the situation is beyond your control, worrying will help nothing.' However, perhaps this situation isn't beyond my control. Whether or not it's my place, I make a mental note to discuss Florence's disposition with Nurse Martin this afternoon.

"Florence, I'm leaving now; my appointment with Dr. Clark is at one-thirty."

Without looking at me, she replies, "Of course. You go on ahead."

I take a few steps toward her. "I have an idea. Why don't you bring your book or your knitting and I'll meet you in the library after my appointment, let's say two o'clock?"

Her eyes remain fixed on the landscape beyond the window. "I'm rather tired right now. I think I'll have a little nap."

"Okay then, you do that. When my appointment's over, I'll look for you in the library. If you're not there, I'll come and get you, okay?"

She nods ever so slightly. I wonder if she even registered what I said. I stow the brush in the dresser drawer and rush to my appointment.

Normally, Dr. Clark is very punctual, but today he's still with another patient. I take a seat in the waiting room. I'm jittery, and I'm chilled. To take my mind off Florence, I rehearse the next chapter of my story.

May, 1922

I live in a tortured state of confusion. I ask myself the same questions, over and over. *Should a house's physical appearance matter if it is filled it with love? Would life on a small farm be so bad? Could I be content as a farmwife, or would I regret not becoming a nurse?*

Depending on my state of mind, the answers to those three questions vary. And believe me when I say, *vary.*

And then there is my key question: *Am I worthy of someone as honourable as Charles?*

I have only one answer to that question: *No.*

Still, it doesn't stop me from seeing him.

It's a lovely spring day and Charles surprises me with a picnic after church. Strolling through the yard, his father winks at us and calls, "You two lovebirds behave yourselves."

Charles reaches for my hand and whispers, "Ignore him. He's only having a bit of fun with us. He means nothing by it."

"I didn't take any offence," I murmur as I smile at Dacre. "I really like your father. And your mother. You're lucky to have them." My gaze travels past Dacre to the old house. Charles' younger sister, Lottie, stands at the kitchen window. She's waving goodbye to us, her lips drawn into a pretty smile. "And Lottie," I add. "She's a sweetheart."

"Yes, she truly is. She packed this picnic lunch for us today."

"Hmm, I wondered who was responsible for it."

"I hope someday soon you'll meet my other sisters, Ellen and Clara."

Charles speaks of his married sisters often. Ellen lives on a farm near Leaside and Clara lives in the United States.

"I look forward to that."

We stroll along, hand in hand, down the fenced lane to the bush lot on his father's farm. He carries the wicker basket over one arm and a large plaid blanket over his shoulder, and as we walk, he explains, "I thought we best take advantage of such a beautiful day. Within a few weeks, the cattle will have free range in the woodlot and then, in another couple months, we'll turn the bull in with them. There'll be no more picnics in the forest for us then."

"But your bull seems friendly enough," I say, considering the time I had rubbed his nose over the barnyard fence.

"Oh, he is. But you can never trust a bull during breeding season. They get territorial with their women, you know."

I fight back a smile. "Don't most males?"

In response, Charles blushes and squeezes my hand.

Upon reaching the forest, I breathe in the cool, moist air of the woodland. The day is soft, the filtered sun spilling through the trees, their new leaves uncurling toward the warm light. I watch as Charles spreads the blanket on the ground, carefully choosing the location, being ever so mindful of the trilliums and violets in bloom.

"Come, sit." He runs his hand across the blanket beside him.

I'm in absolute awe of this man—a man so kind-hearted he shows consideration for the wild spring flowers. Each time he exhibits such thoughtfulness or selflessness, my key question surfaces, niggling at my mind. *Am I worthy of him?* I smooth my skirt, sit, and turn my face from him, embarrassed he might see the tears gathering in my eyes. *Good Lord, why must I always cry?*

He reaches for my hand. "Mary, what is it?"

I withdraw my hand and brush a tear as it slips down my cheek.

"Mary, talk to me."

I look at him. "You're far too good for me, you know."

Charles takes my hand again and kisses my knuckles. "No, that's not true."

My heart flutters at the touch of his lips on my fingers. "Yes, you are. But you don't know that because you don't really know me."

"Then, tell me. I've been asking you for months now and all you ever say is you're a Home Child and you've been moved around a lot. I'm sorry you had a childhood like that, but I don't care." He shakes his head. "No, that's not what I mean. Of course I care. What I'm trying to say is I don't care you were a Home Child—that doesn't matter one bit to me. I'm not ashamed of who you are and you shouldn't be either. I want to know *you*, the girl that's inside *here*." With that, he covers my hand with his and hesitantly places it on my heart. "No matter what happened to you, *you* are a good person. How can I make you believe that?"

I stare at his hand, still holding mine. I've never talked about my past to anyone. Over the years, I've grown so used to getting negative reactions when I tell someone I'm a Home Child, I avoid it at all costs. Until Charles, nobody has ever cared enough to ask. Even Mrs. Randall has asked very little, as if she's afraid of what she might learn. So, where do I start?

He adds, "I'm sure there isn't anything you could tell me that would change my opinion of you."

I think about his words. He's right; I've done little of which to be ashamed. Yet, it doesn't change how I perceive myself. But if I were to share it all with him, every bit, and he still loves me, would I feel differently?

But not this day. Not today.

"I will, but not now. Let's not spoil this perfect day with talk of my past."

Still holding my hands, he gazes into my eyes. "Was it all that bad?"

"No," I say, "not anything like some stories I've heard of other Barnardo children. Considering what could have happened to me, I suppose I've been fortunate." I take a moment. "How about today, while we eat our lunch, I'll tell you about my early life when I was a wee girl living in England? But I'm not ready to talk about my life here in Canada. Not yet. Okay?"

"Of course. You can tell me whatever you want whenever you're ready. There'll be no pressure from me."

We eat our lunch, enjoying each other's company, and I share stories of my happy life with my foster family in England. We laugh as I reminisce, but when my story is nearing the end, the memory of my last day with my foster family hits me hard. I choke on my words. Charles slides across the blanket and pulls me into his lap.

He holds me to him, his left hand cradling my head. Tenderness radiates from his touch. It's been so long since anyone touched me with pure kindness, I had forgotten what it felt like to be loved. Charles strokes my hair.

And I think, *now I know the difference between lust and love.* I drape my arms around his neck and bury my face in his chest, my sobs muffled in his flannel shirt. When I have regained control of myself, I raise a hand to his face and graze his lips with my thumb. I long to feel them on mine.

Charles loosens a curl stuck to my tear-stained cheek. He kisses my forehead. "Feel better now?" he asks.

I don't answer. I draw his face to mine and kiss his eyes, his cheekbones, and then my lips find his.

A soft moan escapes his parted lips. He gently pulls away from me, but I boldly clasp his head in my hands. Every inch of my body tingles with desire. I suck in my lower lip. I can still taste his kiss.

He raises his eyebrows, his eyes wide. His face wears a conflicted blend of confusion and desire. He cocks his head and whispers, "Mary?"

I raise my forefinger to my moist lips. "Shh," I whisper as I press my body against him, forcing him to the blanket.

Afterward, we lay together, my head cradled on his shoulder. We're silent, lost in our own emotions. Charles absentmindedly twirls a lock of my hair around his finger.

I stare off over his flannel-covered chest to the forest, unsure of what to do or say. My mind is a muddled mask of uncertainty. I wonder what he's thinking. He must have some experience with women; being older and having been in the army. He's so quiet now. Perhaps he's disappointed.

And why wouldn't he be?

I am. The act was nothing I had fantasized it would be. It all happened so quickly—the spark kindled, the passion rising, the urgency, the exquisite pain—the conclusion coming far too soon. Surely there's more to lovemaking than that.

It wasn't enough.

Maybe *I* wasn't enough.

I roll onto my back and consider my actions. It only takes me a second to realize where I went wrong—I was too forward. But how was I to know how to act? I simply followed my instincts. Were they wrong?

Of course they were. What kind of girl pulls up her skirt and shimmies out of her panties? In broad daylight? Not a proper one, that's for sure.

Shame rises to my cheeks.

I sense Charles is staring at me. I don't dare look at him; I can't bear to look into those eyes. Gazing into the overhead branches, I listen to the cheerful song of the spring birds. A female robin flits from tree to tree, and then flies out of sight.

Oh, to be that free.

Charles places his fingers under my chin and tilts my face toward him. He blushes as he whispers, "Will you permit me to try again? Do it right this time?" He doesn't wait for an answer. He lowers his lips to mine and kisses me, tenderly at first, and then, gradually, his passion increases. That delicious, aching sensation stirs in me once again as he slowly unbuttons my dress. He slips it and my chemise straps over my shoulders, leaving my breasts exposed. His hand skims down my neck, over my collarbone, and cups my breast. I shiver as a trail of kisses follows. My sensitive nipples harden under his touch and I whimper as his lips close around one. I wrap my arms around his shoulders and hold on as one shock wave after another ripples through me.

This time, I hold back and allow him to take the lead. I follow his example as he takes his time undressing me, touching me, and kissing me. I marvel at his muscular body while undressing him, my desire increasing with each passing moment. And, finally, when I can wait no longer, he holds himself over me. His gaze is intense. I arch toward him, and as he enters me, he murmurs, "Marry me."

I stifle a cry as I reach the peak of my climax and ride out the aftershocks.

I'm dressed. Smoothing the wrinkles from my dress, I run my hand through my tousled hair. Charles lies bare chested on the blanket. He's watching me, his face troubled. "Mary, I'm sorry. That wasn't a proper proposal."

No, it wasn't. I avoid his eyes as I slip into my shoes.

I wonder why he proposed. Was he feeling remorse? Obligation? I think he loves me, but he has never said so. Shouldn't that declaration have come first?

To save my pride, I say, "That's okay. Don't worry about it—you were just caught up in the moment."

He's quick with a comeback. "That's true; I was caught up in the moment. How could I help but not be? But I meant it. I want you to be my wife."

Still not a proper proposal and no declaration of love. I busy myself repacking the picnic basket.

He rises and kneels beside me. He looks perplexed. "Mary, believe me. I meant it. But I'm not pressing you to give me an answer right away. You don't have to, if you don't want to."

That's good; I don't have one. I finally look at him. He stuffs his arms into his shirtsleeves while still watching me. I screw the lid on the thermos and place it in the basket. *Good Lord, why isn't he getting it? Why hasn't he realized what he missed?* It isn't enough he wants to marry me, and, by the way, saying 'Marry me' is not a request, it's an order. However, putting that aside, there are other words I need to hear—words I haven't heard in years.

All I need from him are three simple words: "I love you."

"Take your time," he says. "There's still several months before you're free from Barnardo and, besides, I don't have a home yet to offer you. We've all the time in the world." He buttons his shirt. "Give me your answer when you're ready. There's no rush."

Being apart from Charles the next day gives me time to reflect. I find no fault in his actions and take full responsibility for what happened. I seduced him. If I hadn't, we would have never had relations, nor would Charles have proposed marriage. Obviously, he feels obliged to marry me.

My mind is a whirlwind of indecision, even more than it was before. In my confused state, I conclude I have three choices: I can accept Charles' offer of marriage, I can become a nurse, or I can leave.

It's Monday evening. I sit at the desk in my bedroom, a sheet of paper before me. I pen a letter to Mama Annie, my hand frantically scribbling across the paper. *What,* I ask, *do I do?* I tell her about Charles—not everything, of course—only the things she needs to know. I say Dr. Randall has offered to pave the way for me to become a nurse. But Charles wants a wife, not a girlfriend training as a nurse. And what would be the point of all that training only to give it up and marry Charles? It's nursing or marriage—I can't have both. The pencil stalls mid-air as I remember my pipedream of not only becoming a nurse, but marrying a doctor, living in a beautiful brick home with a housemaid of my own.

I don't write that down.

I've daydreamed about marrying a prosperous farmer, like she did, but not once have I ever fantasized scraping out an existence on a small farm, living in a dated, four-room frame dwelling. Although born into poverty, I have no memory of living in hardship—I was only three months old when I became a ward of the Barnardo Home. Why would I want to start now? Mind you, the Thistles are not impoverished, but they have so little, evidenced by the condition of their home. If I married Charles, chances are I would still have very little, like Lotheria. I don't want what Lotheria has; I want what Mama Annie has.

I don't write that down either.

I imagine my life without Charles, if I were to remain in Ridgeland. There would be times I would encounter him, by chance, in a store, post office, or a restaurant. I would still see him every Sunday morning and Wednesday evening at church. I try to imagine standing in the choir loft with him standing behind me, the proximity of his body to mine, hearing his voice as he sings, feeling his breath on my neck. Even now, as I imagine it, that delicious ache stirs in me. No, that would be far too difficult.

I certainly don't write that down.

I reread some of the letter. It strikes me bizarre how I wrote Charles wants a wife, not a girlfriend who is training to be a nurse. *How do I know that?* Not only have I never told him of my past, I have not talked about my future. I have never told him about my dream of becoming a nurse.

I have never told him anything.

I reason with myself I haven't lied to him—I just haven't confided in him. With that thought, my inner voice shrieks, *For goodness' sake, you're even lying to yourself. There's no difference between a straight-out lie and a lie by omission!*

I see him again as he carefully spread the blanket on the forest floor. Never have I known anyone like him, a person so completely void of greed, pretense, and vanity. I think of the many kindnesses he has shown me over the past months, his generosity, his selflessness, his accepting and trusting nature. I was correct when I told him he was too good for me. He would be far better off with someone else. Someone who is not deceitful.

Someone who is not me.

There's no need to wait for advice from Mama Annie; I've made my decision. I will take the coward's way out and run away from this problem, just like I ran away from the last. Crumpling the paper, I toss it into the wastebasket. Leaving the Randalls will be heartbreaking; I have grown to love them. Leaving Charles will be even harder.

It seems there is only one reason for leaving that carries any weight. The outcome of this situation would be very different had I been honest with Charles all along. There is only one person to blame—me. I have not been honest, and Charles deserves better.

Placing a fresh sheet of paper before me, I address it to the Barnard Foundation, requesting a hasty relocation. I shove it into my pocketbook, brush the tears from my eyes, and scurry down the street to the post office.

The following Sunday, Charles and I stand together on the church's front lawn. The congregation mills around us. I was cool toward him throughout the service, avoiding eye contact and offering him little more than a weak smile. Lottie, wearing a concerned look, stands off in the distance with her friends, watching. With sad eyes, I look at her. I wish I were her sister, or, at least, her friend.

Charles furrows his brows. "Mary, what's wrong?"

I need to stay strong if I'm to get through this. I hold my head high, and take a deep breath. "I'm moving again."

"What? I don't understand?"

"What's to understand?" I say, a touch of bitterness in my tone. "I don't get a say in these things, you know."

He shakes his head, disbelieving. "But I thought you were happy here."

"I am."

"Mary, this makes no sense. You get along so well with the Randalls—I know they wouldn't have requested a transfer. Why would Barnardo move you if both parties are happy with the arrangement?"

"I don't know. They didn't say," I lie.

He lifts my left hand and holds it, his thumb stroking my bare ring finger. I know he isn't doing it intentionally, but I can't help but think how ironic it is. We stand there a moment in silence. Eventually, he whispers, "It's me, isn't it?"

My heart physically aches for him. My chin trembles; I lower my face so he can't see it. "No. Believe me, it's not you." I can at least give him that.

"So, why are you leaving?"

Too many reasons, too many things I have not told him, hang between us. I say nothing.

"When do you leave?"

"Soon. Within the next week or two."

I hear his sharp intake of breath and then the stillness as he holds it. He exhales. "Will you come back to me when you're twenty-one?"

Looking up, I stare across the street. "I don't know." I pause for a moment and put myself in his shoes. It would be heartless to lead him on. "Not likely," I whisper, "You deserve someone better than me." I turn and finally look at him.

His face wears a stunned expression, his eyes vacant, his lips set in a cruel, hard line.

I sense a great distance spread between us in truths not spoken.

I pack my trunk and bid farewell to the Randalls. I will miss them; they've been the best part of my Barnardo life in Canada. I board a train for Toronto, a place where no one knows my story.

Except Miss Silas.

Yes, Miss Silas. Once again, she's my shadow. When I heard that, I actually winced. *Will I ever shed that woman? I wish I could, just like a snake sheds its skin.*

Mrs. Little, my new mistress, is a dear, sweet-tempered widow. My duties are to care for her and keep her lovely home. My goodness, the tiny woman can't weigh more than one hundred pounds, soaking wet. It saddened me to learn she has a terminal illness with a life expectancy of two years. I've never cared for anyone this old, nor this ill, but at least now I'm implementing some of the nursing knowledge I had gleaned from Dr. Randall's books.

To everyone I meet, I am nothing more than Mrs. Little's housemaid and nurse—a young woman with no past and a very unstable future.

Chapter 12

I flush, recalling my last memory. "Good Lord, Dr. Clark doesn't need to know everything," I whisper to myself. I glance at the large black and white industrial clock hanging on the wall. It's two o'clock, and he is still occupied with another patient, their muted voices seeping through the door. I take a deep breath and still my twitching hands. I was supposed to meet Florence at two o'clock. *Has she finished her nap? Has she gone to the library? Is she alright?* I've got to stop thinking about her—I'll go back to my other thoughts.

Shortly after I arrived in Toronto, my health, along with Mrs. Little's, deteriorates and, as each day passes, I slip deeper and deeper into melancholia. I have no direction, social life, or purpose other than to care for my mistress. I do my utmost to appear content and pleasant in her presence—surely with her own failing health, she has enough on her mind. She has a keen eye, though, and often she has remarked, "Listen to your body, Mary. It'll tell you what it needs." If that's so, I really wish it would speak a little louder.

I'm weary all the time. I have trouble sleeping and my appetite has waned. In the mornings, I'm light-headed and nauseous. It occurs to me there could be a chance I'm pregnant, but Charles and I had only been together once . . . well, technically twice. Because my appetite is so poor, I tell myself it's a fluke, my body is reacting from a lack of nutrition, sleep, and loneliness. But as the days and weeks slip by, my concern grows.

I wait for my monthly. It doesn't come.

I'm horrified. *Should I write Charles?* No, I can't do that, not after the way I treated him. If he hadn't felt obliged to marry me before, surely he would now. I don't want him to marry me because he's duty-bound. Instead, I pray nightly for God to make this baby go away.

A few more weeks pass, along with the nausea. Physically, I'm feeling somewhat better, but psychologically I'm tormented. My waist thickens. Now the prayer is on my lips, day, and night. It's all I can think about, and I wonder if there isn't some small way I can assist God in this task.

I wake to cramps and lower back pain and, while relieving myself in the bathroom, I notice a pink mucus discharge. Later, while lifting Mrs. Little into her wheelchair, hot fluid seeps into my bloomers and trickles down my legs.

I race to the bathroom. The cramping starts again, only this time it's much stronger. I hold my head and clamp my mouth shut, stifling my moans. Finally, the pain recedes. I peer into the toilet bowl and watch as a dark red, shiny tissue, resembling a small piece of liver, sinks through the surface of blood and water.

I sigh in relief; my prayers have been answered.

A tear of remorse slides down my cheek, only one tear for my unborn child. Deep shame washes over me, but I harden my heart and straighten my shoulders. I got what I asked for, didn't I? Now there is no need for anyone to know of my indiscretion, nor Charles to know of the baby.

I flush the toilet.

The weeks and months crawl by.

Winter descends on the city. I'm surprised to receive a Christmas card and letter from Charles. Dr. Randall had given him my address. The letter is brief, factual, and newsy. Charles apologizes, vaguely, for what had transpired between us and for his clumsy proposal. Perhaps he was hoping I regretted my decision to leave. Perhaps, in his own way, he was opening the door for me to explain myself. But it is not a love letter, nor an invitation to return next spring. If it were, if he had written those three words, I believe I could find the courage to bare my soul and tell him all. Instead, I respond to his letter in a similar form.

It's true, the old saying, 'Absence makes the heart grow fonder.' Those words come to mind often these days. Being in Toronto with only Mrs. Little for company has given me time to take a good, hard look at myself. I spend hours considering my future and what I hope to reap out of this life. I no longer wish to become a nurse, I only want Charles. It took months of being separated from him for me to realize how much I love him and what a fine offer he had made me in his proposal of marriage.

It seems as my life progresses, my shame multiplies. I was born an unwanted bastard child, an orphan taken in by the Barnardo Home. Since coming to Canada, I've been a servant to others. I am no longer a virgin, and I have shunned and hurt a good man. But I believe the worst of my disgraces is my lack of remorse over the loss of my first child.

I set my pride aside. I have made a terrible mistake. The days and weeks go by while I wait for another letter from Charles. It doesn't come. I consider writing him, but I don't; I still have a speck of pride. I won't grovel before him, and I don't want him to think I'm aggressive and brazen again. I want him to take the lead, like he did that day in the forest. I want him to be the first to write, to be the first to say, "I love you."

But if I stall much longer, Charles will move on. He's wanting a wife and, if it isn't me, he will find someone else. If I have learned anything from my past, it is that I am replaceable.

Miss Silas will be pleased. I have finally learned my place.

Time creeps by on reluctant feet, and still, no letter arrives.

Mrs. Little and I have survived the long, cold winter and spring will soon be upon us. My days are filled with cleaning and cooking and grooming and dressing an ever-failing elderly woman. My nights consist of reasoning and reflecting and tossing and turning. Sometimes I wonder how a body can function on so little sleep.

Dragging my weary frame out of bed, I stuff my feet into my slippers and pad down the hall to the bathroom. I stop once again and gaze at one of Mrs. Little's reproduction oil paintings hanging on the wall: Picasso's Woman with Crossed Arms. I don't care for this painting; it always disturbs me. But this time, as I gaze deeply into the vacant eyes of this woman, I don't back away. This time, I am filled with empathy. I finally understand her. She, too, has lost faith. I leave the forlorn painting and go about my morning ritual. Mrs. Little will be awake soon and will require my services, and Miss Silas is expected at ten o'clock to complete her annual report on my well-being. Thank goodness, today will be my final meeting with her; I turned twenty-one a few weeks ago.

After readying myself and then Mrs. Little for the day, I prepare breakfast and serve her in bed—she doesn't feel well enough to rise.

The teaspoon tinkles against the side of the china cup. I drag my wandering mind back to the here and now. Miss Silas sits on a chair across from me, a small ornate table set between us. She picks up her cup of tea, blows daintily and sips.

"So, Mary, it's hard to imagine we've been together for ten years and today is the last time I will interview you. Perhaps the last time I will ever see you. Tell me, how have you been?"

No, actually it's easy to imagine; those ten years feel like a lifetime. I hesitate a moment before answering her with a lie, "I'm fine."

"Really? Because you don't look fine. As a matter of fact, I don't think you're looking well at all; certainly not as well as you looked a year ago. Now, let's be honest here, shall we? Something is bothering you. Is it Mrs. Little? Is she treating you well?"

"Mrs. Little treats me very well, thank you. Actually, she's the one who is not well," I reply, attempting to steer the conversation in a different direction.

"I'm sorry to hear that." She pauses, and tapping her foot, she looks me in the eye. "But, back to you," she says, smiling. Yes, she's still wearing that permanent, pasted-on smile.

What is it about this woman that brings out the worst in me? I stare at her, and when I offer her nothing, she presses. "You're pale and thin and there are dark circles under your eyes. There must be something going on with you. Tell me now, what's wrong?"

She will not let go of this; she's like a dog worrying away at an old piece of leather. I do not want to discuss my personal concerns with her, this nasty woman who has trailed me for nearly half my life. The cup and saucer rattle in my hands. I sit them on the table.

Fine, I'll give her something, anything to make her believe I have my future planned.

Taking a breath, I begin, "Miss Silas, the truth of the matter is—." I pause at the irony of my words—there is no truth in this matter. I swallow. "The truth of the matter is," I repeat, "I want to move back to Ridgeland. Now I know I won't be able to take up service again with Dr. and Mrs. Randall, but I'll have my accumulated savings from my Barnardo account, which should be more than sufficient to hold me over until I can find suitable employment. You likely read in my file I requested a transfer because I wanted to put some distance between myself and a man who was sweet on me. Anyway, he wrote me around Christmas, and ever since then we've been corresponding," I lie, "and now I've changed my mind. I don't want to be separated from him. You see, he has proposed to me."

She glances at my hands spread on my lap. "Hmm, I don't see a ring on your finger."

I grip my hands together, willing myself to remain composed. I swallow. "I don't have one yet. We've only been corresponding through the mail—no one in their right mind would send an engagement ring by mail, now would they?"

"No, of course they wouldn't." She sips her tea. "Well, Mary, to me, this sounds like good news, so I don't understand. Where *is* the problem?"

Good grief, this woman gets under my skin. So much for composure. "I never said there was a problem. You did," I blurt. "And I never said I wasn't well. I told you, Mrs. Little is the one who is not well!"

"Well," Miss Silas huffs, "you're still that same saucy little brat, aren't you? How is it, after all this time, you haven't learned your place?" She stares at me over her raised cup.

My cheeks flush as I recall the last time she said those words to me. A reply curdles in my gut, like sour milk. I want to scream, *I have learned my place! You made sure of that—you broke me!* But I hold my tongue; I can't give her the pleasure of hearing those words.

I take a calming breath. "It's very simple," I say. "I've grown to love Mrs. Little, and I'm worried about her. She requires so much care and she relies on me for everything." I keep my voice soft and level. "She's such a dear, sweet woman. I couldn't possibly think of leaving her unless I was sure she had someone who could care for her the way I do."

Miss Silas gazes at me. A wily smirk forms on those thin lips. "Oh, I see. How very noble of you." She glances away for a second, then turns her cold eyes on me. "Mary, I don't see why that concerns you. Surely you know by now it's never been difficult to fill your shoes. We have several girls who would be *perfect* for this position. One comes to mind right now." Her smile widens. "She's a *meek, polite,* girl—seventeen or eighteen years old, I believe. I'm sure Mrs. Little will flourish under her gentle care."

I struggle to maintain composed as another blush rises to my neck. It's beyond me how this woman can fit so many hurtful, stinging words into a few breaths.

Miss Silas places her cup and saucer on the table and reaches for her leather case. She removes the same manila folder, now creased and tattered, which holds my life story. While she scratches notes, she asks,

"So tell me all about this young man of yours. What's his name? Have you set the date?"

I drink my tepid tea while I consider my next lie. As much as I had anticipated Miss Silas' validation that I am replaceable, it has set me on edge. Oh, I do hope Charles doesn't feel that way. Regardless, I will not involve him in my lie.

"His name is Lawrence," I say, stumbling on my words, "Lawrence Metcalfe. And no, we haven't set a date." My breath becomes shallow; deceit always made me nervous.

"Metcalfe? Why does that name sound familiar?" She drops her eyes from my face, which is turning a bright shade of pink, to the paper on her lap. "Why, yes, here it is. You lived with a family by that name years ago." Her pencil taps a slow rhythm on the paper.

I swallow as I realize my error. Another old saying comes to mind, 'One lie begets another.' Fine. Let's see how many I can add to my discretions today. "Yes, of course, you're correct. The Metcalfe farm was my second placement here in Canada. But I'm sure there's no family connection. Char . . . I mean Lawrence, has never spoken of any relatives in the Arthur area." *Good Lord, this isn't just a little white lie—Miss Silas is actually taking notes.*

"You should ask him, this Char-Lawrence of yours, about it sometime," she says, that permanent grin frozen on her face. "Nevertheless, quite a coincidence you started out with a Metcalfe family and are now engaged to one." She stares at me, egging me on for another lie.

"Yes, it is." There's a note of finality in my voice; I'm done playing this game with her.

Miss Silas slides the paper inside the folder and returns it to her case. "I should be going." We rise, her heeled shoes clicking on the hardwood floor as she follows me to the door. "I'll be in touch with you soon to advise when you can expect your replacement. Don't worry, like I said, it shouldn't take long. And I'll have a cheque drawn in your name for your accumulated service pay. I expect all the arrangements should be accomplished within a couple of weeks. In the meantime, you can make your own arrangements to return to Ridgeland."

I open the front door and step back, leaving her a wide berth. Miss Silas, my ten-year-shadow, breaks away from me and glides through the door. She turns and our eyes meet. I hold my gaze, unblinking. She's well aware I have lied to her, but I'm determined she will not see me squirm.

She blinks. Her tongue darts over her lower lip, wetting it. In a monotone, she recites her parting words. "Congratulations, Mary, you are no longer a ward of the Barnardo Home. Your life, from here on in, is your own. Make it what you will."

I have no words for her—none she would want to hear. I give her a slight nod and close the door.

"Mary, Dr. Clark will see you now."

I glance at the clock. It's now two-thirty. I rush past Nurse Martin into the office, closing the door behind me. Dr. Clark sits behind his massive desk, a stack of folders piled in one corner. He pulls the top one off, places it on the blotter before him, and studies the papers inside as I lower myself into the comfortable chair.

"I apologize for the delay, Mary."

"That's alright, Doctor. It's given me time to think."

"And how have you been?"

"Very well, thank you."

"Good. Shall we continue? The last time we spoke, you were with Dr. and Mrs. Randall in Ridgeland and you had met a young man, Charles. Correct?"

"Yes, that's right."

"And from reading your records, your next of kin is Charles Thistle. So, obviously, you married him."

"Yes, I did, but not right away. Actually, I didn't marry Charles for several years after that."

"Is that so?"

I inhale and hold it, my mind scrambling to condense my feelings and memories. *How can I speed this session up?* I need to find Florence. So I tell him a few things, withholding the important details. I find myself starting to prattle and ramble, so I rein myself in. "Anyway, Charles proposed. I panicked and requested a move, which I regretted almost immediately."

"I see. Why don't you tell me in your own words what happened during those years? Or at least the important events."

"Oh my goodness, there's far too much to compile it into in a few moments. Besides, I haven't thought that far ahead. So if you like, I could fill in the period from that time until I turned twenty-one. That's when I became a free person."

And so I relay the memory to him, still so fresh in my mind, having rehearsed it outside his office. I'm still evading all my truths. Other than Charles, no one knows about our lost baby, and I have no intention of that changing.

When I have finished, Dr. Clark lays his pencil down, closes the manila folder, and gazes at me.

"And how did it feel? No longer being a Barnardo Home Child?"

I should have expected that question. My emotions seek a hiding spot, but I chase them down, drag them out, and feel them once again. "It was exhilarating and terrifying at the same time. I wanted to put those ten years behind me, to never think about them again, to lose the shame of who I was. I thought I should go somewhere where no one knew me and start a new life—a life with no past. But I had difficulty moving on; I couldn't get Charles out of my mind. I realized I loved him and I had to go back to see if he still felt the same way about me."

Dr. Clark smiles, compassion written on his face.

I look back at him. My opinion of him has drastically changed since my first session. He is not the aloof, impersonal man I judged him to be.

"Mary, you certainly didn't have an ideal childhood, and I am sorry for that. It's not surprising you suffer from melancholia. The electroconvulsive treatments, along with confronting your memories, will help you work through this and move on. Soon, you should feel much better about yourself and your life. So, tell me, do you think we're making headway?"

My hands lie still, clasped in my lap. When was the last time I shed a tear? Two days ago, at bedtime, when I prayed for my boys and Charles. I miss them so. But overall, I am much happier. "Yes," I say honestly. "We are making very good headway."

"Wonderful. That's exactly what I wanted to hear." His chair creaks as he slowly rises. He dismisses me with, "It looks like we'll pick up from here next Tuesday afternoon."

I glance at the small clock on his desk. It's now three o'clock, one hour past the time I had asked Florence to meet me. I rush to the library, hoping to find her waiting for me in our favourite little corner. Her seat is empty. A sense of foreboding dread rises in my throat. I swallow. Perhaps she's still napping, or she grew tired of waiting for me. There could be many reasons she's not here.

I pass the front reception. The secretary rises from her desk as I approach. "Mary, there's a letter here for you."

I'm not expecting a letter from Charles yet; he won't be visiting for at least another week. I suppose Jean may have written, or Charles may have forwarded mail from England. I make the slight detour to her desk.

She studies my face as she hands me the envelope. "Not expecting anything?"

"No." I turn it over in my hand. It is from Charles. I race to the nearest chair and sit. The paper flutters in my hand as I read.

Chapter 13

My breathing slows and my body calms. Charles is coming sooner than expected. He'll be here this Sunday, two days from now, arriving on the noon train and spending the entire afternoon with me.

In the sixty seconds it took to read Charles' letter, my mood has changed from anxiety to elation. Thoughts and plans spill through my mind—I can't process one before another tumbles over it. Tomorrow I will press my best dress and polish my shoes. I will take extra care to groom myself to perfection: showered, nails cleaned and filed, my hair done in his favourite style, my lips lightly glossed as he requested. I want him to see how much I've improved. My heart flutters in joyful anticipation. I need to share my happiness with someone.

Florence.

I gasp; in my excitement, I had forgotten her. I envision introducing Charles to her and Helen. Perhaps they'll enjoy a cup of tea with us. And maybe, just maybe, it will give Florence something to look forward to. In the six weeks I've been here, she has had only one visit from her brother, who lives relatively close to the hospital. *Why does he neglect her so?*

I fold the letter, stuff it into my dress pocket and go in search of her.

I slip into our room. Helen is on her bed, her reed-thin arms wrapped around her legs, her forehead pressed into her knees. She's rocking and humming that same haunting tune. There's no sign of Florence. My scalp prickles.

I walk over to Helen and rest my hand on her shoulder. She flinches and her head jerks up. A smile quickly replaces her frightened look. Slowly I mouth the words, "Do you know where Florence is?"

She shrugs. I squeeze her shoulder lightly before leaving the room. Proceeding down the hall, I stop at the toilets. The bathroom door is closed. My heartbeat quickens and I take a deep breath. How many times have I been told this door is to remain open? Someone hasn't paid attention or perhaps there's a new patient in this wing. Reaching for the doorknob, I notice my hand is shaking. I flick my hand and whisper, "Stop it!" Gripping the knob firmly, I push the door open. I jam the wooden doorstop into place using the toe of my shoe.

The overhead lights are off, the room dark and deathly quiet, save for a steady drip, drip, drip. Water on tile. Thin winter sunlight dribbles from the only window high on the north wall. "Is anyone here?" I call. To my ears, my voice sounds as weak as the sunlight. I reach for the light switch and flick it upwards. The two hanging pendulum fixtures buzz into life, illuminating the room.

Reluctantly, I creep toward the six stalls. Five of their doors hang open. They're empty. The last stall's door in the corner hangs slightly ajar. I hold my breath, my hands grasping my elbows to still their shaking. I peer through the small crack.

Florence is sitting on the toilet. She's fully dressed, eyes closed, her head resting against the wall. Her face is ghostly white, drained of all colour except for the vivid blotches on her cheeks—the rouge she would have applied this morning. At her sides, her arms hang limp. Below one hand, her sewing scissors lie on the floor. My eyes fixate on her slit wrists and her life's blood as it steadily dribbles onto the floor and disappears down the drain.

Drip, drip, drip.

I hear a weak cry, a whimper of utter sadness, and it breaks my heart. I raise my eyes from the blood-stained floor and frantically scan the room as the whimper becomes a moan and grows in intensity. My sight returns to Florence. She's silent. There's nobody in the room, only Florence and me.

Eyes wide, I stare at the floor. I imagine the sound coming from the drain, gurgling from deep below the surface of the floor. The voice is being choked off by the blood.

The moan strengthens into a terrifying scream. I cover my ears as the freakish wails echo off the porcelain-tiled walls. My focus blurs and the room spins as a wild, shrieking keen, a sound I have never heard before, is wrenched from my throat.

My vision diminishes to a pin-prick hole. And then everything goes black.

I'm in and out of awareness, my head throbbing with every heartbeat. I gingerly raise my hand, my fingertips stroke the bandages bound around the crown of my head. A rough, calloused hand gently draws it away. I feel warm breath and a light kiss on my knuckles. Slowly turning my head, I force my eyelids open.

"There she is. There's my Mary." Charles' voice breaks with emotion.

I offer him a weak smile, the best I can, and close my eyes again.

"Mary. Wake up." Nurse Ryckman's gruff, demanding voice summons me.

The blackness beckons.

"Mary, c'mon now. Time to wake up. Your husband has come a long way to visit you." She slides her arm under my shoulders and props another pillow behind me. "I'll leave you two alone," she says to Charles.

Charles is still holding my hand. His chin quivers. "Mary, I'm so sorry."

I glance across the room to Florence's empty bed. My breath comes quick as the memory surfaces. Later that day, Dr. Clarke had come to my room. According to him, I had saved Florence's life. I found her in the nick of time and now she's recovering in the hospital. He thought knowing this would make me feel better. It doesn't. Instead, I wonder if Florence hates me now.

"I was getting better," I say in a weak, scratchy voice.

"You sounded so, in your letters."

"And I was going to convince you I was ready to come home."

"Ah, Mary, you'll be ready soon. I know this has been a great shock to you, but it's only a minor setback. There's no way you could've seen it coming or prevented it."

"But I saw it coming and I could have prevented it."

"Perhaps. But you're not here to look after others. You need to focus on yourself, okay?"

I look past Charles, past Florence's bed, out to the frozen snow-covered fields. Maybe Charles is right. Maybe it is just a minor setback for me—I don't know—it sure doesn't feel like it right now. Not such a minor setback for Florence, though. She'll likely remain in the hospital for a couple of weeks before returning. Will she ever fully recover or will she simply repeat the attempt until she finally succeeds?

Maybe there isn't any long-term solution. Maybe I will follow the same path as Florence. Maybe I'll never fully recover.

I drag my gaze from the window. "Charles, I want you to promise me something." I squeeze his hand so tightly he winces.

His eyes search mine. "Of course. Anything."

Emotion floods over me and my voice breaks. "I want you to swear that if I get better and come home, you won't ever, *ever*, put me in here again."

Our eyes lock. I gaze deeply into his as I tighten the squeeze on his hand even more.

He lays his left hand on top of our clasped hands and holds them tightly together. "I promise."

I raise my voice. "No. Swear to it, Charles. Even if I relapse, or try to take my life, you'll never do this to me again."

Charles stands and leans over me, still clasping my hands. His voice is calm and reassuring. "I swear to it, Mary. I will never place you in another institution against your will."

Lowering my head to the pillow, I whisper, "Thank you."

Eight weeks in.

I'm sitting in Florence's quiet corner of the library. It's March. A trickle of rain worms its way down the long window. Early this morning, fog shrouded the bare trees, turning slowly to a misty rain.

Florence has not returned, or if she has, she's not visible. Perhaps that's a good thing. I enquired about her a few times, but got nowhere. So, I've kept to myself, focusing on myself, as Charles suggested. That shouldn't be hard to do; there's only Helen and me sharing the room and dining table, and I'm fine with that. For my own well-being, I can't risk becoming attached to anyone else here.

"I'm going to get better and go home. And if I need to play act like I'm totally recovered, then that's exactly what I'll do," I mutter to myself.

I resumed my appointments with Dr. Clark shortly after Florence's episode and my blackout. We spent one entire session discussing Florence's suicide attempt. Dr. Clark says I must come to terms with it, accept it, and move on. Honestly, I don't see how I'll ever do that. How does anyone come to terms with something like that? I dread using the toilets. Every time I pass through that door, my heart races and I envision that ghastly scene once again. Strangely enough, Dr. Clark has assured me that being repeatedly exposed to those surroundings will help me get past the trauma. I guess, in this case, I'll have to take him at his word.

During my sessions with Dr. Clark, he has given me something more to think about—being the witness rather than the victim. Not once, as I contemplated my suicide attempt, went to the workshop and found the rope—not once, when I tied the noose and slid it over my head, and—not once, when I stood on the privy seat, did I consider how my actions would affect Charles when he found me dangling from the rafters. *How could I have been so selfish to, not once, have given him a thought?*

"Maybe I've learned something from it."

Oh, no. Did I say that out loud? Again? This is not a good habit I've developed.

Dr. Clark and I have progressed to the time I like to refer to as The Courtship Years, the period of my life between being a Barnardo Home Child and a wife. Similar to the previous ten, they were a roller coaster of ups and downs. As I relate them to Dr. Clark, I try to condense that period into a factual account of the story.

July, 1923

I secure a room at a boarding house in Ridgeland. It's stark. No, it's worse than stark; it's quite dreadful. It's fitting I should have a room like this now—it's all I deserve, and all I can afford. The only pretty things I have to adorn this ugly room are my Annie doll and the lovely vase Charles gave me.

The following day, I arrange a visit with Dr. and Mrs. Randall. As I'm escorted into the parlour by their new Barnardo girl, I glance up the open staircase. Oh, if only I'd not been so impulsive, I'd still be occupying that beautiful bedroom at the rear of the house overlooking the delightful gardens. Surely the Randalls would have kept me on past my indenture.

A sigh escapes my lips; that ship has sailed. It's obvious they're pleased with their new girl. She's lovely, very conscientious and dependable, so they say. I'm happy for them; truly I am, I tell myself as I choke on my resentment.

Days and weeks slip by and I cannot find employment, plus I worry how I will support myself when my funds are depleted.

I didn't get the reception I'd hoped for from Charles. He's cool, holding me at arm's length. I don't blame him for that; he has good reason not to trust me. He no longer sings in the choir, so I only see him at church on Sundays and the occasional chance meeting in town. My one happiness is Lottie has befriended me. Honestly, I don't know what I'd do without her cheery disposition to brighten my dull life.

When Charles escorts her to town to do the weekly shopping, she always drops in for a quick visit. She's here right now, bursting through my door. "Mary, I can't wait to tell you my exciting news!"

Her face beams—she's practically effervescent. "Go on, spill it," I say, dragging her over to my narrow bed. I do not even have the luxury of a chair in my room.

Once seated, she leans forward. "We were down visiting my sister Ellen yesterday."

"Yes," I say, encouragingly.

"Well, it just so happens she also invited her neighbour to dinner. She's so sneaky, that Ellen—she had it all planned. Anyway, his name is Robert Ashton and his farm is down the road from theirs. He's a bachelor, about the same age as Charles. And Mary, he's ever so handsome and good. I know I hardly know him, and I can't believe I'm going to say this . . ." She pauses for a moment and blurts, "I think I'm in love."

I think back to the first time I laid eyes on Charles, and I squeeze her hand. "Oh, love at first sight! Lottie. I am so happy for you."

Concern flashes across her pretty face. "Shame on me, Mary. Where are my manners? Talking about myself and my happiness without even asking about you? Have you had any luck?"

I shrug my shoulders. "Perhaps," I say. "I spied an advertisement for a clerk's position at the Morriston General Store. There's even a room above the store I could rent."

Lottie's face relaxes. "Well, that sounds hopeful."

"Yes, I suppose it is." I sigh. "I'm being silly; I know. It's only a short distance away, but I don't know anyone there, like I do in this town, and it would feel like I'm starting all over again." I frown. "I'd hardly ever see you."

Lottie smiles mischievously. "Or Charles."

I blush. "That too. But I don't see I have a choice; I've already gone through my savings."

"Ah, Mary. I wish I could help."

"Don't worry about me; I'll be alright. I need the job, so I will apply for it. It's just hard to believe my earnings from ten years of service were only enough to support me for six months. I didn't know it would be so little—such a pittance for so much hard work! You know, I used to dream of all the pretty things I'd buy when I finally received it." I glance around the room. "That didn't happen though, did it?"

Two weeks later, I land the job and rent the room above the store. Lottie has convinced Charles I should still attend Ridgeland church, using the silly excuse my voice would be sorely missed in the choir. I'm sure he saw through her ruse, but nevertheless, Charles and Lottie drive to Morriston every Sunday morning to escort me to church.

June, 1925

Lucy, Charles' horse, draws the buggy down the country road. We're heading to his farm. Yes, that's right, his farm. Where he lives. Alone.

Charles is no longer cool with me—I can almost hear the wedding bells. I should be ecstatic, but I'm not; a great weight burdens my soul. Three years have passed since that day in the forest, the day we made love, the outcome of which was a lost baby. I agonize over keeping my secret from him. I have still told him very little of my Barnardo years, but this is different. This secret involves him.

I should tell him. But if I did, how would he react? He trusts me now, and I'm afraid of losing that trust. Will he hate me for not telling him the moment I found out? Maybe. Will he hate me if he knew I prayed to God to take it from me? Likely. Will he hate me if he knew how relieved I was when I lost it? Of course he would. Anyone would. I shake my head ever so slightly. I don't want to think about it right now.

Charles holds the reins in one hand and reaches for mine. "A penny for your thoughts?"

My face is far too readable. I shake my head again.

"Okay, never mind. Just scoot on over here."

He seldom presses anymore. It seems my mind is a library of old sayings. Mrs. Little was constantly using them, but this adage isn't one of hers. I heard it years ago . . . something about secrets, how they're like calluses on your heart. The more secrets you keep, the thicker the callus grows. And the thicker the callus grows, the more hardened your heart becomes until, eventually, you're unable to feel anything.

I don't want that to happen to me.

"Have you heard from your family?" I ask to lighten my mood. "How's Dacre doing? It must be so hard for him, having recently moved, and then your mother passing so soon. And Lottie? She and Robert must be so excited—her due date is coming up fast."

He releases my hand, wraps his arm around my waist and slides me across the leather seat. "Now, that's better," he says, smiling. "They're all good. Dad's lonely, of course. It'll take him some time to adjust. I think he's still happy they moved, that he lives close to Lottie and Ellen now. And Lottie says she's getting huge—she can't even see her feet anymore." His face breaks into a boyish grin. "What do you say we have a picnic when we get home? It's such a lovely day . . ." His words trail off and his eyes grow thoughtful. "Kind of reminds me of another day we had a picnic in the forest. Do you remember?"

Oh gosh, it's like he can read my mind. I nod.

I should tell him. This is the perfect moment—he's leaving the door wide open.

He's grown accustomed to my silence and continues, "Well, there are several things I remember about that day." He ponders for a few seconds. "I think you know the first."

I glance at him. He's smiling down at me, a hint of mischief on his face. It's so sweet. Heat rises on my neck.

He clears his throat. "Besides that," he says, "there are two other things I remember. The first one is, that was the day you actually told me a little about yourself." He hesitates a moment. "Now, mind you, you still haven't told me much since then, but that was the first time I felt you trusted me enough to give me a glimpse into your life."

I nod, keeping my gaze on the road ahead and the rhythmic sway of Lucy's muscled rump. I find it so odd he felt that way—that I trusted him. Even then, I would have trusted him with my very life. I should trust him now.

I should tell him.

His arm, wrapped around my shoulder, gently presses me closer to him. "Can you guess the second thing?"

Without looking at him, I shake my head. I feel the window closing; the moment slipping away.

He draws the reins in and Lucy, obediently, comes to a stop. "No? Well, okay then, I'll tell you. The second and most important thing is, my Mary—"

I jerk my head up and gaze into his eyes.

He pauses for extra emphasis, and repeats, "The second and most important thing is: I fell in love with you that day."

"What did you say?"

"I said 'I fell in love with you that day.'"

"No, not that. Before that?"

He cocks his head, totally confused. "I said, 'Mary, I fell in love with you that day.' How many times do you need me to say it?"

I wring my hands, my voice impatient. "No, before 'Mary.' Did you call me '*my* Mary?'?"

"Yes, I suppose I did." The boyish grin forms again on his confused face. "You are *my* Mary, aren't you?"

I raise my hands, and pulling his face to mine, I kiss him long and hard. I slowly draw away, happy tears streaming down my face.

Charles searches his suit pocket, pulls out his cotton handkerchief and hands it to me.

I drag the offered hankie across my face and blow my nose. When I've retrieved some measure of composure, I explain. "My foster family used to call me *my Mary* or *our Mary* and when you called me that, it all came rushing back. I loved it then and I love it now." I wipe my eyes. "Yes, I am your Mary," I say between sniffles. "And I love you too."

He slowly exhales. "You do?"

"Of course I do." Knowing he loves me has given me my voice. "Why do you think I came back? I think I loved you from the moment I first saw you, but I didn't know for sure until I had left."

"So, why didn't you write and tell me?"

"How could I, with the way I left? I knew I had hurt you. Plus, I had no way of knowing if you loved me."

He furrows his brows. "You should have known. I thought it was obvious."

For three years I've held these words in, and now they spill from my mouth. "You thought it was obvious? How? Sure, you asked me to marry you and, by the way, saying 'Marry me' is about the worst proposal I can imagine—." I inhale. I'm getting off track. "Anyway, it wasn't enough. You should have known I needed to hear the words 'I love you.' Have you any idea how long it's been since someone said that to me?" I don't wait for an answer but ramble on, "And then when you finally wrote, your letter didn't give me any reason to believe you cared, or that you wanted me back." I gulp in a deep breath.

"I never told you I loved you?"

"No. You didn't."

He no longer looks confused. "No wonder you were upset. Mary, I'm so sorry."

I lean in, and pressing my body against him, I kiss his lips.

When we part, the grin creeps back on his face. "Actually, there's one more thing I remember about that day. It's the way you were with me." He blushes a bright shade of pink and looks away. "The way you wanted me. I loved that you weren't inhibited and shy."

I groan. "Or proper. I was horrible."

He turns to me and holds my face in his hands. "No, you weren't. You were beautiful."

"And inexperienced."

"That you were. But we can remedy that." His lips are on mine. My body responds. I close my eyes and press myself against him. Slowly, Charles pulls away, his voice husky. "You won't go running off on me again, will you?"

"No, I'll never leave you again." I take a quick breath. "No. Not unless you send me away."

His eyebrows draw together. "Now, why would I do that?"

I shake my head. It's too late to tell him now; the window has closed. I stuff the hankie in my bag. "Let's go for that picnic."

He flicks the reins and the buggy jerks as Lucy picks up her pace.

Chapter 14

Nine weeks in.

I'm restless. Sleep is eluding me and it's not because of Helen; she's sleeping like a baby.

I slip into my robe and slippers and pad to the window. The full moon's silvery light streams through the open drapes. With only the two of us sharing this room, the atmosphere has drastically changed from what it was a few weeks ago. At night, we no longer draw the curtains around our beds and we leave the drapes open as we both prefer the natural light over complete darkness.

As much as I tried to keep to myself, Helen has wheedled her way into my heart. I catch her watching me and when our eyes meet, she gives me a shy smile. Lately, she's even attempted to communicate with me through eye contact, facial emotions, or gestures.

I glance back over my shoulder at her, snuggled peacefully beneath her blankets. *Why such a drastic change in such a short while?* Naturally, she was frightened of Margaret. Who wouldn't be? But Margaret was only here for a short period. I can't imagine Helen was afraid of Florence, although she was a ticking bomb. Likely, Helen's fear comes from her past. Maybe she feels safe with me; lately she spends her time shadowing me. Charles has always said I'm a natural caregiver. Is it possible I've contributed to this change in Helen? I smile; I'd sure like to think so.

Like Helen, I should be sleeping. Perhaps a pill would help. I tiptoe out of the room, momentarily blinded by the hallway's bright lights, and head to the nurses' station in search of Nurse Johnson.

She glances up from her desk as I approach. "Mary, what are you doing up at this hour?"

I sigh. "No matter how hard I try, I can't seem to fall asleep. I was hoping you might have something for me."

"Yes, I'm sure I do—I'll just have to check your chart first. Have a seat while I get your file."

I lower myself onto the wooden chair as she rummages through the file cabinet. She removes a folder and opens it, her finger tracing down the paper.

"Certainly, I don't see why not. A very light sedative should help. Is Helen restless tonight, or do you have too much on your mind?"

"No, it's not Helen. She's sleeping like a baby."

Nurse Johnson takes a key from the desk's top drawer and inserts it into the medicine cabinet. She removes a bottle of pills, unscrews the cap, and hands me one.

"Speaking of Helen, I've noticed a big change in her the past little while," I say.

"Yes, she does seem much better," she says as she sits behind her desk again. "I see little of her, being on the night shift and all."

My curiosity gets the best of me. "I wish she could speak. I'd love to know her story. Other than being deaf, she doesn't seem to have anything wrong with her."

Nurse Johnson clicks her tongue. "Now Mary, you know I'm not allowed to discuss one patient's health with another." She contemplates a moment and gives me a sly, conspiratorial smile. "I shouldn't repeat this, but it's not like I'm divulging her medical information." She peers down the hall and leans forward in her chair. "Helen's only been here a short while herself. Her grandmother placed her here to keep her safe."

Safe? She didn't seem very safe when Margaret was attacking her. "I don't understand. Wouldn't she be better off at home?"

"It's a long, complicated story."

I nod, encouragingly.

She glances down the hall again and continues, "Rumour has it that Helen's mother, the daughter of a wealthy business owner, became pregnant at a young age. She was sent to a home for unwed girls, right here in this town, and the pregnancy was . . . well, you know . . . kept hush-hush."

She leans in closer. "Immediately after birth, Helen was placed in foster care, awaiting adoption, but that never happened. She's not an attractive young woman now, and she wasn't a pretty baby then. You know, it's a real shame the prerequisite for a baby girl's quick adoption is for her to be blonde-haired and blue-eyed—those baby girls fare the best. And to make matters worse, she lost her hearing at a young age."

"She wasn't born deaf?"

"Oh, no." Nurse Johnson shakes her head. "It was from neglect. Helen developed a severe ear infection after having the measles. She didn't receive any medical attention and lost her hearing."

I shudder, imagining the suffering the poor little girl endured.

"Helen never found an adoptive home, let alone a safe one. As she grew older, I heard she was not only neglected, but abused. She has spent her entire life being moved from one home to another. You know, Mary, not all foster parents are good people. There are some who will take children in just for the pay cheque."

Or, for the free labour. Obviously, my conversations with Dr. Clark are strictly confidential—Nurse Johnson does not know my history. I remain silent and allow her to continue.

"Anyway, long story short, her grandmother caught wind of how she was being treated. There must be some good in that old woman, for even though the family doesn't acknowledge Helen, she set up a trust fund for her. Helen will live here indefinitely."

I'm lost in the thought of spending an entire life within these walls, and I doubt the pill clasped in my hand will help now. Rising, I say, "I should get back to bed. Thank you for sharing that story with me."

"Goodnight Mary."

I escape the bright lights of the hallway and enter our moonlit room. The pill is bitter on my tongue. I chug it down with a glass of water. Lying down, I draw the covers over my shoulder.

Still, sleep evades me.

Like I did with Florence, I compare my life with Helen's. How strange is it that her birth was my fictionalized origin and how sad is it she has never had a loving home? At least I had that when I was a child. I'm humiliated by my self-pity; I have had a far better life than Helen. I wonder if anyone has ever shown her one speck of love in her entire life. Gazing across the room at her, I realize how well she has adapted to her present circumstances. She is content. She has made this place her home.

Which gives me something else to ponder. After two months of living here, I am becoming comfortable with this arrangement. I believe, like Helen, I could adapt; however, I have no intention of doing that. I'm going home.

I yawn. I need to sleep; Heaven forbid I look tired when I'm in Dr. Clark's office tomorrow morning. Only two more weeks of treatments and less than three weeks to go, and then I'll be released. And that all depends on how well I appear.

I close my eyes. But before I drift off, I realize I haven't prepared the next chapter of my story for Dr. Clark.

September, 1925

Another week slips away. My entire world has taken on a beauty I'd never knew existed. At times, all things are bathed in a soft, sweet glow and I swear my feet float an inch off the ground. I'm giddy, an eternal grin plastered on my face. The days I spend apart from Charles are physically painful; my body aches for his tender touch and kisses.

But the ugly secret I carry eclipses my happiness like the earth's shadow darkening the moon. I don't want that sweet glow to fade, but my heart tells me I won't have peace until I tell Charles.

I recognize the familiar rumbling of Charles' automobile engine as it comes to a stop in front of the store. Bouncing on my toes, I part the lacey window curtain of my second-story room and gaze out. Charles steps out of the vehicle and saunters around the corner of the building toward the back door. I take one more glance in the mirror hanging over my dresser. My face is beaming with happiness, but as I peer into my eyes, I see the turmoil lurking in their depths. Snatching my sweater, I leave the room and fly down the back staircase.

I fling open the door and there he is, and not for one second do I hesitate. I don't care we're in town, or there are watchful eyes in the windows of the surrounding homes and businesses. Throwing myself into his arms, I tip my head up and kiss him. My body melts into his. Too soon, he gently pulls away, his eyes sparkling. "Let's go to the farm. I've a surprise for you." He leads me to his car and opens the passenger door.

There's a bulge in his jacket pocket. I swallow and lay my hand on my chest to calm the butterflies beating against my ribcage. Today's the day. He's going to propose to me again—and this time he's going to do it right. I glance over at him as he opens the driver's door and settles into the seat.

I want to be with him so badly, to spend every day with him for the rest of my life. Maybe I shouldn't tell him today. Maybe I should wait until after he proposes.

Expertly, he backs the vehicle away from the store-front and heads in the farm's direction. I take a deep breath through the open window, inhaling the sweet, fresh June morning. Along the roadside, the goldenrod, loosestrife and asters bloom.

No, I should tell him. I don't want any shadows hanging over me or secrets to come between us later. He has a right to know.

"How was your week?" His voice breaks into my thoughts.

I seductively smile. "Long."

He reaches for my hand and raises it to his lips. The touch of his lips sends flickers of excitement through me.

"Mine too," he whispers into my knuckles.

I must tell him. Now.

I stall. "So, what are the plans for the day? Any work projects, or are we just going to have fun?"

He winks at me. "Can't tell you. Like I said, it's a surprise." He turns his face toward the road ahead. His eyes twinkle with mirth, the corners of his mouth drawn up into a contented, boyish smile. He's happy, filled with a serenity which comes from having lived a clean life. A life with no secrets.

I glance off without really seeing anything. As bright and beautiful as this day is, the shadow hangs over me and it won't go away until it is no longer my secret. *Charles is a good man,* I tell myself. *He'll understand.*

I will not keep it to myself any longer. I will tell him everything. Every. Last. Thing.

I close my eyes and offer a silent prayer for forgiveness.

Before my courage wavers, I shift my body on the leather seat and lay my hand on his shirtsleeve. My voice sound reedy, unsteady. "Charles, could you pull over for a few minutes? There's something I must tell you."

The tone of my voice startles him. "Of course." He steers the car off the road, the right wheels cutting through the grass and weeds.

His face is shrouded in concern as he turns and reaches for my hands. "Mary, you're trembling. What's wrong?"

My eyes drop to our hands. Will he still hold them once he knows?

Slowly, I make my confession. I tell him why I left and went to Toronto, how I thought I wanted to be a nurse and felt I could do better than to marry a farmer. I tell him about the pregnancy, how ashamed I was, how I felt I was following in my mother's footsteps. I tell him how I thought of writing him, but decided not to and instead prayed daily for it to be taken from me. I tell him about the miscarriage, how relieved I was when it happened. I tell him how depressed I became, how I felt Barnardo and Miss Silas had finally broken me, how I had finally 'learned my place.' And then I tell him how I knew I would love him forever, only him, and how I needed to come back to him.

I tell him all. Every. Last. Thing.

Charles grows quiet, even somber. A change has come over him. The twinkle has left his eyes, his usually soft mouth is drawn into a hard, straight line. That look he wears on his face is becoming familiar. I've seen it twice now: the first was when I told him I would leave Ridgeland and the second was when he heard his mother had passed. He releases my hands, faces forward, and straightens his stooped shoulders.

Shifting the car into gear, he makes an abrupt turn in the road. We travel back toward Morriston.

My breath is shallow, and my eyes burn with unshed tears. I grasp my hands to still their trembling. I stare at Charles, willing him to look at me, but he's doesn't turn his head. No longer do I hold back the tears. They stream down my cheeks.

And all I can think is: *I was never worthy of him.*

The never-ending days drag on. My feet are not only planted firmly on the ground, I'm dragging them through several inches of sand.

Charles no longer comes for me on Sunday mornings. I spend my time alone, reflecting. I write Lottie a long, sorrowful letter, telling her Charles has left me because I had kept a terrible secret from him. I can't bring myself to tell her what it was, not with her expecting her first baby in a matter of weeks.

I decide to attend the Morriston Presbyterian Church and join the choir, but my heart is not in it. To my ears, my voice sounds dull, flat, off key. I have to be honest with myself—my favourite part of singing in the choir, or going to church for that matter, was being close to Charles. I decide, from here on, I will be honest with myself and with those who come into my life. There will be no more secrets, lies, or omissions. I will not allow my heart to become calloused.

I vow I will be a changed woman: an honest woman, a woman who would be worthy of Charles' love—if he will ever have me back.

The weeks pass. Lottie writes. She has given birth to her first child, James, a big, bouncing baby boy. I mail a gift, a sweet little baby quilt, which I made myself. I enclose a card filled with congratulations and well-wishes for her and the baby's good health, being careful not to disclose my feelings of utter jealousy at her happiness.

Months pass and I become more and more despondent. Rumours are flying around Morriston; Charles is courting another woman who recently moved to Ridgeland. Lottie confirms the rumours are true. It appears he has moved on. My heart is fractured, damaged beyond repair, and each day I'm dragged further into a bottomless, black pit.

February, 1926

It's another dreary Monday morning. A mixture of sleet and light snow drizzle from the leaden sky. The bell hanging above the front door tinkles as Jack, the mailman, enters with his canvas sack thrown over his shoulder. Regardless of how low I feel, the sight of this portly little gentleman always lifts my spirits. If he wore a red suit rather than his mailman's uniform, he could be Santa Claus.

"Good mornin', Mary!" his cheery voice calls as he wipes his boots on the entry mat and saunters to the counter. He rests the bag on the floor. Opening it, he retrieves a stack of envelopes and newspapers tied together with a twine and hands them to me.

"Is it?" I ask as I untie the twine.

He turns and gazes out the front windows. "I suppose it could be better," he says, chuckling. "Actually, it really isn't all that nice outdoors today."

"No, it's not," I agree, "but then I wasn't referring to the weather."

"Ah, Mary, a pretty face like yours shouldn't be wearing a frown. Tell me, what's troubling you?"

I force a smile as I sort the letters into the residents' mail slots. "It's nothing Jack. Feeling a little low, that's all."

"Yeah, it's hard not to in this weather. But let's not forget—spring's only a month away." He turns and ambles toward the door. Looking over his shoulder, he calls, "Put a smile on that pretty face, okay, Mary?"

"I'll try." I hold an envelope addressed to me. The delicate script is familiar. I quickly break the seal.

Dear Mary:

I hope this letter finds you well, or at least as well as can be expected.

I've been so worried about you lately and I hope what I am about to tell you will help your situation. I have secured a new station for you, if you want it. It's a clerk's position at a local store in Leaside. The owner, George Smith, is a good friend of Robert's. I believe the pay he is offering is a little higher than what you are receiving now.

I have also arranged for you to board at a home within walking distance of the store. The woman who owns this house is Mrs. Hartwick. She's a dear, older lady—I'm sure the two of you will get along wonderfully.

I know the past months have been very difficult for you without Charles, so please say you'll come. We all agree we would love for you to be closer to our family, especially Father.

Please write back as soon as possible with your decision.

Your loyal friend,

Lottie

My next thought is sad enough to silence a song-bird. *There's no reason I can't go; there's nothing left here for me.*

I wake the next morning before the nurse enters the room, my mouth pasty from the sleeping pill. I take a sip from the glass on my bedside table and swish the cool water around my parched mouth.

My mind is foggy, the memory of my last thoughts before I fell asleep still lingering. I had made my confession to Charles. I see him, like it was yesterday, shifting the car into gear and making an abrupt turn-about in the road. Pulling up in front of the Morriston General Store, he marched over to the passenger door and assisted me out. He would be a gentleman to the end. He said not a word. His eyes never met mine. And as he drove away, I stood alone on the street and watched, through blurry eyes, until the Model T was nothing but a black speck on the eastern horizon.

I shake off those feelings. "Stop it, that's not how this chapter ended," I whisper to myself.

My chat with Nurse Johnson is the second memory that surfaces. Somehow, while I was ascending from a deep sleep, I had made a plan. I will attempt to engage Helen in conversation. If anyone in this world deserves a friend, it is her. I will be that friend.

My gaze travels across the room to her bed. She's beginning to stir, her long legs stretching beneath the covers. Her eyes slowly open and she looks my way.

"Good morning, Helen," I say, slowly articulating the words.

She rises in her bed and smiles brightly at me.

Chapter 15

Late September, 1926

The church service is over, and Mrs. Hartwick and I stroll down the tree-lined walk toward home. My new home.

"Good morning, Grandma Hartwick!" A group of young women seated on a park bench wave at us.

Mrs. Hartwick waves and calls back, "Good morning, girls!"

I turn to her. "Does everyone in town call you Grandma Hartwick?"

"No, not everyone," she says. "You don't."

"Should I?"

Without looking at me, she reaches for my hand. "I'm actually quite surprised you haven't picked up on that yet. You've been living with me for over six months now."

I squeeze her hand and smile. Lottie was right; Grandma Hartwick is a dear lady. I've never had a grandma and it would be an honour to call her Grandma Hartwick. She and the Thistles have given me a genuine sense of belonging to a family once again.

Her soft voice cuts into my thoughts. "Will you be spending the afternoon with the Thistles?"

"No, not today," I say, sighing. "They're expecting Charles for dinner."

"Oh, I see," she says, understandingly. She halts her step, a bright smile crinkling around her eyes. She inclines her head toward me. "Hey, no frowns though; it's far too beautiful of a day for any of that nonsense. And don't you fret. We'll find something to fill our time. Something fun."

I nod and return her smile. She has a way of filling the void in my heart, as I have helped fill hers. Her husband of fifty-four years passed one year ago. If she can be brave, well then, so can I.

Later that day, alone in my room, I consider this new life I have made for myself in Leaside. Ellen, Lottie, and Dacre seem pleased to have me here. Over the past months, I have grown to love Dacre, despite his rough-around-the-edges-old-farmer ways. He's the closest thing to a father I have had since I left England. I know he's fond of me too and, when I catch him watching me, I like to imagine he's wishing I am his daughter-in-law.

Or, perhaps that's me—still holding out hope.

Charles was right—Dacre is lonesome without Lotheria. Sometimes I wonder if he questions whether he did the right thing by moving here and leaving Charles alone on the farm. It must seem surreal for him, at times, considering he spent his entire life on that farm. But if there's one thing I've learned—circumstances change. In order to survive, a person must learn to adapt. It appears Dacre is doing that, and I suppose I should too.

But I find this new life bittersweet—being close to Charles' family but not to him. I lie on my bed, imagining the happy hours the Thistle family would have spent at Lottie's home today. I picture Charles giving baby James, now a sturdy one-year-old, a horsey ride on his knee. And then when evening fell, Charles and what's-her-name (I can't even bring myself to think it) would have said their goodbyes and driven home. I envision her snuggling up beside him on the seat, his arm draped over her shoulders.

I close my eyes tight, willing the image away as vile jealousy rises like bile in my throat.

If I truly loved Charles, I would wish for his happiness, would I not? I wish, with my whole heart, for him to be happy.

But only with me.

Another work week has begun. I enjoy my new position and work, my employer being a fair man. The store is amazing, carrying everything one could ever need, plus many luxury items very few do need. And daily as I work, serving patrons, stocking shelves, tidying and dusting, I fantasize one day the bell above the door will tinkle and Charles will be standing there.

Constantly, I tell myself to stop dreaming about him. Stop hoping. Move on, because, obviously, he has. It doesn't seem to be working.

By now, I know many of the store patrons by name, and when I think of moving on, there is one gentleman who comes to mind. Mr. Williams. He's a handsome travelling salesman, who, over the past month, stops into the store more and more often.

I'm attending Lottie as she admires the new arrivals of winter woolen fabric. It's on the tip of my tongue to ask her about Charles' visit yesterday. I'm loaded with questions: did what's-her-name accompany him, or did he come alone? Did he stay overnight? Is he still here?

I clamp my mouth shut and push those questions from my mind. Of course she came with him, and do I really want to hear that woman's name spoken and have more images of them together thrown at me? No, I don't. What I need to do is move on. I take down another bolt of cloth, a beautiful emerald colour, and hold it on the counter before her. She fingers a corner of it with one hand while her other arm cradles James, sleeping on her shoulder.

The heavy oak door squeaks on its hinges and the bell above it tinkles. Again, a flutter of hope fills my chest. I look up. His tall frame fills the doorway. He tips his stylish fedora at me and winks. My heart sinks.

I have never encouraged Mr. Williams' flirtatious attentions, but perhaps it's time I did. I force the corners of my lips into a smile. "Excuse me, Lottie, I'll be back with you in a moment." I move out from behind the counter and stroll toward him.

He removes his hat. His grey eyes flicker as they roam over my hair, face, dress, calves, and shoes. "My, oh my, don't you look exquisite today, Miss Mary?"

I've had little experience with flirting, but I'm game to give it a whirl. I incline my head and brush a loose curl from my forehead. "Why thank you, Mr. Williams. Funny you should come in right now . . . I was just thinking of you."

He smiles wickedly. "I hope they were pleasurable thoughts. And please, call me Tom."

I finger the long strand of costume pearls around my neck.

It appears I've given him the green light. He steps in close, leaning over me. He's a full head taller than I. My sight rests on the starched white collar peeping out under his tweed overcoat. His black hair gleams, he smells of hair tonic and aftershave, his teeth are straight and white. His clothing is well made, cut to accentuate his lean, masculine body.

"I was thinking of you, too, when I arrived in town a while ago. I've a few business calls to make this afternoon, but I was hoping if you didn't have plans this evening, you might join me for dinner."

For a second, I'm flattered, excited, and then I see Charles' playful, boyish smile, his bashful blush. *How can I accept Mr. Williams' invitation when I'm still in love with Charles?* I shift from one foot to another. It's been well over a year since he broke it off with me. Nothing has changed. Nothing except the fact he has a new girlfriend. So, why can't I accept the fact he has moved on? If I'm ever to get over him, I must do the same. Mr. Williams, I mean Tom, is strikingly handsome. It wouldn't be hard to look at him across a table. He's friendly and has a good sense of humour. Yet there's something about him, something I can't lay my finger on. He's so very different from Charles. Yes, that's it—he's different from Charles. He's not Charles. I'm still looking and waiting for Charles.

Tom's low voice disrupts my thoughts. "It can get awful lonely on the road and there's nothing worse than eating dinner all alone, night after night." He studies me through lowered lashes, a sad pout tugging at his mouth.

Oh, don't I know? I don't eat dinners alone anymore, but over the years I've spent many evenings eating by myself—in my mistresses' kitchens, in boarding houses, in restaurants. I suck in my bottom lip with my next breath. It's time I put Charles behind me. It's time I moved on. "I believe I might be free this evening."

"Perfect!" His forced pout quickly disappears. "Shall we meet in the dining room at the Leaside Inn at, let's say, seven o'clock?"

A blush creeps up my neck, and I raise my hand to cover it. I nod.

He reaches one hand to my face, the tip of his fingers trailing down my cheek and chin. He picks up the string of pearls and closes the distance between us. "I'll be waiting for you," he purrs.

I slowly turn with the uneasy sensation of being watched. Lottie's glaring at me.

The great door groans as it closes.

She rushes toward me, placing her back to the door, and hisses, "What do you think you're doing?"

I shrug and attempt to keep my voice calm, but it still sounds shrill to my ears. "What does it look like? If you were eavesdropping, which apparently you were, you must know I accepted an invitation to dinner."

"Dinner? Just dinner? Are you sure about that? Because from what I saw, it looks like the two of you were getting pretty cozy with each other. Have you been out with him before?" Her outburst awakens James. He whimpers and squirms in her arms.

My blush deepens. "No, this is the first time he's asked."

"Humph," she huffs, her voice even louder. "So, now you'll date just any man who asks you out?" She bounces James on her shoulder. His whimpers turn to cries.

Why is she so upset? I'm a grown woman now, I'm not her responsibility, and, really, this is none of her damn business. "What are you talking about? Of course I won't date *any* man. That should be obvious—I haven't dated *anyone* in over a year now and you know it!"

"Well, you might want to ask around, learn a little about a man's character before you decide to go out with him."

"What do you mean?"

Lottie studies me. Her face softens. She takes a deep breath and, in a level voice, she asks, "Mary, do you even know Mr. Williams at all?"

"Of course I do," I say defensively. "He's a travelling salesman—sells perfumes, colognes and such. I believe he comes from the London area. But he's been in the store several times now and I've had a few brief conversations with him."

Lottie listens to me while she gently bounces James in her arms. When he has calmed, she brushes the tears off his cheeks with her thumb. Pulling her gaze back to me, she prompts, "Anything else?"

"No, not really." I stall for a second and add, "He seems nice, though. I thought we'd get to know each other over dinner."

"Hmm . . . no, that's where you're wrong. There'd be little he'd tell you about himself." She pauses for a moment while she shifts James to her other arm. "But I suspect Mr. Williams had plans to get to know you much better after dinner."

My goodness, that's presumptuous of her. I'm not sure I'm more angry or hurt she thinks I would let something like that happen on a first date.

"Ah, can't you see? Mr. Williams is a cake-eater."

I snort as I inhale. "A what?"

Lottie smiles and shakes her head. "Oh, sweetheart, where have you been? Have you never heard of a cake-eater?"

I feel very naïve. "N-no."

"He's a lady's man, Mary, a playboy. I overhead George, I mean your employer, Mr. Smith, gossiping about him one day with another man. Mr. Williams was just leaving the store when I came in." Her brow creases. "I would have thought you knew—practically everyone in town does. Anyway, what makes it even worse is he's married. Sure, he's handsome and charming, that's why he's got a girl in every town. Now, you really don't want to be one of them, do you?"

I whisper, "No, of course not."

I glance through the window glass. Mr. Williams is crossing the street, a self-confident swagger in his step. Suddenly I see him for what he is—the type of man who looks at a picture on the wall and, instead of seeing the photograph behind the glass, admires his own reflection.

And it occurs to me why I am attracted to him. He reminds me of Sam.

After my workday has finished, I return to Grandma Hartwick's home. On the mantelpiece, a letter lies waiting for me. I snatch it, and run to my room.

October 1, 1926

Dear Mary:

Perhaps you've spoken with Lottie since my visit last Sunday. Perhaps you have not and this letter will come as a surprise to you.

I gasp. Lottie has said nothing to me. *Oh, no, surely Charles hasn't proposed to what's-her-name?* The paper shivers in my hand. I've had an aversion to letters since I was a little girl, always expecting bad news to arrive with them. Gripping the paper, I take a deep breath.

I tried to put you out of my mind. I dated another woman, a good woman, a woman who would have made a fine wife, but she's not you. I had hoped being with her would help me forget you. It didn't and so I've broken things off with her. I feel terrible about that—it wasn't fair to lead her on and cause her pain, but it wouldn't be fair to marry her either, feeling the way I do for you. I need to make things right.

I want you to know I forgive you. For everything. I forgave you a long time ago for up and leaving me—you were young, not ready to give up on your dreams and settle down. It was harder to forgive you for not writing and telling me right away about our baby. But, in time, I came to understand your reasoning. The most difficult thing to forgive was you didn't want my child. It was a hard blow—it took me a long time to reason that one out in my mind. But when I put myself in your shoes, I'm not sure I wouldn't have felt the same way. I understand how frightened and alone you must have felt.

Now, I realize the person you are. It must have been very difficult for you to make your confession. You must have known I was about to propose and yet you took that chance, knowing very well what the consequences might be. You have shown immense courage and strong character. And Mary, I want you to know you are a good woman, too.

I'm sorry for not being more understanding. I realize now I turned my back on you when you finally felt you could trust me with your secrets.

Will you now find it in your heart to forgive me?

Lottie has led me to believe you still have feelings for me. If it is true, will you, once again, be My Mary?

Will you please come back to me so I can propose to you properly?

Charles

It doesn't take me long to answer that letter and pack my bags. Within a few short weeks, Charles has arranged a room for me at another boarding house in Ridgeland. We set the date for our wedding, May 28, 1927, which will give us ample time to plan the wedding, plus do a few updates on the farmhouse.

The months glide by in a flurry of contented bliss. May is upon us; the special day fast approaching. Arrangements have been made: the invitations mailed, the church booked, the small banquet and flowers ordered, my dress complete.

There is only one thing missing.

I'm early to the church this fine Sunday morning, seated in the choir loft. The organist plays soft music as the congregation proceeds through the front doors. I raise my eyes from my hymn book and there he is, exactly where he had stood five years ago. I make eye contact with him, my hazel eyes locked with his halcyon blue. Our gaze holds as he walks toward me and takes his place. The church fills, the minister arrives and, after a short salutation and prayer, he calls out the number for the first hymn. After the organ prelude, our voices rise, my soft alto melding with Charles' strong tenor. To my ears, they're the only two voices filling the sanctuary, and they blend beautifully together.

Finally, we are singing from the same hymn sheet.

After the service, we drive to the farm. Pulling up beside the farmhouse, I admire the transformation. The grey clapboard siding is now a bright, fresh white. Inside, we've painted the kitchen cabinets a soft butter yellow. The trim throughout the house has been freshened up with a coat of white paint, and the living room has been wallpapered. The hardwood floors gleam with two coats of varnish. Even though it's Sunday, I change out of my best dress and don my work clothes.

We sit at the table and enjoy a quick lunch, while I open my notebook and go over the wedding arrangements with Charles one more time. He's ever so patient as he listens to all the details. When I come to the end of my list, I grow quiet, staring at the pages.

Charles stands and clears the dishes. "Something wrong?"

"No, nothing's wrong. Something's missing, that's all."

He chuckles. "How could anything be missing? You've been going over these plans for weeks now."

I flat-out say, "Shows how much you know about weddings. Something *is* missing. You know, normally, a girl would have her father give her away."

Charles' face sobers as he sits again. "I'm sorry. I hadn't thought about that." He thinks for a moment. "I have an idea. I'll bet Dr. Randall would be honoured to walk you up the aisle."

I furrow my brows. "I had thought of him too, but I've spent so little time with them over the past few years. It just doesn't feel right."

"Well, you're a strong, independent woman. You could always walk up the aisle alone. Lots of women have done that."

"Yeah, I thought of that too, but that's about the last thing I want to do. I've felt like I walked alone enough of my life without walking up the aisle alone too. No, I know who I want—it's highly unusual—I'm just not sure I should ask him."

Charles inclines his head.

I look him straight on. "I want your dad to walk me down the aisle."

Charles arches his eyebrows. He leans over and kisses me. "Go ahead and ask. He'll be delighted."

After lunch, Charles carries in two saw horses, an old plank door, a wooden stepladder and a pail of warm water, rags, and scissors. We slide the bed and dresser into the middle of the room and create a makeshift table with the sawhorses and door.

I open a brown paper sack and remove one roll. It's a lovely paper, water-coloured wisteria blossoms, vines and leaves on a cream background. Simply looking at it makes me happy; it's so dainty and feminine. I unroll a length and hold it up against the dingy-grey plastered wall. "What do you think? Isn't it beautiful?"

Charles raises an eyebrow, a slight frown on his face. "Yep, it's definitely beautiful."

I detect a hint of sarcasm in his voice. "So, is . . . is there a problem?"

"No, no problem."

"Then why are you looking like that?"

"Like what?"

"Like that!"

"Well, okay, since you asked—don't you think it looks a wee bit girly?"

Oh, Good Lord. I didn't think of that. This room will not only be my bedroom—it will be *our* bedroom. He's right; I should have chosen a more neutral paper. My shoulders slump in disappointment.

"Ah, Mary, I'm sorry. I shouldn't have said that."

"No, don't apologize. It's my fault. I should have picked a more neutral paper—something suitable for a married couple's bedroom."

Charles is deep in thought. After a moment he says, "I don't know for certain, but I doubt you've ever been able to decorate a bedroom the way you would want, have you?"

I shake my head. "No, of course not. I've never had any say about my bedrooms."

"No, I didn't think so. Now, I've no idea how to make a home attractive; my parents never had extra money for niceties." He considers his thoughts and continues, "You've lived in grand homes and it appears you have the know-how. So, why don't you make this room as pretty as you'd like?"

"Really, Charles? Because I can exchange the paper. I don't want you to feel uncomfortable in your own home."

He gazes at me, a mischievous grin forming on his lips. He blushes. "Honestly, I don't expect I'll be staring at the walls very much in this room anyhow." He regains his composure and continues, "No, don't give it another thought. I'll never feel uncomfortable in this house—it's always been my home. What I really want is for you to make this house feel like it's your home."

Sitting the roll of paper on the table, I move to him and wrap my arms around his neck. I feel his heat through the light cotton fabric of my work dress as I press my body against his. I marvel at how our bodies fit together perfectly, my soft curves melting into his hard frame. He slips his arms around my waist, his hands resting on my lower back.

I'm lost in his embrace, my only thought being I want to be held by him forever. My fingers snake through his short hair as I press my lips to his.

I step backwards, guiding us toward the bed.

The next morning, I relay The Courtship Years to Dr. Clark, as concisely as I can, although I omit the parts which are too private to repeat. I'm jittery this morning, likely on account of my sleepless night.

When I am finished, he looks up at me. "It appears you finally got your man."

I nod my head. "I most certainly did."

"Mary, you're coming along nicely. I'm going to recommend you finish your final treatments this week and then we'll follow up with a few more sessions. I believe, if all continues the way it has, you should be ready to go home in another two weeks, give or take a day or two. How does that sound?"

Enthusiastically, I give him my best and brightest smile. "It sounds perfect. I can hardly wait."

Chapter 16

June, 1927

Two weeks have passed since we were married. Two amazing weeks. I never imagined life could be so unbearably sweet or I could be this happy. We have transformed our four-room home into a sweet little doll house. Each day I'm playing make-believe, like Mrs. Metcalfe's children did in their playhouse. I dust and sweep, cook and clean. Until now, those chores were simply chores, tasks requiring much effort. Now I sing and hum while completing them. For once, I am doing for myself and I am blissfully content.

My closest neighbour, Jean Sherman, is a lovely woman, only a few years my senior. She and Bob have one son, little Georgie, a busy two-year-old. On our wedding day, I knew Jean and I would become good friends. She offered cuttings and shoots from her rose bushes, hydrangeas, and lilac bushes. I transplanted the rosebushes along the front and east side of the house so, with the white backdrop of the building, they would be clearly visible from the road and laneway. I planted the hydrangea in the centre of the front yard, with the lilac bush off to one side of the front door.

My vegetable plot, which I started early this spring, is well on its way to producing a bountiful crop. My other duties include cleaning and sorting the eggs, straining the milk, separating the cream, and churning the butter. I intend to be an excellent farmwife.

And at the end of each day, there is Charles.

It is morning and I am in my tiny kitchen making breakfast. I remove the cast iron frying pan from the wall and place it on the hot cooktop. When it has heated, I lay five strips of thick bacon in it. They sizzle and snap, the ends curling, and the sides fluting like fancy ribbon candy. Charles sneaks up behind me and wraps his powerful arms around my waist, his lips grazing the back of my neck. My body responds to his touch and I turn.

Immediately, my stomach churns, sweat beading on my upper lip. I break from his embrace and race for the back door. Throwing it open, I step off the porch, drop to my knees and retch.

I wait for the nausea to pass, my arms wrapped around my stomach, my eyes closed, inhaling through my nose and exhaling through my mouth. This feeling is not entirely new to me—the nausea that appears in an instant. If my guess is right, I'm pregnant. My pulse races, along with my thoughts. *When it comes, what will everyone think?* You can be sure they'll all be counting the months. I shake off those thoughts. *Why do I care what people think?* I'm a happily married woman now and I desperately want this baby.

When the sensation has passed, I wipe my mouth with the corner of my apron, turn my head in the house's direction and open my eyes. Beside me, I see Charles' blue jean overalls and work boots. He bends over, slips his hands under my arms and helps me to my feet.

I gaze into his face, the face I love more than anything on this earth. How could I have ever thought he was just an average guy? He is everything good in this world.

He is my world.

Happy tears stream from my eyes. I take his hands in mine and kiss them. "So, are you ready to be a daddy?"

His wide grin tells me everything I need to know.

Helen and I sit in the library chairs Florence and I used to occupy. It's not so very different being here with Helen—Florence was a quiet companion, too—but when Helen and I converse, I do all the talking.

Helen is a very attentive listener, plus I've realized she can read lips. And even though she contributes very little other than the occasional smile, sigh or frown, it appears she enjoys my narratives. I wonder if I should tell her I'm aware of her past, maybe drop a few hints. Perhaps then she'll share her story with me. She hums, so I'm sure she can speak. She must choose not to.

Lately, I've been rehearsing my stories with her before relating them to the doctor. I have no intention of becoming emotional again with Dr. Clark—I'm a healed woman, ready to go home.

I'd rather talk than sit here stewing. "Helen, would you like to hear the story about my babies?"

She lowers her book, her eyes peeking over the top, and nods.

"Good. This is the story I'll be telling Dr. Clark tomorrow. It goes like this: Ernest, my firstborn, was born on a blustery, bitter day. It was January 29, 1928. He was an exceptionally large baby for an eight-month preemie, weighing in at almost nine pounds. At least that's what I told the curious ones with their raised eyebrows and pursed lips as they studied my plump baby boy, all rosy and dimpled. His little brother, Tommy, followed along less than two years later, on December 20, 1929. I always thought of him as our special Christmas present."

I wink at Helen. "Maybe I won't mention their birthdates and how I lied to everyone about Ernest being premature. Dr. Clark really doesn't need to know all that, does he?"

Helen smiles mischievously.

"No, I don't think so either."

I continue. "They were wonderful years, full of promise." I'm in a story-telling mood, so I'll expand on this part, and although I won't share it all with Dr. Clark, Helen might enjoy it. "Charles and I worked hard on the farm, making improvements and buying more stock when we could afford. Now, today we have five horses, four of them workhorses, and one for riding. One workhorse is an old mare named Hettie. She's given us three foals over the years. We have an automobile, but Charles stores it in the barn for the winter—the roads out our way are hard to navigate in the winter snows and early spring thaws. We also have eight milking cows." I chuckle as I picture Charles milking them.

Helen raises her eyebrows.

"Okay, I'll tell you. It's ever so funny to watch Charles as he milks. You've probably seen someone milk a cow, right?"

Helen shakes her head.

"No? Oh, I suppose you wouldn't have, living in the city. Anyway, you don't know what you're missing! Now, when Charles milks, he sidles up to the cow and rests his head in her flank, no different from anyone else. But, what's funny is all the barn cats and kittens, which are usually quite a few, sit off to the side. He milks the cow, the warm milk streaming into the bucket, and then he squirts milk into each of the cats' mouths—one by one, down the line—without missing a beat. His aim is always true because the cats never move. They just sit there, waiting their turn."

Helen smiles and nods for me to continue.

"We also have pigs and hens. The income from the extra milk, eggs, and butter pretty much pays for all our other necessities.

"When the boys were very young, we got a collie pup from a litter born to our neighbour's dog. They named her Ruby. My, how they loved that dog."

The smile slides from my face; I'm speaking of Ruby in the past tense. My eyes sting as my last memory of her surfaces. I need to push through this feeling and carry on. I take a deep breath and steady my voice. "They had so much fun with her. When Ruby was full grown, Charles made a small harness for her and she would pull the boys on their sleigh. That dog was so smart. You know, my boys actually trained her to climb the loft ladder in the barn."

Helen's face is skeptical.

I incline my head. "I can see you don't believe me."

She shrugs.

"I tell you, it's true." I hesitate a moment. "Have you been in a barn loft before?"

She shakes her head again.

"Of course not. There are no barns left in the city." I continue, using plenty of hand gestures, speaking slowly and clearly. "Fine, let me paint you a picture. A loft ladder runs vertically up the wall of a barn loft into its highest peak. Tommy would head on up first. Ernest would get Ruby started on the ladder, placing her front paws on the rungs and boosting her up by her hind quarters. Ruby would follow Tommy and then Ernest would follow right behind her, steadying her or giving her a little help if she needed it. The three would congregate on the small wooden landing, and then they would jump off, one by one, into a huge, loose haystack below them." My face and voice are soft with the memory. "My, oh my, Ruby was quite the dog. There'll never be another like her."

Helen's face beams. She inclines forward, hanging on every word.

I've become sidetracked. This story is supposed to be about my babies. "Anyway, in the early part of our marriage, Charles and I planned to build a new home. It was apparent we would need more room in the coming years to accommodate our expanding family. My goodness, Charles only had to look at me with that mischievous twinkle in his eye, and I became pregnant."

"I wanted our home to be just like I remembered my Mama Annie's: full of children's laughter, the sound of little feet padding on the floors."

My voice hardens. "Those years didn't last. My boys were born at the tail end of the Roaring Twenties. The good years were behind us, swept away by the gales of the Great Depression." I shake my head; those last few sentences were dramatic. My story-telling skills are definitely improving. "I imagine you have memories of that time while living in foster care, although you would have been rather young then."

She nods her head and mouths, "I remember a little."

My eyes widen in surprise. She mouthed those words.

"I don't know what you endured, but for us, it seemed there was never enough. Not enough time, not enough to eat, not enough clothing, not enough anything. Charles was right—we were lucky to live on a farm, growing our own produce, eggs, meat, and milk—at least we weren't standing in food lines like the city dwellers. There were so many men out of work, so many families were homeless. Thankfully, Charles had never taken out a mortgage and our farm was in Ontario and not in the western provinces where years of drought, hail, and grasshopper plagues caused some residents to pack up and leave, their homesteads left to their bankers or buried in blizzards of dust.

"It was hard to stay positive during those times. It felt as if we had put our lives on hold. My very body sympathized with the plight of Canada—my womb had become a dust bowl. It seemed I could not conceive and if I did, I lost the baby within the first few months. In the five years after Tommy was born, I lost four babies. I grieved terribly for the first two." I pause and take a deep breath. "After that, I no longer cared.

"Charles and I ceased to speak of the *new home*. We struggled, like most, to survive. And, yet, as little as we had, Charles remained a generous man. He insisted we help others who were worse off than ourselves with gifts of eggs, milk, and butter. That was my household income we gave away to the needy, but I didn't mind; there was nobody left with cash to buy it anyhow.

"Oh, and one Sunday, at church, we had a terrible shock. Tommy was about seven years old, sitting beside me on the pew. He looked up at me, his hand held to his chest. His face was pale, his lips were turning blue. I remember him saying, 'Mama, it hurts'. Our doctor lived right in town, near to the church, but luckily that Sunday morning he was right there in the congregation. He quickly checked him over and called an ambulance and Tommy was raced to the hospital. My poor boy has a heart condition. Luckily, he's had no episodes since then, but we're very careful with him.

"Anyway, back to my story. On the heels of the Depression, the Great War began. When I was able, I would scrounge together care packages, jams, pickles, canned meat and such, and mail it to my foster family in England. I tucked letters into the packages, begging them to come to Canada where I could keep them safe. They never came."

I swallow my grief. Papa is gone. I will never see him again. Not that I really expected to, but I had always hoped I might. But death changes everything. If my faith were stronger, I might believe I will be reunited with him again, but honestly, I question if there is anything after this life. And if there is, I'm not sure I want any part of it. Which brings me to the subject of religion. It confuses me. With hundreds of different man-made theories of God, reason tells me they can't all be true. Most times I don't know what to believe.

I shift my attention back to my story. "I received a letter from England only days before I came here, telling me my foster father had passed. That was the day before Ruby died." I hang my head. "I suppose I'll have to tell Dr. Clark about that—about Papa and Ruby." I sit quietly for a moment, thinking. "I think it's important he knows. You see, Helen, I killed Ruby."

I hear a gasp and look up. Helen's eyes and mouth are open in shock.

I shake my head. "No, not directly Helen. It doesn't matter though, my boys still blamed me for her death. I heard her outside scratching at the door and I just couldn't be bothered to get out of bed and let her in. So, I left her out in the cold and she froze to death. Those days, before I came here, I was so sad. It'd been coming on for a long time, years actually. I didn't understand what was happening to me or how to deal with my feelings, and it got so bad I just wanted it to end. I didn't care about anyone or anything. All I could think was how wretched I felt."

Helen nods her head as if she understands those emotions.

I'm deep in thought and sit in silence for a moment. "Now, after being here, I know it wasn't my fault Ruby died, but I still feel shame for the person I had become. I was jealous over what other people had, I coveted my best friend's home, and I was mean to Charles. Self-pity consumed me." My eyes fill with tears and I turn my face. "I hate who I had become."

I've shocked myself with my brutal honesty. Taking a deep breath, I rise, and walk to the window. These memories have put me on a roller coaster of emotions, but better to be doing it here with Helen than with Dr. Clark tomorrow morning.

Through bleary eyes, I note the grass is greening at the edges of the walkways, pale sunlight casting shadows over the dirty lawns. The daffodils' green shoots are emerging through the wet soil, poking their sharp heads toward the sun. Spring is almost here—the time for rebirth and new beginnings.

A timid touch on my shoulder startles me. I turn. Helen's face is drawn in sadness. Her eyes search mine, bidding permission before awkwardly wrapping her scrawny arms around me.

I hold her thin frame tightly and allow my tears to flow freely, for myself and for her. Her body relaxes as she lays her head on my shoulder, and in each other's arms, we cry for our lost childhoods and for all that is cruel in this world.

We separate and return to our seats. Helen wipes her eyes and blows her nose. She picks up her book, *The Heart is a Lonely Hunter*, and resumes reading. I read that book a while back and when I saw it here on the shelf, I handed it to her. Engrossed in the story of a lonely, deaf-mute in the Deep South, she hums.

In a flash of recognition, I know the song. It's the one my little friend, Emma, sang at the Girls Village Home in Ilford and on the steamer from England. I recall the words—something about two lovers and a fair.

I rise again and, sitting on my heels in front of Helen, I ask, "Do you know the title of that song?"

She shrugs.

I sigh. "No? Do you know any of the words?"

She smiles and nods.

Excitement rises in me. I'm about to ask her to mouth them for me, but I've got a better idea. "Can you sing them for me?"

Her eyes widen and her fingers rise to her lips. "M-m-me, sing?"

To stabilize myself, I rest one hand on her knee. She doesn't flinch. "You can speak and sing, can't you?"

She gazes into my eyes, once again looking for validation.

I nod and give her an encouraging smile. "You can, can't you?"

She nods again.

"Okay, let's hear you," I encourage. "Go on."

She takes a moment, clears her throat, and begins. Her voice is weak and unsteady from lack of use, the tune off-key.

"M-m-my young love said to me,
M-my mother won't mind
And my father won't slight you
For your lack of kind.
She stepped away from me
And this she did say,
"It will not be long love
Till our wedding day."

She pauses for a second. I nod and she continues on with the second verse. Her voice steadies into the rhythm.

"She stepped away from me
And she moved through the fair
And fondly I watched her move here
And move there.
And she went her way homeward
With one star awake,
As the swan in the evening
Moved over the lake."

I turn my face up to her and listen with rapt awe. There's another verse to this song—it's all coming back to me—the words, the tune. It's an old, old song entitled, She Moved through the Fair. While Helen sings, I see another girl's face and hear her sweet voice as she sang this ballad. Once again, I nod encouragement at Helen. She continues in a clear voice, carrying the tune perfectly.

"L-last night she came to me,
My young love came in.
So softly she entered,
That her feet made no din.
And she came close beside me
And this she did say,

"It will not be long love
Till our wedding day."

The song is finished. I remember the first time I heard Emma sing it; the words puzzled me and I had asked her if she could explain the last verse to me. "You silly girl," she had said. "You're older than me, you should get it." She explained the young woman died tragically, and she returned to her lover as a ghost at night, repeating the words 'it will not be long, love, till our wedding day'—the day they would reunite in the afterlife.

Helen's voice breaks. She appears as if she is about to cry, but she giggles. It is one of the sweetest sounds I have ever heard.

I squeeze her knee. "Where did you learn it?"

"At, a, hospital . . . a long, t-t-t-time ago," she stutters. Her words are thick and slurry.

I glance up at her in shock. I'm surprised she could sing so fluently and, yet, she stutters. My heart pains as I imagine the ridicule and abuse she likely endured because of it. Little wonder she's only hummed until now. "Yes, before you lost your hearing. Do you remember who taught it to you?"

She nods. "Yes, Emma, t-t-the cl-cl-cleaning lady. She sang it all the t-t-t-time."

What are the chances it could be the same Emma? Singing the same song? I'll never know for sure, but it gives me hope Emma survived Hazelbrae and is still living. I move to my chair and sit. Closing my eyes, I offer a silent prayer for Emma; for even though I question if there is an afterlife, prayer still comforts me.

I open my eyes and study Helen. It's amazing how far she's come in two months' time, how she has blossomed living in a safe environment. I suppose what her grandmother did for her has turned out to be a blessing. Still, how much better would her life have been if her birth mother had kept her? I wonder what my life would have been if mine had kept me? Miss Silas was likely correct—I, most likely, would not have survived.

Helen stares back at me, our eyes reading each other's faces.

"What a gift you are, Helen."

She tilts her head, her eyebrows drawn together.

"Well, you are," I say, laughing.

The following day, I spend my allotted half hour with Dr. Clark. I am not nearly as honest with him as I was with Helen.

One more treatment and three more sessions, and then I'm done. I am much better now, but I don't suspect I'm fully recovered. It's difficult to describe, but something is not quite right. My mind seems muddled—no, that's not what I mean—it's not muddled, it's vague. Some memories are hazy now and I know they weren't that way before I came here.

So, that's another thing I won't tell Dr. Clark. I can't have him thinking something else is wrong with me. My goal is to get through the next two weeks and go home to my waiting family.

Chapter 17

Twelve weeks in—my last week.
I'm in the laundry, pressing a mountain of linen. Inwardly I sigh; there seems to be no end to it, when Helen carries another basketful of white kitchen aprons toward me. "My goodness, girl! Could you slow up a wee bit?"

A mischievous smirk plays on her lips.

"Don't think for a minute I don't know what you're up to. You're trying to show me up, aren't you?"

She shrugs and grins.

Sprinkling an apron with water, I glide the heated iron across it. The wrinkles disappear, wiped away with one stroke of the hot appliance. The threads in the cloth retain no memory of them. I furrow my brows. *Could the shock treatments be erasing my memory?*

As I work, my mind returns to another day several years ago.

Winter, 1937
With index and middle fingers, I puncture the bowl of bread dough. I watch it deflate like a punctured rubber tire. Turning it onto the floured table top, I divide it in half with a sharp knife and form four identical

loaves. Placing each loaf in a greased pan, I cover them with a clean tea towel and set them on the warming tray of the cookstove to rise.

The mantel clock in the parlour chimes three times.

The back door of the entry bursts open. I peer through the glass of the kitchen door at their rosy faces. Charles grins at me as he enters the warm kitchen. "Is the tea ready, my Mary?" He chafes his hands together to warm them before tackling the buttons of his coat.

Ernest bursts into the kitchen. "Sure smells good in here, Ma. What are you making for supper?"

"Nothing you would like," I say, chuckling. That boy of ours has a bigger appetite than the pigs in the barn.

While they remove their coats and boots, I wipe the table and set out mugs for tea. "Tommy, c'mon now, it's time for tea."

Seconds later, seven-year-old Tommy bounds into the kitchen, dressed in flour sack overalls. "Hey, slow down," I remind him. "You know what the doctor said."

"Jeez, Ma. I'm all better now." He wiggles into his chair at the table.

He seems as if he is, but I still worry about him. Pouring the tea, I think, *they never need to be called twice.* Two young boys with hollow legs—sometimes it's a struggle to keep their bellies full. Charles is so right, we should be thankful we live on a farm. We're far better off than some city folk.

"What's the matter, Ma?" asks Tommy.

"Nothing, sweetheart. What makes you ask?"

"'Cause you look sad." He quickly adds, "Did you make gingersnaps like you said you would?"

"No, I'm sorry, sweetie. There wasn't enough flour left after I finished making the bread. We'll get more next time we go to town." Tommy frowns, and I tousle his curly, blond hair. "Ah, now you look sad."

We drink our tea, the children's diluted with milk and honey, while they devour thick slices of bread and jam. When we've finished, Charles says to Ernest, "Well, son, let's go back to the barn and finish stacking that wood."

"Can I help?" asks Tommy.

I inhale sharply and turn to Charles.

He gives me a slight nod, assuring me Tommy will be alright. "Of course you can."

"No, Dad, he doesn't work. He'll just be in the way," grumbles Ernest. For a boy of nine, he can work as hard as some men, and he likes to think of himself as his father's right-hand man.

He's growing up so fast, I think. *Far too fast.*

Charles narrows his eyes as his eldest son as he stands. "C'mon Tommy. We can always use another pair of helping hands, isn't that right Ernest?"

"Yeah, I suppose," Ernest says, reluctantly.

Once again, they don their outerwear and hustle out the door. I watch the three through the frosted window glass until they disappear through the barn door. Turning, I spot Charles' glove on the floor. I pick it up and turn it over in my hands, studying it. It's one of the brown leather gloves I gave him ten years ago, our first Christmas together. Now it's worn and tattered, the palms faded and wrinkled, a large hole in the thumb's ball.

I slump into a chair. That's just like him; he never once complains. A sob catches in my throat while a tear escapes and slides down my cheek. For a few moments, I sit, lost in my thoughts. I imagine a better world: a world where Canada is not in a depression, where children have cookies with their tea, and leather gloves can be replaced. A world where I am not always so exhausted.

The mantel clock chimes once, indicating half past the hour. I finger his glove once again. This just won't do—I'll start knitting him a new pair tonight. I rouse myself and brush the tears from my eyes.

The loaves of bread have doubled in size. I open the oven door and place them beside the pot of stew. Knowing the bread will take an hour to bake, I pull on my warm outer clothing and tuck the old glove inside my pocket.

Charles did say they could always use another pair of helping hands. I step outside and, leaning into the raw, biting wind, I plod over the bare, frozen ground to the barn.

Helen taps me gently on the shoulder and points at the iron held in my hand. Her nose crinkles and she sniffs the air. "M-M-Mary, you're d-d-daydreaming again."

"Oh, good grief!" A telltale brown imprint of the iron witnesses my inattentiveness.

"Oops," Helen says, chuckling.

My last memory still lingers and with it another one, much further back, slowly surfaces. The vision is murky, the memory obscure, difficult to grasp. Somehow, I sense the act of bread-making has triggered it and so I concentrate on that thought.

My mind clears, as if a heavy veil was slowly drawn away.

I'm very young, perhaps four or five years old. I'm standing on a stool, watching a woman's long slender fingers poke into a big crockery bowl of raised dough. The dough expels its built-up gases and deflates. I suck in a breath, hold it, and puff out my cheeks as big as I can make them. Hands on my belly, I slowly blow the air out. It whistles through my teeth and I giggle. My giggles turn to snorts. A woman's musical laughter fills the room and then I hear her say, "Oh, my Mary, you're such a silly little goose."

In my mind's eye, I see the woman's hands, but not her face. Yet I know she is someone very special to me. I close my eyes and concentrate. Suddenly I gasp. I was only a small child, so it has to be Mama Annie. I was watching her as she made bread. The hairs on my arms bristle. I have memories I would gladly forget, but not those of Mama Annie, Papa, and my foster family. *Please God, not those.*

I should write a journal about my early years—those memories are jewels and I must hold on to them, somehow, if only on paper.

It's strange, isn't it, how memories alter as time passes? During the years we struggled the most, it seemed like it was the worst of times and yet, now, those same periods of time have turned into golden memories.

I am so ready to go home and make things right again—to make more golden memories with Charles.

Dr. Clark settles into his chair. "Mary, this is your second to last session with me."

I hold my hands in my lap. "I'm sure hoping that's the case."

"How are you feeling?"

"Very well, thank you."

"Good." He takes a good long moment, studying the papers fanned out before him.

It makes me nervous. I chew on my bottom lip.

Finally he speaks. "Mary, I've spent some time rereading my notes." He stalls again, which makes me even more uneasy.

"Most of our sessions focused on your childhood." His finger trails down the paper as he continues, "Your birth circumstances, being taken away from your foster family, your immigration to Canada, and your domestic placements in various homes. I think we can both agree those events left you feeling vulnerable and ashamed of yourself. Am I correct?"

I cross my ankles and tug them back under the chair. I nod. "Yes. That's true."

"And in our last few sessions we discussed your marriage, your sons, your miscarriages, living through the Great Depression, and wartime." I want to draw my eyes away, but I hold my gaze steady. I know what's coming and I must stay strong. Once again, I nod, encouraging him to continue.

"While most of those things, I'm sure, have been very difficult for you, I'm still trying to understand what drove you to your suicide attempt." He pauses. "We haven't addressed that issue, now have we?"

The leather chair squeaks as I wiggle in it. My thumb finds a tag of skin around a nail and I pick at it. Immediately, I realize what I'm doing. I stop and clutch my hands together.

Dr. Clark's eyes are on me, taking in my every move. "Mary, what are your thoughts on that?"

I take a deep breath. "Yes, you're right. We haven't discussed it."

He presses his lips together and nods. "I didn't think so. Are you ready to discuss it today?"

I sigh. I'm thankful I had rehearsed it with Helen—I think I can get through it again.

And so I tell him how I was, prior to coming here: absorbed in self-pity, envious of my best friend Jean's lovely home, mean-hearted toward Charles, disconnected from my family—from my own life. I tell him about Papa's death and how heartbroken I was, how I didn't care about anyone or anything, except my misery. And then I tell him how I let Ruby freeze to death at the back door, and how my boys blamed me for her death. An earlier memory flashes before my eyes, the one that began my great decline, but I push it aside. I haven't thought about it for a long time and I've no wish to think of it now.

Still, the telling is very difficult and tears spill from my eyes. Dr. Clark rises from his chair, moves around the side of his desk and hands me a handkerchief.

I dab my eyes and blow my nose.

He returns to his seat. "Finally, it appears we've come to the core of your melancholia. We've spent many hours talking about the trauma caused by your childhood circumstances and being a Barnardo Home Child, which left you doubting your self-worth and place in this world. But it appears we should have spent more time concentrating on the more recent years." He pauses for a moment. "Mary, I want to be perfectly clear. I think it would be best if you remained with us a little longer, perhaps another two or three weeks, to discuss the recent issues you brought up today."

I'm deflated and hang my head for a moment, but then anger starts to burn in my gut. Most of my life I've been told what to do, where to be, how to act. Even Charles did that to me when he sent me here.

I'm tired of it.

I don't want to stay here. I've put in the time. I've done the work. I'm ready to go home.

I *am* going home.

In a calm voice, I say, "No, I can't stay. Charles is expecting me at the Ridgeland train depot on Friday."

Dr. Clark inclines his head. "That can be undone; we can send him word."

I shake my head. "No, I'm not staying. I've come to terms with everything in my past. I've faced up to all those hard memories and dealt with them. I am so much better now."

"Yes, I agree. You are much better. However, now we've much more to go over."

I hold my ground. "No, we don't. I swear I'm not that person anymore."

He takes a moment. "Can you honestly tell me you don't feel envy toward your friend, or mean-spirited toward Charles, or disconnected from your life?"

I feel my courage unravelling and strangle the hanky in my hands. "No, not at all. Since I've been here, I've learned a beautiful home is not important. My goodness, look at my roommate, Helen Wood. She's adjusted so well to living here, she has made this hospital her home. Surely if this feels like home to her, my little house will feel like heaven to me." I inhale quickly and continue; I don't want to give Dr. Clark a chance to say a word until I'm finished. "And I don't feel mean-spirited toward anyone and I'm certainly not disconnected. I just want to go home to my family . . . please."

He leans forward, elbows on his desk, his chin resting in his hands. He says nothing for a long moment, all the while his eyes peering at me over his black-rimmed glasses.

Stay calm, I will myself. *Breathe. Don't squirm, don't wring that hankie, and don't pick at your fingernails. Breathe. Just breathe.*

Finally, he picks up his pen. "Okay, Mary, I'll sign your release. I still hold reservations, but if you really feel you're ready to go home, I see no reason to detain you against your will. Now mind you, if you feel you're slipping again, I want you to get in touch right away with your family doctor and he'll arrange for you to return here as soon as possible. Is that understood?"

"Perfectly," I say through a wide smile.

"Okay then. I'll see you again on Thursday and we'll discuss the circumstances prior to your suicide attempt in more detail."

Breathing a sigh of relief, I quickly exit his office.

~

I keep my final meeting with Dr. Clark. We discuss, in detail, my self-pity, my envy, my pulling away from my family, and Papa's and Ruby's death. And, somehow, I convince him to sign my release papers, on the condition I return to the hospital should my melancholia return.

I agree to his terms, but that's never going to happen.

No, not in a million years.

~

My valise lies on my bed. I pack my folded clothing and personal items inside and snap the buckles closed. A taxicab has been called to deliver me to the train station at one o'clock. I skipped lunch; I was far too excited to eat.

I hear Helen's soft footsteps before I see her. She walks through the door and in a hushed, throaty voice she asks, "W-w-where were you?

You didn't come to l-l-lunch." Her gaze falls on the suitcase at my feet before climbing to my face. "You're l-l-leaving now?"

I nod. "Yes."

Her eyes blink in a rapid succession. "You were just g-g-going to g-g-go?"

I shake my head. "No. No, I would never leave without saying goodbye to you."

A frown flits across her face, replaced by a forced smile. She blinks again, forcing back tears.

"Ah, Helen, don't be sad." I skirt past my suitcase toward her.

"I'm n-n-not sad. I'm happy for you."

Reaching, I grasp her hand in mine. "Of course you are," I say, searching her face. "I'll write to you. I promise. I'm a wonderful letter writer. We'll be pen-pals. You can write, can't you?"

Helen scowls. "Of c-c-course."

"Of course you can. I'm sorry for even thinking that. So, we'll write regularly, okay?" I'd like to tell her I'll come and visit her, but I know it will never happen. I'm never coming back to this place and she'll never be leaving it. The reality of the situation is we were nothing more than two people destined to meet at a certain place and time. I smile warmly and wrap my arms around her thin shoulders. I was blessed to have had this time with her. My eyes smart with unshed tears. "I will miss you," I whisper into her hair, although I know she can't hear the words.

I draw away, my hands still on her shoulders. "Will you do something for me?"

Her eyes narrow.

"Don't look so concerned," I say. "It's really a simple request."

She inclines her head, the corners of her mouth tipping up into a genuine smile.

"I want you to find yourself another friend. I'm sure if you made the effort, you'd find there are plenty of other good women in this place . . . you simply have to get to know them. And when you find her, one you think could become a true friend, open up to her, talk to her, let her get to know you. You have a voice. Don't be afraid to use it."

She brushes a tear away and nods.

"Oh, and one other thing. Never stop singing."

I gather my winter coat, drape it over my arm, and slip my fingers around the handle of my valise. Walking toward the door, I glance back over my shoulder. Helen stands at the foot of my bed, looking lost and forlorn, the same look little Emma wore, years ago.

It breaks my heart. I say, "Be brave, Helen. And if you can't be brave, well then pretend." I suck in my lower lip. *Oh my. Where have I heard that saying?* It's not just another one of the old adages I'm always picking up and repeating. I haven't heard this one in years, and yet it feels so personal, like I've been hanging on to it my whole life. The hairs on the back of my neck bristle.

I take a deep breath, straighten my shoulders, and pass through the doorway.

But, as I go, I can't help but feel I'm leaving a piece of me behind.

Chapter 18

A light rain falls. Tiny rivulets meander down the window of the moving train. With my gloved hand, I clear a peephole on the steamed glass. The view has drastically changed over the last three months. Then the landscape was a frozen black and white wintriness buried in snow and ice. Now the fertile brown earth is clearly visible, the fields puddled with run-off from the dirty, shrunken snowbanks yet clinging to the fencerows, and water trickles everywhere. Wisps of early spring delicately colour the edges of the countryside.

Again, my reflection ghosts the moving scenery. Similar to the landscape, this woman has also changed. Her skin is no longer ashen, there are no dark circles under her eyes, and her hair is clean and styled. I offer my reflection a smile, albeit slightly nervous—she and I are on our way home—unaided and unwatched.

My eyelids close and I concentrate on the trance-provoking sounds around me: the murmurs of the other passengers, the chugging engine, the rumbling of steel wheels over the rails. I incline my head against the window and press it to the cool glass.

October, 1940

I smooth my hands over my thickening waist. My stomach muscles clench as I button the front of my green floral housedress, and cinch the belt tightly around my midriff.

In the kitchen, I pump water into the large kettle and place it on the stove. I stare out the window, past the barns and back the lane to the woodlot. The clouds part, and a shaft of sunlight beams on the forest, showcasing its weeping autumn colours, the trees ablaze with the warmth of browns, reds, oranges, and golds. I imagine strolling through a thick bed of fallen leaves, the dry, bitter scents intensifying as my feet shuffle through them. Autumn is my favourite season, although it is far too short. For when it departs, winter descends upon us again—the season I like least—the harsh, bleak one which seems to go on infinitely. But then, eventually and never too soon, springtime steals back, its expanding warmth slowly dissolving the frostiness.

Next to autumn, I love springtime on the farm. There's an excitement in all things new: the trees budding, crops sprouting, cows calving, sheep lambing, pigs farrowing, and chicks hatching.

Will I also be birthing? With my many miscarriages several years ago, this has come as a surprise. I never believed it could happen and yet, here I am, thirty-eight years old and four months along in the pregnancy. The others were lost between two and three months and honestly; I waited to shed this one too, like the rest.

Because of that, I have told no one, not even Charles. But I suppose now I should. And it's time I made an appointment with the doctor. I should have done it earlier, especially with my medical history.

Perhaps this is the little someone I've been waiting for, the one who has been missing from my life, the little girl to gently raise with the same love Mama Annie showered on me. Maybe God will finally bless us with a little girl. I decide, right then and there, we will name her Annie.

As if considering Charles has conjured him up, he's coming to the house, his arms laden with stove kindling. He sees me through the window glass and, puckering, he blows me a kiss.

I feel the first butterfly quiver in my womb.

I close my eyes, and offer a silent, heartfelt prayer for the child's safe arrival. Tonight, I will tell Charles. He always said he wanted a little girl who looked like me—a little girl with auburn curls.

The day has passed. Twelve-year-old Ernest and ten-year-old Tommy are asleep in their beds and Charles and I are retiring for the night. I switch on the small table lamp, its soft glow throwing long shadows across the room, before closing the bedroom door. Charles unbuckles his overall suspenders and removes his clothing. He lays them on the chair and turns back the bedclothes.

I glance over at him, before he crawls into bed: his small stomach paunch, carried high, his thinning upper arms, his slightly dropping shoulders. His body reflects his age of forty-six years and the hard physical labour it has endured. He's not a young man anymore, nor does he have the physique of the strong farmer who made love to me for the first time eighteen years ago. My goodness, he'll be an old man when this child reaches adulthood.

He's watching me as I unbuckle the belt around my waist. I had closed the door to talk privately, but, unexpectedly, a new notion pops into head. With a sense of daring, I slowly unbutton my dress. It puddles on the floor. Turning my back to him, I glance over my shoulder and reaching my arms behind, I undo my brassiere, slip it off my shoulders and drop it. My fingers graze down my sides, slip under the elastic of my panties, and shimmy them over my hips. I flick off the table lamp and join him between the sheets.

The harvest moon streams through the window glass, illumining us. Charles weaves his fingers through my hair and holds my face while he kisses my eyes and cheeks. He presses his lips against my ear. "What's this? No nightie tonight?" He moves his hands downward over my shoulders and tender breasts.

In the semi-darkness, I draw him to me.

Afterwards, we lie facing each other, the sheets pushed to the foot of the bed. Our aging bodies are shadowed and sculpted, bathed in silver moonlight. Charles' fingertips tenderly trace my figure: my head, shoulder, and down my arm. They rest on my ample hip.

Lifting his hand, I roll over onto my back, and lay it, palm down, on my belly. I stare at the ceiling and murmur, "Charles, how would you feel if I told you we're going to have another baby?" I hold my breath and wait for his response.

He raises his upper body and leans on his elbow. He's pensive, saying nothing.

I lay my hand over his. "If all goes well, she'll be born in the early spring. I felt her move for the first time today . . . " My voice trails off and I turn to him, my eyes searching his.

His face looks as if he's forcing himself out of a deep sleep. "She?"

"Yes, *she*. Don't ask me how, but I know it's a girl."

"I don't understand; I didn't think we'd have another child."

"Me neither."

Charles studies me. His hand is still resting on my belly, cradling the unborn. His eyes glass over and he whispers, "Are you okay with this?"

Holding his face in my hands, I softly kiss his lips. "I'll be honest with you—I wasn't until today. I thought I was too old, that it was too late for us to have another child. I didn't want to get my hopes up in case I lost it, like the others. And then, only this morning, I felt her move. Charles, I want this baby." I take a breath. "But I asked you first, how do you feel? Do you want her?"

He draws me close. Our bodies, though changing as we grow older, still fit together perfectly. He kisses my forehead. "Ah, my Mary, you know I do."

We lay together a while, at times quiet, other times whispering about how things will change. We toss around name suggestions, and then I giggle and tell him I'd already decided, earlier in the day, on Annie. We speculate how the boys will dote on their baby sister. And then we talk of practical things, how we will need more space. Perhaps, an addition to the house, which will incorporate a larger bedroom for us, an extension on the kitchen, plus an indoor washroom. I imagine the luxury of indoor plumbing, hot running water, not going to the outdoor privy in the dead of winter. But that will take money—money we don't have. "Don't worry, Mary, we'll manage. I'll figure something out," he murmurs.

My body has cooled. I slip into my cotton nightgown and pull up the bedclothes. I fall asleep, cradled in Charles' arms.

Lower back pain drags me from a deep sleep. The moon sits high in the sky—it's well past midnight. *Lie perfectly still*, I tell myself. *It'll pass.* I close my eyes and drift off.

I'm awoken again with intense lower back pain and abdominal cramps. The moon has scarcely moved. I press my hands against my belly, grit my teeth, and groan with the onslaught of another gnawing contraction.

Charles stirs.

A trickle of hot liquid seeps between my legs. "No, God, please," I whimper. I clamp my lips shut, silencing my cries.

Charles raises himself and leans over me. "Mary, what's wrong?"

Pulling myself into a sitting position, I clutch the front of my nightgown, pressing the cloth between my legs as if doing so will prevent it from passing. "The baby." I choke on the words.

Charles dashes around the bed and switches on the lamp. I double over in pain as another contraction grips me. A stream of hot liquid gushes from my body along with a small, solid mass. I push back the covers and we watch as a pool of blood stains the white sheet below me. My hands shake as I tug on my nightgown, raising it to my waist.

I stare in awe at the fetus embraced between my slick thighs.

"Oh my God, Mary."

I lift the babe and hold it in the palm of my hand. It's no bigger than a newborn kitten and yet she's perfectly formed. I marvel at her delicate fingers and toes, her miniscule eyelashes, and eyebrows, her paper thin, translucent eyelids. I take the hem of my nightgown and tenderly wipe the blood and fluid from her tiny body. Her legs part, and yes, *she* is a girl.

That was the death of my baby girl. And the birth of my deep decline.

The train pulls into the station. I rise and follow the other passengers to the door. My breath comes fast and my heart thuds in my chest. Throughout our entire marriage, Charles and I have only been apart this once. Will our reunion be awkward? Will we act as strangers? I'm through the door and down the steps, my eyes scanning the small crowd.

He steps politely through the crowd and draws me into his arms. Eventually, he pulls away from me, his eyes watery. "Aren't you a sight for sore eyes?" he says, beaming. Charles finds my suitcase and grasps my hand. "C'mon. Let's go home. The boys are waiting for you."

I exhale, and my shoulders relax. The light rain has stopped and thin sunlight is breaking through the gaps in the heavy cloud cover. It's springtime. I am home. And I am wanted.

"I thought you would have brought the car today," I say as we walk to the buggy.

"No, our road is barely navigable right now. Besides, I thought it'd be a treat for you to ride in the open air on such a beautiful afternoon."

"You're so right," I say enthusiastically. I notice Charles' favourite workhouse, Daisy, harnessed to the buggy. "Where's Winny?"

Charles helps me into the buggy. He's silent, pretending he didn't hear me. He flicks the reins. "Giddup, Daisy."

"Charles?"

Without turning, he softly says, "Mary, I'm sorry. Winny's gone. I sold her to help pay the hospital bills."

I gasp. "No, surely you didn't have to do that. She was the boys' favourite." I don't know what I was thinking when he wrote he was making sales from the barn, but I never thought he'd sell Winny. I furrow my brows. "Hold on a minute. You said 'help?' What else did you sell?"

He faces me. "Well, you're gonna find out soon enough. I sold Winny, two of the workhorses, and four of the milk cows."

My shoulders fall. "Oh, no. How much did it cost for me to be there? That's too much. I should've never let you do that."

"Ah, Mary, never mind the costs. I'm glad you went. Look at how much better you are now. And I don't want you feeling bad about it either—you needed help, and that cost money. So, I sold the animals and now we're square with the world once again. We don't owe one cent to anyone. And the war's over now. Pretty soon, things will be booming. You wait and see. We'll be back on top in no time."

I gaze at him in awe. Of course we will be. We may never get ahead, yet somehow we always manage.

As we drive out of Ridgeland and enter the countryside, Charles says, "You said little in your letters about your treatments or your stay at the hospital and, of course, we didn't talk about too much the day I came to visit. Do you want to talk about it or is it something you want to put behind you?"

If I've learned one thing from Dr. Clark, it's how to talk about myself. "No, I'll talk about it with you, but I'm not sure how much I want to tell the boys. Eventually, though, I will want to put it all behind me."

Charles smiles encouragingly. "I understand."

I stall for a moment. "Charles, I don't know where to start."

"Start anywhere. But, like I said, if you'd rather not talk about it, I understand."

"No, I do," I reply. "Okay, I found my sessions with Dr. Clark to be very enlightening—he had me tell him my life story, right from the very beginning."

Charles raises a brow. "I'm thinking maybe this Dr. Clark knows you better now than I do."

"No, that's not true. I may have told him more about the years I'd rather forget, you know, those before I met you, but, in all honesty, there's no one who knows me as well as you do." I lower my face, another untruth to hide. 'In all honesty'—it's funny how carelessly I use those words. Dr. Clark knows me better; at least the early version of me.

"So, you told him all about your happy childhood in England with your foster family?"

"Yes, of course. Like I said, I started from the beginning."

"With your Papa recently passed, I imagine it was hard for you to talk about them. There's so many of them too, your Papa, Mama Annie, Henry, Kathleen, Dorothy, and all the rest." He hesitates a moment. "I'm sorry. Since I've met none of them, I have trouble remembering all their names."

I expected the brain fog would be a temporary side effect from the treatments, but it seems to be getting worse. "What was the name you said after Mama Annie?"

Charles pauses in thought. "Henry. He's the oldest, isn't he?"

That's strange, I don't remember a Henry. Rubbing my gloved hand over my temple, I try to recall their names. Some are not coming to me. That life feels like such a long time ago and as I piece it together, the memories wane. It's no longer clear and I know it was a few months ago. Good Lord, it's terrifying. If I recorded those memories on paper, like I said I would do, could I even trust them to be accurate? Could I even remember enough to write anything down?

Eventually, and without certainty, I answer, "Yes, you're right, Henry was the oldest."

Charles glances at me and reaches for my hand. "I'm sorry. I shouldn't have pressed; I can see you're tired." He pulls on the reins and Daisy plods onto the South Centre Road.

He's so understanding. I swear, I am the luckiest woman in the world. "Going to the hospital and having the treatments did me good, but I never want to do it again. I'm always going to hold you to your promise."

He furrows his brow. I can tell he doesn't know what I'm talking about.

"You remember. The day you came to visit. You promised you would never commit me again."

"Yes, I remember now." Charles nods his head. "You can hold me to it."

We ride along in silence while I gaze fondly at the familiar landscape. Daisy strains as she drags the buggy along the rutted dirt road.

Charles dips his head toward Hilltop Farm. "Jean says she sent you a get-well card while you were at the hospital." The Sherman home sits proudly on the knoll. It is beautiful, but I no longer covet it.

"Yes, she did. It was lovely to hear from her. How are they?"

"Oh, they're good. I told them you were coming home today. Jean said she'll be around to see you in a day or two."

I incline my head. "That'll be nice. I miss her."

He's still holding my hand and gives it a tender squeeze. "I thought you'd like that. By the way, the boys have a surprise waiting for you at home."

"And what might that be?"

"Well, you're gonna have to wait and see."

The reins are slack, but Daisy knows home. Without instruction, she turns off the road. I study our farm as we drive up the mucky lane. The four-room house has changed little over the past years, decades. It was Charles' great-grandfather's home, the land purchased by him from the Crown and held in the Thistle family name ever since. The old clapboard siding remains, the white paint faded so much it looks like whitewash. Two red brick chimneys poke through the weathered shingles. The old barn stands firm and square on a good red brick foundation, however, the pasture fence and posts are showing their age and need of repair. The most magnificent feature on this farm is the ancient butternut tree positioned at the southeast corner of the house—older than the deed of land on which it stands. If Charles is correct about the economy improving, we'll start making improvements again.

Daisy comes to a stop as Tommy and Ernest vault out the back door.

"Ma!" Tommy dashes toward the moving buggy.

Charles draws back on the reins and Daisy comes to a halt. I take a deep breath and step down from the buggy, and as I turn to the boys, they stop. They look as if they've had their reins pulled in too.

Tommy tentatively approaches me. "Ma, you're home." He looks shy, awkward, standing there before me. Ernest walks around to the back of the buggy and retrieves my valise.

I grab Tommy by his shoulders and pull him into my arms. "Get on over here and give your mother a hug."

He wraps his arms around me. "Are you all better now?" he murmurs into my hair.

"Yes, I am. And you? Have you been okay?"

"Yeah, I'm fine," he says, pulling away from me. "What did they do to you there?"

"Tommy!" Charles' voice is stern. "Don't be pestering your mother with questions right away. If she wants to tell you about her stay later on, she can."

I tilt my head toward Ernest. I believe he's grown another two inches in the past three months. He's so tall and handsome. "And do I get a hug from my first born?"

"Of course you do, Ma," he says as he sets the case down on the grass. He takes me in his arms and gives me a gentle squeeze. "Welcome home."

Charles drives off to put the buggy away and Daisy to pasture while the boys and I go to the house. I'm overwhelmed with relief and happiness. Walking through the door into the entry, the aroma of roasting meat and vegetables emanates from the kitchen.

I remove my hat, gloves and coat. I sniff. "Mmm . . . what's this I smell?"

"Ernest and I wanted to surprise you by having a welcome-home dinner tonight," Tommy says. "It's roast beef and vegetables. We've even baked a butterscotch pudding cake for dessert."

"Oh my goodness, you boys are too much! Your Dad told me you were turning into real good cooks."

Ernest carries my bag to the bedroom while Tommy and I remain in the kitchen. I take it all in: the orderliness, the cleanliness, the properly set table.

"Not me, Ma. Ernest did most of the cooking while you were in the psychi...." Tommy stumbles on the word and drops it, like a hot poker.

I pretend not to notice. "I'm sure you did your fair share."

Ernest laughs as he returns to the kitchen. "Not quite his fair share, but he helped. And yeah, I did most of the cooking, but I sure won't mind giving that task back to you."

"And I'll be glad to take it off your hands," I say, beaming.

"C'mon Tom, we should get to the barn and give Dad a hand with the chores. You'll be okay here for a bit, Ma? Supper should be ready within an hour."

"Of course I will be," I reply. "I'm just going to change my clothes and freshen up a bit."

"There's hot water in the kettle on the stove." Ernest says as he dons his outerwear and heads outdoors, Tommy in his wake. I watch as they slog along the muddy lane to the barn.

In their absence, the house falls eerily silent. I move through the kitchen into the parlour. Everything is in perfect order, floors gleaming, rugs shaken clean, furniture polished. I enter my boys' bedroom. It's tidy, like the rest of the house. I wonder if they've kept it this way while I was gone, or did they work all day to make it spotless for my arrival? I'm hoping it's the latter. If not, it doesn't appear I'm needed as much as I thought I was. "Stop it," I say. "You're proud of them for this. You taught them to be self-sufficient, remember?" I'm speaking aloud again and clamp my mouth shut.

Back in the kitchen, I remove the kettle from the stovetop, carry it to my bedroom, and pour water into the basin. I sigh. No more indoor toilets and running water for me. I take my time performing my toilette and change into my everyday dress.

As I unpack my valise and hang my clothes in the closet, I recall Nurse Ryckman's comments the day I arrived at the hospital. I scowl as I imitate her curt, harsh voice. "You sure didn't bring much with you."

I remember thinking; I didn't have much to bring, and this was the best I had. *Why didn't I say those words to her face instead of only thinking them?* For the life of me, I can't fathom why she wanted to make me feel even worse about myself when I was in such a vulnerable state. It seems some people in this world are just naturally cruel.

As I shut the closet door, I mutter, "And a good riddance to you, Nurse Ryckman. May I never lay eyes on the likes of you again."

Chapter 19

Placing the egg in my basket, I move to the next nesting box. Matilda, my favourite hen, fluffs herself and emits a broody growl. She looks like my feather duster hanging on the wall in the kitchen. "Oh, you're setting, are you? How many eggs have you under there? Don't mind me; I'm just going to check, okay?" She's harmless—she won't peck. Slipping my hand under her, I run my fingers over the eggs, counting them. "Only five. That's not enough." I slip three still-warm eggs underneath her. "Here, have a few more."

Everyone says it's been a hard winter, but I've hardly noticed. Stepping out of the henhouse, I raise my face to the April sky. My, but it feels good. It's barely discernable, but there's a promise of heat in that sun. A brisk wind races around the corner of the building and I draw my cardigan across my ample bosom and head for the house.

Bob Sherman's red Ford pickup truck turns in our lane. He's the first of our neighbours to own a truck. Luckily for him, he purchased it before the war started—there have been no pickups available to civilians over the past four years. Jean's pert silhouette sits tall in the passenger seat. I sigh as I look down at my everyday dress hidden beneath my apron, my ratty old cardigan, and my rubber boots slick with mud.

Jean rolls down her window as the truck pulls up beside me. She's the same as always, dressed in her classic timeless fashions, her hair neatly styled, lips glossed. "Mary, I'm so happy you're home. You look wonderful!"

A gust of wind tosses my loose curls across my face. I brush them from my eyes. "You've got to be kidding. Look at me."

"I am. You're beautiful—you're the picture of health."

"Where are you off to this morning?"

"Here, I hope. Bob has a couple of errands to run in town, and I was thinking I would visit with you while he's away. Is this a bad time, or do you have an hour to spend with an old friend?"

I glance at my attire one more time. The fraction of a second pause is long enough for Jean to sense my reluctance.

"If you're busy, I understand," she says. "I know I've caught you by surprise."

I reach for the door handle. "No, not at all. Of course I have time."

"Are you sure? I know it's early for a visit, but I just couldn't wait to see you."

I give her a genuine, warm smile. "C'mon in."

Jean rolls up the window and steps out. Bob's long, wiry frame leans across the bench seat. "It's good to have you home, Mary. Can I fetch you anything from town?"

"Thank you, Bob. It's good to be home. No, we don't need anything, but thanks for the offer. Charles stocked the larder before I came home."

"Okay, then. I'll be back in a bit, Jean. I doubt I'll even be an hour."

Jean laces her arm through mine as we walk to the house. "Oh, Mary, I'm so glad you're home. Have you any idea how lonely this road is without you?"

"Now I know you're not serious."

"But I am. Anyway, Bob says Charles and your boys did a fine job of looking after things while you were away."

"They most certainly did—you'd hardly know I was gone." I shake my head and add, "Actually, it scares me a little; I think they may keep a better house than I do."

"Oh, I can't imagine that," Jean says, laughing.

As we cross the threshold and enter the house, I step out of my dirty boots and hang my old cardigan on a hook. "C'mon in, Jean, I'll put the kettle on." My heart swells with gratitude for my family's thoughtfulness as I glance around the orderly, clean room.

"Oh, don't go to any bother for me."

I give Jean a sideways glance as I set the basket of eggs on the counter beside the milk pail. "Are you honestly going to pretend you don't want a cup of tea?"

Jean laughs once again. "Ah, you know me better than that. No one makes a cup of tea like you do."

"I'll tell you again, probably for the hundredth time—it's not me—it's the pot." I grab the kettle, pump a small amount of water into it, and place it on the stove. "Do you mind if I tend to the eggs and milk while the kettle boils?"

"No, of course not. Can I help you with anything?"

"No, just make yourself comfortable. This will only take a minute or so."

Jean sits at the table, in her usual spot. My heart warms toward her; she's comfortable in my home. She's always said a lovely house doesn't make a home, and she was right. Even if it's small and shabby, I've made this house a home. *Why did I not see that before?* I make eye contact with her and smile. "I've missed you."

Her face softens and her eyes mist. "I've missed you too," she whispers.

As I strain the milk through cheesecloth, and sort and clean the eggs, Jean catches me up on the local news and gossip. I carry the teapot and mugs to the table and sit. She's not one to pry, never has been, but after I sit, an awkward silence falls over us. It's unusual as Jean's never at a loss for the right words. Finally, she says, "Would you like to talk about it?"

I take a deep breath. I can either talk about it, or I can bottle it all up again and, eventually, I'll be right back where I was before, with that hard callus over my heart. I'll tell Jean and later, I'll tell Charles. I'll tell them everything.

I openly divulge my stay at the hospital, my consultations with Dr. Clark, and the treatments. When I describe my first shock treatment, her eyes well up with tears, and when I tell her of Florence's suicide attempt, she reaches across the table for my hands.

"Mary, I'm so sorry you had to go through that."

"Really, Jean, it's okay. It was worth it. I'd do . . ." I stop mid-sentence; I had almost said "I'd do it all again," but that would be a lie. I won't do it again. I'll never do it again. "It doesn't matter," I continue. "I'm better now and Charles has promised he'll never send me back there again."

She squeezes my hand. "You do feel much better, though?"

I hesitate a second. "Actually, I haven't felt this good in years."

"That's wonderful," she says, smiling. She studies me for a moment. "You said you told Dr. Clark everything? Even your early life?"

"Yes. He said he needed to know my entire story so he could understand what my life had been like and what led me to . . . well . . . you know."

Jean shakes her head. "Mary, you don't have to say it."

My eyes drop, and I glance away. "Thanks. Anyway, that's why."

"Yes, I understand all that. However, I can't help but wonder—" Her words trail off.

"Wonder what?"

She hesitates a moment, chewing her lower lip. "Mary, may I ask you something?"

I raise my eyebrows. "Of course you can."

"I'm your friend, right?"

"Of course you are." I detect a note of indignation in my voice. I soften it. "You're my best friend, Jean. You've been my best friend since Charles and I were married."

Her hand is still holding mine. She strokes her thumb over my knuckles. “So, if I’m your best friend, why have you never told me?”

I gaze into her kind eyes. *Why have I never told her? What’s even worse—why have I never told Charles or my boys?* I lightly pull my hand from hers and pick up my teacup. My lips tremor on the rim of the cup as I press it to my lips. I blink rapidly as I battle the tears burning in my eyes. She’s right. I should share it with her. She’s a local girl, born and raised in this area. I know her family, her siblings, and her history. *Why shouldn’t she know mine?*

“You’re perfectly right, Jean. There’s no reason I haven’t told you. I suppose I haven’t talked about it because it always made me feel ashamed.”

“Ah, Mary. If it hurts to talk about it, then don’t.” She pauses. “I shouldn’t have asked. I’m sorry.”

“No. I want to tell you,” I insist. “My early memories with my foster family in England are my happiest. I had a wonderful life with them. I’ll start there, like I did with Dr. Clark.” I look into my tea cup and give myself a moment to think. My mind scrambles as I attempt to remember that time. I stall. “Just give me a minute, okay?”

“Of course.” Jean raises her teacup and drinks, her eyes watching me over the rim of the cup.

Memories flash before me in bits and pieces, obscure fragments of a dream. Try as I might, I can’t hold on to them; they vaporize as swiftly as they settle. I set my teacup down and shake my head, trying to clear my thoughts. My breaths come quick and shallow—those memories are gone.

Our faces turn toward the window at the sound of the truck engine. Charles comes through the barn door and saunters toward it. He leans on the fender and talks with Bob.

Jean rises. She lays an understanding hand on my shoulder. “It’s okay, Mary. Maybe another time.”

I nod.

"Anyway, I best be going. Thanks for the visit and the tea." At the back door, she slips her arms into her jacket. "You take care of yourself," she murmurs as she lets herself out.

I sit there, rubbing my temples and staring into my cup. I struggle to remember my earliest, clear memory. It slowly surfaces. I'm eleven years old, standing on the stone steps of the cottage holding my Annie doll, all my other earthly belongings packed in two cloth sacks beside me. A strange woman speaks to Papa. Mama Annie wraps her arms protectively around my shoulders. It makes me feel safe, but I know it won't last. The woman looks down at me and says, "Time to go, Mary." Mama releases me, her hand trailing across my shoulders as she drags herself away. Papa kneels before me and, holding me tightly in his arms, he whispers, "Be brave, my Mary and if you can't be brave, pretend." He stands and Mama falls into his arms. She's crying now, I can tell by the shaking of her shoulders. I can't see her face; it's buried in the crook of Papa's neck. He's smiles at me, but it's not a happy smile—it's a be-brave smile, a keep-your-chin-up kind of smile, and tears glisten in his eyes.

I didn't know it then, but that would be the last time I would ever see them. I gasp and cover my mouth, silencing my cry.

With no memory of anything before that time, I've lost everything good from my childhood. The pickup truck slowly backs out the lane. Jean's been watching from the truck, her troubled eyes fixed on the kitchen window. She waves.

I dab the corners of my eyes with a napkin. "Damn it! What a sacrifice I've made." Will this memory loss be permanent or, heaven forbid, will it progress until I lose even more of my past?

Be brave, he had said to me.

"I've tried, Papa, I really have." My thoughts go back to my suicide attempt. I know most people consider suicide an act of pure cowardice, but in my eyes, it isn't. For even when I had given up on life, when I believed I was a burden on those I loved, it took incredible courage to do what I did. And what about all I went through at the hospital—the treatments, the scrutiny, the analyzing? Surely that was courageous. "I was brave, Papa. I did what you told me to do."

And because of my bravery, I've lost all memory of you.

The tea in my cup is cold. A slight scum, sediment from the minerals in the hard well water, floats on the surface of the dark liquid. Today is Saturday. I glance at the electric clock hanging on the wall. Charles and my boys will be in shortly for their mid-morning tea break. I rise and carry the cups to the sink.

I will move forward and make the best of the years remaining to me. Because, if there's one thing I'm certain of, it's time will continue to slip by, one day after another, one year after another.

I will be brave. For Papa.

They burst through the door, the tiny kitchen reduced by their male presence. I push my melancholy thoughts and feelings aside and allow my heart to fill with contentment. It's pointless to dwell on what I've lost—I have all the family I need right here in this room. I refill the huge crockery pot with boiling water and another two tablespoons of tea leaves and set it on the table.

Our first full day together passes comfortably, almost as if I hadn't been away. Charles and our sons are busy outdoors, the typical Saturday chores taking up all their time.

I wander aimlessly about the house, running my hands over the tabletops, fingering my lace curtains. My gaze falls on my African violets lining the deep windowsills. Poking a finger under the leaves of one plant, I test the soil. It's moist. Someone even tended to them; there's not a wilted leaf or flower in sight.

My brief tour finishes in my bedroom, my thoughts a patchwork of fragmented memories and jumbled hazy images. I still have one possession from my early days, and opening the closet door, I lean deep inside and drag out a small wooden trunk. The lid is coated in a thick layer of dust—so thick it reminds me of winter's early-morning hoar frost. I fumble with the pitted latch, rusty from years of neglect, before it finally releases.

The hinges creak as I open it and dust pools on the floor. I scrunch my nose up as the mouldy scent of years past rises from its dark corners. In its shadowy interior, my gaze falls on a few books, one being the Bible I received from the Barnardo Home in England. I open the cover and read the inscription on the first page: The National Incorporated Waifs Association . . . *This Bible is Presented to . . . Mary Clifton . . . With Best Wishes for Her Future Welfare and Prosperity from her friend.* Underneath the inscription is Dr. Barnardo's signature, in his very own hand. The date is September 23, 1913.

I clench my jaw and snap the Bible closed. "Some friend you were," I hiss. "What kind of friend plucks an eleven-year-old girl from a loving home and ships her overseas to an unknown life?" I want to scream and tear the insipid inscription to bits. Instead, I hurl it against the wall. It hits with a loud thud and falling to the floor, a tattered black-and-white photograph tumbles out. Picking it up, I study it, allowing my fingers to trace the figures in the photo. I know they're my family. I recognize Papa and Mama Annie. The children's faces are ghostly familiar, but their names elude me.

I turn it over, and there, written in ink, faded, yet still legible, are the names of my family members.

I set the photograph aside and reach further into the box, removing my baby doll. Her auburn curls, now faded with time, hang lank on her shoulders and her white eyelet bonnet and nightgown are yellowed with age. I tenderly pick her up, holding her in my arms.

"Hello Annie," I say as I run the back of my fingers over her porcelain face. "You're looking a little rough around the edges, a little older—just like me." I remember her well; she's the one and only childhood toy I carried with me from England. I've kept her all these years hoping to pass her down to a daughter. That will never happen now. But who knows? Maybe someday I'll be blessed with a little granddaughter who will love and play with her.

I raise the photograph again and look into Mama Annie's face. I recall naming my dolly after her. Tiny fragments of that day drift through my mind, vague and filmy. I remember icy hands and cheeks, walking home from school with someone . . . a girl. My eyes leave Mama Annie and I stare at the others in the photo, the boys, and the girls. I gaze into their faces; I study their smiles.

There's nothing. It's all gone.

It's too late now to write that journal.

I toss the Bible into the trunk. Reaching up, I pull an old shawl off a hanger and, picking up my Annie doll, I place the photo under her arms before gently wrapping the shawl around her. "Goodbye, Annie." I hold her to my breast for a moment before laying her on the trunk's bottom.

Tommy's voice quavers. "Ma, why are you talking to a doll?"

I jerk, and look up into Tommy's face. It's incredulous, his eyes wide. My heart clenches. Poor Tommy. How long has he been standing there, watching? Not only have I scarred him by being in a psychiatric hospital, now he finds me talking to a ratty, old doll. My brain scrambles for words. "I-I-I . . ."

Tommy backs away and rushes through the house. The back door bangs.

I scramble to my knees and shove the trunk back into the dark recess of the closet.

I rise and step away, but then I stop. Why have I hung on to that old trunk all these years? And that despicable Bible? I should get rid of it all.

I leave my bedroom and go in search of my son. I have some explaining to do.

Chapter 20

September, 1952

Time seeps away, like water between my cupped hands. It's perplexing, really, how it advances at an ever-increasing rate the older I get. And as difficult as it is for me to grasp, I'm fifty years old now and Charles is fifty-eight.

I'm standing at the base of the Eastgate United Church's wide concrete steps. A slight breeze ruffles the hem of my new forest-green silk dress. I incline my head, inhaling the citrusy scent of the orchid pinned below my shoulder. I've never seen such an exotic flower, let alone worn one. Charles stands beside me, looking handsome in his new brown tweed suit. I glance around the gathered crowd: the photographer and the other wedding guests. Thank goodness, they don't appear to be watching me. Sometimes I wonder if, just by looking at me, they can see the chaos whirling in my mind; how these days I'm living more in my head and in my memories than in this world.

One Sunday morning, before Charles and I were married, we attended services at this church. When I stepped inside, the interior beauty positively took my breath away. The round, red brick building is a work of art, with the morning sunlight spilling through the long stained-glass windows, and the lacquered oak hardwood floors, wainscoting, pews, and furniture gleaming in the pastel light. Beautiful antique pendant lights hang from the beams, but beyond them is the most spectacular feature of this building—the arched oak hardwood ceiling with a large stained-glass dome. Maybe it's just me, but I find it difficult to focus on the service when all I want to do is admire the beauty above my head. Anyway, I decided, right then and there, this church is where I wanted to be married.

We're patiently waiting for the bride and groom, along with their attendants, to appear through the open double doors. If only Dacre were here to witness our happiness; he would be so proud of his grandson. It's been five long years since Dacre left us, yet today I feel his presence.

With my gloved middle finger, I carefully dab a tear from the corner of my eye. This day is going to be a roller coaster of emotions; grief and joy intermingled become very complicated.

I glance up and there they are, in the same spot Charles and I stood twenty-five years ago. Ernest stands tall and handsome, Ada by his side. In contrast to my son, Ada is petite. She's wearing a sweet little white gown, lace cape, and short-layered veil. My goodness, I swear that girl's smile is as big as she is. Her bouquet is one large orchid surrounded by white hydrangeas taken from the bush in my front yard. Standing behind them is the wedding party, the best man, the maid of honour and two little flower girls, their baskets overflowing with roses and carnations. Ernest and Ada pose for a couple of photos and then I hear her call, "Get ready, girls!" She laughs, turns and tosses her bouquet over her shoulder. The young women, standing in the crowd's forefront, push, and shove, as they try to catch the bouquet flying high over their heads.

Feelings of extreme happiness, tamped down with a touch of melancholy, wash over me. With one less man, our tiny house won't seem so crowded. Oh, I know—it's high time Ernest moved out; my goodness, he's twenty-four years old. When he had finished his schooling, he elected to remain at home, helping Charles on the farm, and working full time at a local trucking company, squirrelling away his earnings to buy his own farm. After all, that's all he's ever wanted.

Mark my word, one day he'll be the proud owner of one of the finest plots in the township.

And that Ada. She's a spunky little girl with a great sense of humour. She's a clerk at the bank in Eastgate. I chuckle, thinking of all she puts up with. That Ernest can be such a tease. She takes it all in stride, though. To this day, he tells everyone he had no choice but to choose her—she was the only girl left in the village. Another story he likes to tell is how, at the end of every long workweek, he would take his paycheque into the bank. Ada would stand there, batting her eyes, and giving him a coy look which clearly said, 'I could help you spend that.' Now, there's not one word of truth in any of it—everyone knows he's had his eye on her for a long while. It appears Ernest has a bit of his father in him; it took him almost as long to marry her as it did for Charles to marry me. Ada knew, like I did with Charles, that Ernest was worth the wait.

The wedding party follows the newlyweds down the stairs to the waiting car, decorated with tissue-paper flowers, a *Just Married* sign tied to its bumper, and strings of empty tin cans trailing behind. Naturally, Ernest's best man is Tom. I don't call him Tommy anymore. How many times did he say, 'Ma, a real man over the age of twenty should never have a name that ends with a *y*?' More times than I care to remember. So, I call him Tom, like everyone else.

Marilyn, the maid of honour is Tom's fiancée. I'm so glad Tom chose her; she's such a nice girl. Unlike Ernest, who according to him had no choice, Tom actually did have a choice. I smile as I remember the story. Tom had been seeing Marilyn's sister, long enough that she invited Tom home to meet her parents. Now, from the way Marilyn tells the story, it was love at first sight. He was seated across the table from her, and while they ate their dinner, Marilyn gazed at my Tommy and said to herself, *"He's all mine."* Now, you can imagine the kerfuffle that started. A muddled Tom finally came to his father for advice. Charles had laughed, his bright blue eyes twinkling, and simply said, "Well, boy, you're going to have to decide . . . you can't have them both." They've set their wedding date for next August.

My goodness, two weddings, two years in a row.

Tom has a good factory job in London. He boards at a house in the city during the week and comes home on the weekends. He's had two more scares over the past year, not necessarily heart attacks, however his doctor suggested he reduce his stress. I suspect a quieter lifestyle on the farm is exactly what he needs and now that Ernest is married, Tom is returning home to help his father. He's already purchased a farm, the original Sherman homestead, right across the road from us, with a closing date this coming December. The house on this farm needs many repairs, if not a total rebuild, but the land and barns are good. It'll be nice having him and Marilyn so close. She loves to cook and bake and she's already asked me if I would teach her how to quilt. I have a strong feeling we're going to get along splendidly.

I wave, along with the other guests, as the newly married couple drive away. They'll circle the town a few times, beeping the horn, the tin cans rattling behind the automobile, before returning to the church for the reception. Ada is waving out the window. Tom and Marilyn appear to be snuggling in the back seat, the little flower girls wedged in beside them.

A hand brushes my arm. I turn and see Jean's pleasant face. "Mary, you must be so proud. You're positively beaming today." Her hand rests on my arm.

I lay my hand on hers. "I am."

"And Ada's such a sweet girl. She'll make a fine daughter-in-law."

"Yes, I'm sure she will." I pause for a moment and think. "I haven't talked to you since you've moved. How are you adjusting to town life?"

"Good," she says, too quickly. Apprehension casts a shadow over her face. "To tell you the truth, not really all that good. I'm adjusting okay, but Bob's having a hard go of it. He still goes to the farm every single morning." Her face softens. "George is twenty-six now, you know; it's time for him to take over. I'm sure both he and Judith wish Bob would stay home at least once in a while. Plus, I keep telling him it's never going to feel like their home if he keeps hanging around there all the time. "

I frown. "Poor Bob." I consider how lost Charles would be in Bob's situation. "I don't think Charles could adjust to living in town."

"No, I can't see him doing that either. He's like Bob—lived on the same farm his entire life. Neither of them has ever had to adjust to a different home, a different life."

I reflect on the many houses I've lived in, the different lifestyles I've experienced. I inhale deeply as I'm reminded, once again, that I can't even remember a significant portion of my young life.

Jean's voice interrupts my thoughts. "With Tom buying the old homestead across the road from you, hopefully, Charles will never have to move. You'll always have a son close by to help. With Bob's heart condition, I'd hoped leaving the farm might get him to slow down a little, take things easy, but it hasn't made a difference."

I nod in agreement. "Still, you did the right thing, Jean."

"I hope so, but sometimes I wonder. Anyway, you and Charles should come by for a visit real soon, now that we're settled."

"That'd be nice. I can't wait to see your new home; I'm sure it's beautiful."

"It's nice," she humbly replies. "Not nearly as big as the farmhouse, but then we don't need all that room. And it's so much more convenient with everything all on one floor . . . like your house."

Years ago, I would have felt envy over Jean's convenient, modern home. Not anymore. Now, I can honestly say I'm content, even happy, in my modest, tiny home.

Helen comes to mind right now, the way she adjusted to hospital life and made it her home. According to her letters, she's still doing well, making new friends all the time; some for a short period, and others that stay. I'll have to remember to write her with news of this glorious day.

Jean's my dearest, truest friend. After returning home from the hospital and over several visits, I told her my story, at least the parts I could remember. I pulled out my trunk and showed her my few keepsakes. I told her of my ocean voyage, and I summarized the stories of my many placements by the fragmented memories I still had. And then I told her the things I'd rather forget. Contrary to my beliefs, Jean's opinion of me never changed, nor did her love for me waver. I learned something very important—sharing your life, the good and the bad, with someone who loves you will only bring you closer.

Jean speaks again, her words drawing me back. I gaze into her eyes and, once again, marvel at the depth of compassion and understanding. "Mary, do you know what I miss the most about living on the farm?"

I incline my head. "No. What?"

"Having my best friend as my neighbour." She pulls me into a soft embrace. "Come soon," she whispers.

As she strolls away to visit with others, I lay my hand on my chest. My heart physically aches as if it might simply burst; it is so filled with love. I spot Charles visiting with some of our neighbours and join him. Silently I stand beside him, listening to the men discuss the upcoming harvest. My mind drifts again.

Looking back, the past several years have been excellent years. Financially, we're doing so much better. Charles was right; when the war was over, the economy boomed. He purchased his first tractor, a John Deere Model B, a year after my stay in the hospital. It was a used tractor, but still it was an exciting day when he climbed onto the seat and, looking over his shoulder, he watched as a three-furrow plough effortlessly turned the soil. Until then, he had always followed, on foot, a workhorse dragging a one-furrow plough. In awe, I stood at the edge of the field and observed. I listened to the growl of the tractor's engine, and smelled the distinct aroma of the fresh, moist soil as Charles worked off in the distance. And I thought of what a momentous day this was—this being the very first time in history a tractor had ever turned soil on this piece of earth.

A year later, we repainted the house, once again a bright white, the perfect backdrop to my lovely red rosebushes. We extended the kitchen and installed running water. I can't describe how thrilled I was to have an indoor bathroom and no more trips to the cold outhouse. Now, I still keep the outhouse clean and maintained; it's convenient when we're working outdoors or for the occasional time when company is around and one bathroom is simply not enough.

The past years have been good, happy times. Golden times, except for Dacre's death in 1947. My, but that was a hard blow, coming so unexpectedly. He was 'here one moment and gone the next,' just like the saying. I mourned his death for a long time. No, that's not entirely true; even yet I'm mourning. Sometimes, I wonder if I grieve my losses more than others. Could it be because I've lost so many? And not all of them through death. I've simply lost them.

And with every loss, I lose a piece of myself.

I hear Charles speak, but I pay no mind. My thoughts have wandered to my foster family, my first significant loss. I don't remember them much and I don't think of them often anymore. I shouldn't be thinking of them now; it will only upset me.

Charles lays a hand on my shoulder. "Mary?"

I blink, startled. "I'm sorry, Charles. Did you say something?"

"Yes, I did. We should go. Everyone's moving back inside the church."

"Oh, okay."

"Where were you?"

"Nowhere. Just thinking."

"Well, you sure looked like you were a long way off." He runs his forefinger over his chin. "You know, you're doing a lot more of that lately . . . thinking, daydreaming." He quickly checks himself and clamps his mouth shut.

I gaze at him, my face soft. I know him so well. He's never been one to start a discussion about the hard topics. He'd rather leave it alone, trusting it will resolve on its own. And this would certainly not be the time or place to start a conversation such as that.

"Never mind," he says. "It's time we get back inside for the reception. The wedding party returned a few moments ago."

I glance around the churchyard. Very few people linger outside. Charles takes my hand and leads me into the church reception hall.

We're settled in the round basement hall of the church, the linen-covered tables set up for a farm-style feast. At the head table Ernest and Ada stand and kiss, at increasingly regular intervals, to the tinkling of water glasses. My thoughts return to my simple wedding twenty-five years ago. I had thought it was a beautiful ceremony and reception, but this one has put mine to shame. My goodness, close to one hundred souls are congregated here.

The ladies of the church carry platters and bowls laden with meat, vegetables, and salads and set them at intervals on the long tables. The room is abuzz with laughter and chatter. Charles carries on a jovial conversation with those nearest. Occasionally I join in, but even with all the cheerful commotion surrounding me, I'm distracted by thoughts of those who are gone.

Later that night, I lie awake. A gentle September breeze sifts in the partially opened window, lightly fluttering the sheer curtains. A three-quarter moon hangs in the sky, illuminating the room. Charles is asleep, lying on his back, his rhythmic breathing relaxes me. Now and then he makes a little snoring sound. No, it's more like a little sputter. I've noticed he's doing that more often, the older he gets.

I glance at the walls, freshly papered in a neutral beige and brown damask—a paper fitting for a married couple's bedroom. Oh, how I hated to cover up the faded wisteria paper. I tried to remove it by soaking a small area before lifting it. But when the old plaster became moistened, the surface crumbled and came off with the paper. So, I layered the new over the old, content to leave the old paper as a reminder of the past, and with every strip I hung, I thought of the beautiful spring day Charles and I first papered the room.

That was the day Ernest was conceived. And now he is a married man with a wife, a home, and a life of his own.

The back screen door squeaks on its hinges. I hear Tom's quiet footfalls through the entry to the bathroom. A few moments later, he pads to his bedroom and closes the door. Wire hangers jingle as he hangs his suit in the closet. The bedsprings squeak as he settles.

And the house falls silent.

Less than a year from now, he'll move into the house across the road, with Marilyn as his new bride. In the blink of an eye, Charles and I will be alone in this old house once again.

The house is static, bathed in an eerie hush. I listen for a sound. Any sound. I glance at the window. The curtain hangs limp; there's not a breath of a breeze. Not a breath.

Not one breath.

I turn my head on my pillow. Charles has not moved—he is still lying on his back. I raise myself on my elbow and lean over him, my ear a few inches above his face.

He lies motionless.

Deathly silent.

I hold my breath . . . waiting.

Finally, he gasps, sputters, and inhales. He rolls over onto his side.

Chapter 21

July, 1967

I move around the table, arranging plates and silverware. The back door opens. "Be sure to wash up before you come to the table," I yell.

It's summer vacation and the children are out of school. Ada is employed as a part-time clerk at the Township Office and Ernest is travelling the countryside today measuring tobacco acreage for the Ontario Burley Tobacco Growers' Marketing Board. Their children are spending the day with Charles and me.

I catch my eldest grandson, twelve-year-old Eddie, roll his eyes as he and his younger brother, Danny march to the bathroom. His grumbling voice is low, but not so low my sharp ears can't pick up his words. "Jeez, it's a wonder we have any skin left on our hands with the amount of washing she makes us do."

I chuckle to myself. I back up, just enough to see them. They're standing before the sink in the bathroom, their backs to me. Danny reaches for the bar of soap. "I know. And they weren't even dirty. Do you see any dirt on my hands?"

"Nope." Eddie holds out his hands, palms up. "Mine?"

"Nope."

"D'ya see what I'm saying?"

"Yep."

I lift my three-year-old granddaughter and place her in the antique highchair. She squirms in my arms. "Grandma, no! Not the highchair. I'm not a baby anymore."

Her full name is Samantha, but that's way too much of a mouthful, so her father nicknamed her Sam. Now and then, I have mixed-up feelings or memories of another Sam, but they're elusive, impossible to put my finger on. And I don't know how I feel about pegging a little girl with a name like that, but I guess it's not my place to say. Anyway, none of that matters.

Now Sam, she's a bright little whip, that one. I press her down into the chair. "I know you're not, sweetie, but this way you'll sit up nice and big at the table . . . like everyone else. Besides, it's not really a highchair as there's no tray—it's just a small, high chair." I untie my apron. I use it to secure the little ones in the chair. It's a novel idea as it works two-fold—it holds them in, plus it works as a bib.

"No, don't put that on me," she whines.

I place my hand under her chin and raise her face. She stares up at me with her steely grey-blue eyes, her father's eyes. "Okay, but do you promise to sit still? I don't want you falling and hurting yourself. Not on my watch."

She nods.

"Okay then." I tie the apron once again around my thick midriff and push her chair up to the table.

"Hurry, boys! Dinner's almost on the table."

Eddie sighs loudly. I hear him grumble once again. "C'mon, Danny."

I imagine them running their dripping hands over the hand towel or wiping them on their blue-jeaned bottoms.

"Where's your grandpa?" I ask as they slip into their chairs.

Danny reaches for his glass of milk. "When you called us, I ran out and told him dinner was ready. He said he'd be right along."

"You must have misunderstood me; that's not what I asked. I asked you where your grandpa is."

Danny's shoulders slump. He stares at his empty plate.

Eddie picks up where his chicken-liver brother left off. "He's back the lane, about half way to the bush."

"And . . . what's he doing?"

"Fixin' the fence. There's some posts rotted off at the bottom and he's replacing them."

I walk over to the kitchen window. "Weren't you two supposed to be helping him this morning?"

Danny shakes his head sheepishly. Eddie explains, "We asked, but he said he didn't need any help."

"Besides," added Danny, "we could hear the cousins out playing in their yard, so we went over there for a while."

Eddie glares at his big-mouthed brother.

I peer at my grandsons. "I don't remember you asking me if you could go play with them." They both lower their eyes.

Sam squirms, and stands in the chair. "Sam, I told you to sit still in your chair!" I rush to her and settle her again in the highchair.

My voice sounds tetchy. It grates on my ears.

"But I'm hungry, Grandma."

An unsettling feeling creeps over me. I inhale a calming breath and hand her a small glass of milk. "I know you are, sweetie. We'll eat as soon as Grandpa comes. He'll be here in a minute."

I pace to the window and gaze down the lane, my fingertips drumming on the kitchen counter. I see Charles off in the distance. He flips the spade over, end for end, and using the rounded top of the wooden handle, he tamps down the loose earth around the newly installed fence post. He turns the spade over again and shovels more earth around the post before tramping it down firmly with the heel of his work boot. Satisfied the post is firmly in place, he rests the spade handle on his shoulder and trudges to the house. His steps are sluggish, his heels dragging in the laneway dirt.

I retrieve a platter of sliced ham and a bowl of potato salad from the refrigerator and carry it to the table as Charles appears through the back screen door.

"Dinner ready, Mary?"

I remove a bowl of salad greens and a dish of pickles. "Yes, just putting it on the table."

After washing up, Charles joins us at the table. We bow our heads as he offers the blessing and then we pass the platter and bowls around. I gaze around the table, studying my family. Charles, at seventy-three years old, shows his age. His neatly trimmed hair is silver and there are deep creases in his brow and around his mouth. He glances up and catches me staring at him. The wrinkles around his eyes deepen into smile lines.

I drag my gaze from his and allow it to rest on Eddie. He's blond-haired and blue-eyed, and while lanky, he won't be a tall man when he's grown. My, but he's a talker, that one. He brings to mind someone else I knew a long time ago. I remember, back then wondering how much glue it would take to keep that man's mouth shut. Yes, Eddie's a lot like that man—whoever he was.

Now, Danny, he's stockier than Eddie, with curly brunette hair and blue eyes. He'll be a good-sized man when he's grown. Like Eddie, he's a bit of a talker too. But he has a pleasant disposition, he's thoughtful, and gentle. A good boy.

And then there's Sam, the baby, the afterthought, the surprise. She's fair, her dirty-blond hair straight as an arrow. Of the three children, she's the one who favours her father the most. The boys are both outgoing, sociable children—they've got a lot of their mother in them. In comparison, Sam's shy, although I admit she didn't get that from her father. Ernest has never been timid—no, not by a long shot. Listening to the boys chatter with their grandfather, it's easy to understand why she's so quiet. In their household, it'd be difficult for her to get a word in edge-wise.

I scoop potatoes on her plate and pass the bowl to Danny.

It's funny how both my sons' families are the opposite of each other. Tom and Marilyn also have three children. Vashti was the first to come, she's almost thirteen years old now. When they told me her name, I wondered where in the blazes that came from. Marilyn said she found it in her old family Bible. I didn't say, but if you ask me, she should have left it there. I tried shortening it, or altering it into something softer and prettier, but what can you do with a name like Vashti? No one seems to mind it but me, so I guess I'll live with it. I admit I was relieved when they christened their other babies with common, sensible names. After Vashti came Barbara, nine. Both girls are blonde, blue-eyed cuties. There's no doubt who their father is—each carries a strong resemblance to Tom. And then, like Ernest and Ada, Tom, and Marilyn had a baby much later. Karl will turn one in September.

And not a one of them with auburn curls.

I place a slice of ham on Sam's plate, cut it into bite-sized pieces, and pass the platter to Eddie.

I remember when Vashti was about four years old; we were playing a game of Chutes and Ladders on the floor in the living room, just her and me, and out of the blue I remembered my Annie doll tucked away in the closet. "Come with me Vashti. I've a surprise for you." I took her by the hand and led her into my bedroom. She climbed upon the bed, lay on her belly, head hanging over the end of the bed, and watched while I dragged the dusty old trunk out. I opened the lid and carefully lifted the doll. I unwrapped the tattered shawl from around her.

My heart plunged when I saw the doll's condition. I reached for the old photograph, yet lying in her arms. It crumbled at my touch. I heard a cry and glanced up at my granddaughter. Vashti's small hands cupped her cheeks, her mouth hung open. She closed her mouth, and swallowed hard. "Oh, Grandma, I don't want that dirty old doll. She's ugly."

Time had not been kind, and the moths had been hungry. Annie's eyelet nightgown and bonnet were yellowed and riddled with holes. The crevices in her face were dust-filled.

"She's not ugly, sweetie—she's only dirty. We can clean her up. This is Annie—she was my baby doll when I was a wee girl, like you are now."

Her eyes grew enormous. "You were a little girl?"

"Of course I was. Everyone was little once upon a time."

She gazed at me, her eyes still doubtful. "Did you have a mommy?"

I blinked. "Of course I did. Everyone has a mommy."

Her eyes were disbelieving yet. "Where is she?"

My sight returned to my doll, while my mind searched for a plausible answer. It'd been years since I'd been asked about my history, but children have curious minds. Will the young ones pester me with questions I cannot answer? Perhaps I should take the few wisps of memories I still have, and weave them into a story. But, then, it wouldn't be factual, the lines blurring between truth and fiction. Best to say nothing. My heart felt heavy. "I don't know, sweetie. She's just gone, that's all." I ran my thumb gently across my doll's cheek before laying her back to rest.

And I had thought, *if I can't remember this past, then why do I hang on to these things?* They have never given me an ounce of joy, and whenever I've looked at them, they only bring me heartache. I decided, from then on, I would only hang on to memories and possessions which brought me joy.

Later that day, after Vashti's mother had come for her, I hauled the trunk outside. Charles and Tom had been cleaning fencerows all afternoon, a hot brush fire ablaze in the field behind the house. I looked back at them. Charles was on the tractor, a flat-bed wagon hitched behind it. Tom was operating the chainsaw and throwing the scrub brush onto the wagon. They were focused on their work. No one was watching me.

With every ounce of strength I could muster, I hurled the trunk into the fire, and I watched as the last memories of my childhood went up in flames.

"Mary?"

I'm staring at my plate. My head snaps up and I look at Charles. "Sorry, did you say something?"

His eyes are kind. He's forever patient with me. "Yes. I asked what your plans are for this afternoon. I have to finish repairing the fence so I can let the cattle back out of the barnyard."

"Could you use some help?"

"No, I'm not looking for help. I took the barbed-wire down that side of the fence and I'll be using the tractor and the come-along to stretch it back on again. Actually, I was asking because I'd rather you kept the boys up here with you. I don't want to risk anyone being hurt should the wire snap."

I nod. "Of course." I think for a moment. With the gap in their ages, how will I keep them all occupied at the same time? What I should do is stop being so irritable with them and have more fun. Heaven forbid they remember me as a grouchy old grandma. "Okay, kids. What do you say we invite Vashti and Barbara over here this afternoon? We could play board and card games outside."

Eddie and Danny nod in agreement, but there's no enthusiasm in their eyes. I run my hand over my damp neck. "And it's so hot today. How about we make ice cream, too?"

Their eyes light up and Sam shouts, "Yay!"

I tickle her under her chubby chin. "You finally got a chance to say something, did you, sweetie?" I tweak her earlobe.

She beams, and her little body shivers with excitement. "Play ear soup too, Grandma."

"No, not today." My eyes dart at the faces around the table. Charles and the boys look at me questioningly. Why did I ever start that with her? It's a silly game we play, a sort of hide-and-seek except I've added, "When I catch you, I'm going to make ear soup!" It's creepy, I admit, but she seems to love it.

But, where did that dreadful game come from? A hazy memory of another time flickers before my eyes: a girl chasing her shrieking younger siblings under a large shade tree.

I change the subject. "Maybe your big-girl cousins will help you make a daisy chain for your hair." I shake my head and continue, "I don't know why they call them daisy chains—you can't call them daisy chains when you use hydrangea blossoms. But then again, I suppose hydrangea chains are a bit of a tongue-twister. Anyway, it doesn't matter; Vashti loved doing that when she was a little girl."

Charles and the boys stare at me, patiently waiting, while Sam grins at my chatter.

"Okay then. When we're finished up here, you boys can walk across and invite the girls over while I get the dishes done." As an afterthought, I quickly add, "Don't let them bring Karl along, though . . . that'll be too much. Then, when you get back, you kids can carry the picnic table into the shade of the butternut tree. We'll make the ice cream there." My mind races. "Charles, how long will you be?"

"Oh, not more than an hour at the most."

My brow creases. "It's too hot to be out working in the sun today. Why don't you leave it until this evening? Maybe Tom or Ernest could help you then."

"No, I want to get it done now."

I learned a long time ago that there's no sense arguing with the man. "Okay, but don't be too long and please don't let yourself get overheated." My thoughts go back a couple of years. It was a scorcher that day, not unlike today, when we got the news. Bob and his son, George, were baling straw when Bob had a massive stroke and collapsed in the wheat field. It was such a shock to everyone, especially Jean. She's doing okay though, living alone in her modern rancher in town.

Charles' voice disturbs my thoughts. "Stop your fretting, Mary. The tractor will do the hard work, not me."

I nod, but the anxious feeling still niggles at me.

Later that afternoon, Charles and I sit in lawn chairs watching the older four children playing cards at the picnic table. Sam sleeps at our feet on an old plaid blanket spread on the ground, her daisy chain broken and wilted beside her. For a while, I had played cards with the children, but I could see Eddie's hackles were rising. He's got a bit more of me in him than he'd like to admit—we're both very competitive and hate to lose.

The nerve of those children, though; they accused me of cheating! Now, as far as I'm concerned, cheating isn't cheating unless you get caught and, you can bet your bottom dollar, I make sure I never get caught. But, since I'm the adult and it's up to me to keep the peace, I backed away from the table and joined Charles.

With age, Charles has taken up whittling. He's leaning forward in his chair right now, legs spread apart, his hands gripping a jackknife and a small piece of cherry wood. I watch the shavings fly while the figure of a fat little red hen slowly appears. One child, likely Sam, will leave today with that little treasure.

I glance across the road at Tom and Marilyn's new home, a modern, three-bedroom brick rancher. It's about time they built one; that old farmhouse of theirs was beyond repair. Unlike our little house, theirs didn't sit on a solid foundation. I'm happy for them, truly I am. Once in a while, I envision the pretty home of my imaginings—the one Charles and I had planned to build years ago, had times been better. But it never happened, and it's far too late now.

Several years back, though, when the boys were still at home, Charles had surprised me. He asked me to get in the car and go for a short drive with him; he had something he wanted to show me. We drove into the town of Eastgate, turned right, and headed east bound. About a mile or so out of town, he pulled the car into the lane of a farm, one I had always admired. At the corner of the lane was a 'For Sale' sign. I glanced up the long lane. On a knoll sat a handsome Victorian brick farmhouse and tall, sturdy barns. I pulled my gaze away and looked at Charles.

He raised his eyebrows. "Well?"

"I don't understand. What do you mean—well?"

"If you want, I'll sell our farm and buy this one. It's got everything we could ever want: more land, good barns, a silo and a beautiful house. And I checked out the listing—the price is very reasonable. We could swing it."

Stunned, my thoughts clambered as I tried to digest this idea. "Swing it? So, what you're saying is, we'd have to mortgage, right?"

"Yes. But, the way I figure, we'd only need a little one."

"Why only a little one? With that house and all those buildings, plus more land?"

He shrugged his shoulders. "Because our land's worth more per acre."

What a dear man. He had obviously given this much thought. He'd sell the farm his family has held since Crown Land just to give me the home I always thought I wanted. I gazed again, up the lane to the farmyard. It reminded me a little of Bob and Jean's, sitting up there all pretty and proud on a rise of land, however, unlike theirs, this yard had no big, old shade trees, nor a cedar windbreak. I gave myself a moment and tried to imaging living here. To do that, we'd sell our farm and leave our home. Someone else would live in it, or, heaven forbid, demolish it.

"No," I said, firmly.

His brows drew together. "What do you mean—no?"

I chuckled. It didn't appear we were communicating well. "I mean, I don't want it."

"Why? I thought this is what you've always wanted."

I had thought it was too, until I had spent time in the hospital. Sitting in the car, with a beautiful home placed on offer at my feet, I now fully understood how wrong I had always been. I took a moment to mull over this realization. Before speaking, I formed my words so my meaning would be crystal clear. "I was wrong. I don't need a big, beautiful home to make me happy." I was quiet for another moment. "I'm happy where we are. You and the boys are all I need. You're the reason I love living there, and I don't want to leave it." I shook my head. "Besides, when the boys are grown and move out, we won't need a big house." A practical thought ran through my mind and, with it, another question. "You said our land is worth more per acre. So, what type of soil is this?"

"Well, you can see the land is high and dry here. The soil is lighter, sandier. It's not loam like ours."

"That's what I thought. That's why it's such a reasonable price. So, in the spring, when the winds blow, I'll be spending all my time cleaning dust out of that big house." I gazed at him and reached for his hand. "No. Thank you for the offer, Charles, but I'd rather keep our little house."

We drove home. And never again did we speak of it.

A fly buzzes around Sam's sweaty head and she stirs. I lean over and swoosh it away. "What time is it, Charles?" I murmur.

He twists his arm and reads his wristwatch. "Coming on to five o'clock now."

I nod. Ada should be off work and along shortly for her kids. My thoughts drift in her direction.

Just as I had predicted, Ernest and Ada purchased their farm a few years after they married. It's a show-piece, that farm, and only a mile or so away. The huge, five-bedroom solid brick farmhouse stands stately, back off the road, four stories counting the basement and walk-up attic. It's not unlike many of the farmhouses I served in as a young girl.

When Ernest left this house, I overheard him saying, "I've lived in a cramped house my entire life—I'll never live in one again." I suppose he won't either; he usually gets what he wants and settles for nothing less.

Would you look at that; Ada's not coming for her children after all. Ernest's brand-spanking-new, red-and-white Ford pickup is turning in the lane. I haul myself from the webbed lawn chair and kneel on the blanket beside Sam. I gently touch her forehead, smoothing the damp, fine hairs from her brow. "Sam, time to wake up . . . your Daddy's here."

Her eyelids flutter open and close once again.

"C'mon, sweetie. Time to wake up."

She rolls into a sitting position on her fat little bottom. Charles is holding out his hand to her, his fingers rolled into a fist. "I've got something for you, Sammy."

She stands and rubs her eyes. "What is it, Grandpa?"

"Come see."

She toddles to him, still fuzzy with sleep, as he uncurls his fingers. "Oh look! It's a baby chickie!" she squeals. The pickup comes to a stop, the driver's door opens. Sam is fully awake now, running toward it. "Daddy! Daddy! Look what Grandpa made for me!"

Ernest strides around the front of the pickup, his gait long and sure. Tall, standing over six feet, he's one fine specimen of a man. His brown hair, always short and neat, is combed straight back from his forehead. Even late in the day, it's held perfectly in place with a little dab of Brylcreem . . . . you know, like the commercial says, 'a little dab will do ya.' He's a take-charge kind of man, runs a tight ship. Sam races to him. He bends over and takes her in his arms. She's the light of his life—a Daddy's little girl. Wrapping one chubby arm around his neck, she displays her treasure. "Look what Grandpa made for me!" she repeats.

He removes it from her hand and admires it. "Wow! Grandpa's getting really good at whittling." He sets her back down on the ground. "Had a couple of extras here today, did you, Mother? Were they all good for you?"

"Yes, of course they were," I reply. "The cousins were only here for the afternoon."

I listen as Ernest converses with his father. He asks Charles about his day, if the boys were of help to him. Ernest talks of where his travels had taken him, the gossip he heard around the county, the usual end-of-day conversation. Sam stands at his feet, peering up at him, raptly listening.

After a few moments, he announces, "Okay, finish up your game, boys. It's time to get home and start chores. Your mom should be home from work by now." He glances at his nieces. "That goes for you, girls, too. It's time you both headed on home. Vashti, I'm sure your Dad will be expecting you in the barn shortly."

The four children reluctantly stack their playing cards. Vashti sighs. "C'mon Barb, we better get going."

When they reach the lane, Barbara calls over her shoulder, "Thanks for the ice cream, Grandma."

"You're welcome, sweetie."

Ernest raises his eyebrows. “Ice cream? Sounds like Grandma spoiled you today.”

Sam dances on her toes. “It was s-chocolate. It was yummy!”

Ernest bends over, lifts Sam and marches to the truck. “C’mon, boys. Let’s go.” They race to the truck and pile in the passenger door. Sam stands on the bench seat beside Ernest, her chubby little arm circling his neck. He turns the truck around behind the barn, and, as he drives past us, he calls, “Thanks again for watching the kids.”

Sitting in the shade of the butternut tree, we watch the truck drive out of sight, and our granddaughters tramp up their lane. Charles turns to me and reaches for my hand, and those eyes, yet so startling blue, gaze into mine. In a soft voice, he says, “And then there’s two. Just you and me, my Mary.”

Chapter 22

Spring, 1969

Now, what in tarnation has got into that kid?

"Darn his hide anyhow," I mutter as I slam the door behind me. "You get out of that puddle right now, you hear me?" The shrillness of my voice offends my ears.

Karl's head jerks up. He stares at me, wide-eyed, as I stomp toward him. He's splattered with dirty water to his waist, his arms are muddy to his dimpled elbows, and his brown curls drip filthy water onto his shoulders. Fighting the urge to give his bottom a good, hard smack, I clench and unclench my tingling hands. He can be such a little devil, that one. Lucky for him, the puddle is a good distance from the house, and as I march across the lawn, my anger ebbs. I don't spank, his mother wouldn't approve. Instead, I snatch his hand and drag him to the house.

He stands inside the entry while I fill the washtub. Water pools around his feet on my clean floor. "You're such a bad boy," I scold. I strip him naked, yank off his dripping, filthy socks, and plop him in the tub. "Look at these socks! How am I ever to get them clean?" Reaching for a bar of soap, I lather it up between my hands. "And look at all the extra work you've made for me. All your clothes need to be washed and dried now before your mother gets home." My pulse is slowing, but it seems I haven't quite run out of steam; my voice is still stern. "Karl, whatever made you think it was okay to splash in that puddle?"

I wait for his reply. His brown liquid eyes stare up at me, wide-eyed. Normally they remind me of our Jersey cow's eyes: placid, innocent, and trusting. Right now, they look scared. A huge tear spills over the rim and courses down his mud-spattered cheek. He draws his shoulders in, and lowers his head to his chest.

Oh . . . my. I'm overcome with remorse. I bite my bottom lip to still its trembling. Tears sting my eyes and I blink, fighting them back. How could I have been so short-tempered with my youngest grandson? Good Lord, he's scarcely more than a baby, not even three years old. Besides, it's only natural for a child to splash in puddles. And what was I doing when he slipped, unnoticed, out the back door?

Nothing. I was doing nothing. Nothing but thinking. And daydreaming.

Tenderly, I place my fingers under his chin and tip his face up, forcing him to look at me. "I'm sorry, sweetie. Grandma shouldn't have lost her temper with you." I run my thumb gently over his dirty cheek. "And you're not a bad boy. Not a bad boy at all—I'm a bad grandma."

His eyes grow larger, if that's even possible, and the corners of his mouth curl into a timorous smile. "Gamma's bad?"

I nod. "Yes, today Grandma was bad. I shouldn't have yelled at you. I'm sorry. But you should never go outside without asking me. Don't do it again, okay?"

He doesn't answer my question. Instead, he giggles and says, "Gamma's bad."

I sigh. "Fine. But let's not tell Mama, okay?"

If I don't watch myself, my grandchildren won't even want to come around anymore, nor will their mothers leave the younger ones in my care. Didn't I prove I'm not a trustworthy babysitter? What if he had wandered further, into the barns, or got lost in the fields? What if he had thought about going home and got out on the road? My heart lurches; this road is getting so busy.

Lately, the older four spend less time here; they don't need to be minded anymore. Come to think of it, Eddie already acts like it's a punishment to spend ten minutes alone with me. But then he's a boy and boys can be like that. Perhaps if I had wheels instead of legs or a motor instead of a heart, he might find me interesting.

I'm beginning to wonder if they think I'm weird; they've caught me talking to myself more than a few times. And they can pretend all they like they're not rolling their eyes or sniggering behind my back, but I've seen them doing it.

Sometimes, I wonder what they'd be like as adults if they'd lived a life like mine. They've no idea how fortunate they are to have been born in these prosperous times, to families who love them. Unlike my generation, they're growing up without a want or care in the world. Now, Ernest and Tom's generation went through some tough years when they were young—they remember what hard times are like, and so they appreciate these good times. But the younger ones take it for granted.

Now, mind you, the first four grandkids are hard workers—I'll give them that. Their parents made sure they help with all the farm and household chores. But these last two, well, I hate to admit it, they've been spoiled. I'm not saying it's wrong; after all, they are the babies. Besides, did I not do the same thing myself? Was I not a little gentler in Tommy's rearing than I was with Ernest? And because of Tommy's heart condition, did I not coddle and shelter him from as much physical labour and stress as I could? My goodness, I'm still doing it. Even in my thoughts, he's still my baby, my Tommy. And he's forty years old.

Now, isn't that funny? Not once, not even when he was a newborn babe, did I ever think of Ernest as Ernie. No, he's always been Ernest—serious, reliable, and assertive—someone you can count on to get things done.

I suds up the face cloth and rub it over Karl's curly brunette head and face. I fill a cup with clear, warm water. "Close your eyes tight, sweetie, while I rinse your hair. I don't want to get any soap in your eyes."

Karl squeezes his eyes closed. I laugh; his face resembles one of those trendy, folksy, dried-apple dolls. The water sluices over his head and the suds glide down his shoulders and gather in the murky water around his little round belly. I wring out the cloth and wipe his eyes dry.

"C'mon, baby, let's get you out of this dirty water." I lift him from the slippery tub, wrap a terry towel around his sturdy little body, and hold him close to my chest. "I love you," I say, and in a sudden outpouring of love, I smack a big kiss on his rosy cheek.

I long for a kiss in return. Or a hug, a giggle, or at least a smile. At the best of times, Karl's not an affectionate child with me; he's a mama's boy. He screws his eyes shut and, wiggling one arm free from the towel, he wipes the last remaining trace of my kiss off with his damp palm.

Summer, 1969

It's another humid day. I've finished up the lunch dishes and have retired to the parlour. Charles is having his usual after-every-meal nap on the sofa. I nestle myself in my chair, don my glasses, and open a novel to the bookmarked page. For a page or two, it holds my concentration, but then, as usual, my thoughts stray.

Time carries on, much the same, day after day. These days, Charles and I spend more time alone. Our sons' families are caught up in their own busy lives, their farming operations continually expanding. It's been relatively easy for them though, with the farming sector being as stable and prosperous as it has been the past decade. At times, I wonder what Charles and I might have accomplished, if we had been given the same opportunities.

The world is changing all around us, and it's changing fast. It seems only yesterday—the old days—that time would stand still. I could feel it most in the late afternoons when the heat would rise in waves over the fields and pastures. Nothing moved, save the flies droning. A dead calm would hang over the farm.

Nowadays, you'd have to be blind and deaf not to notice time shifting. Never is there complete silence, not with the constant hum of vehicles on the paved road out front. There are farm machines working the fields, heavy machinery excavating the gravel pit behind our farm, and airplanes crisscrossing the skies.

For today's farmer to keep up with the changing times, he must be prepared to expand, and there doesn't appear to be any end to how big the farms are getting. Pretty soon, the small family farm will become as extinct as the dinosaur. And to expand, today's farmers borrow; it's big business now. Would Charles and I have kept up to the times by borrowing to build a new house, a machinery shed, purchase more land, and expand our livestock holdings?

No, I can't imagine Charles borrowing money to build up a farming enterprise to the extent that, let's say, Ernest has. Charles and Ernest are simply not cut from the same cloth.

They are good men though, my sons, always ensuring Charles has help when, and if he needs it, although I've yet to hear Charles ask for help. True, he's the first to aid anyone in need, but he's the last to ask. And he's not getting any younger, that's for sure. He'll be seventy-five in October.

Now, just how did we get to be that old? I'm not the same young bride Charles carried over the threshold some forty-some odd years ago. Ha! I'd like to see him do that now! My hair has more grey strands than auburn, my heavy breasts sag and my waist and ankles have grown thick. But my bones are sturdy and, at sixty-seven years old, I'm still strong. I'll bet I could outwork most young women today.

Charles worries me, though. I've offered to make him a doctor's appointment, but he'll hear nothing of it. His reply is always, "I'm fine, Mary. Stop your fussing." But it's hard to stop something I've been doing for well over ten years. I've been fussing over him ever since Bob passed—fretting he'll leave me in an instant. The thought terrifies me. I look over at him lying on the sofa. His silver head rests on a cushion, his eyes are closed, his mouth relaxed. His chest rises and falls rhythmically under his blue short-sleeved cotton shirt, tucked neatly inside his blue-and-white striped carpenter overalls, his legs crossed at the ankles.

What would I do if he were not here? Would I stay on the farm? And if I didn't, where would I go? I suppose I could find a small place in town like Jean. But then, how would I fill my time without having him to cook for? Clean for? Do for?

What would I do without him? What would I *be* without him?

My hands tremble. The pages of the book shiver in my hands as if a light breeze had passed over them.

I've been hiding it well, these feelings of anxiety and despondency building the past several months. I tell myself times are good, my life is good, I have no reason, *not one reason*, to validate these feelings. They're nothing new, the familiar old enemies lurking in the shadows: the heavy rain feeling, the melancholy leaden-sky feeling. I've been applying the same old technique I used long ago, focusing on the good thoughts and pushing the others aside, but it's not working any better now than it did some twenty-five years ago. For it seems every time the house falls silent or my mind becomes idle, the familiar old enemies are there.

Waiting for me.

If only I could find peace while I sleep but, in the darkest hours, I'm awoken by obscure dreams. Some are formless, and yet they are tender and soothing. The rest, although vague, are intense and disturbing. I've dreamed I'm nauseous on a roiling ship, or I'm travelling to a new placement, another new home to clean, another new family to serve. It seems I'm constantly being scolded by sharp-faced, heartless women and, as hard as I try, my efforts are never enough. I know these are not merely dreams, but glimpses into my forgotten past.

And I don't need someone like Dr. Clark to listen to my stories again and analyze my life. Because I know what he'll say: the dark feelings I'm experiencing are because I'm now haunted by a past I can't remember. Well, Dr. Clark, whose fault is that? So, thank you very much but, *no*, I don't need you or any of your progressive treatments.

The clock chimes once. Charles stirs. Thank heavens Ada will be along soon with Sam—she'll be spending the afternoon with me while Ada's at work. Sweet little Sam. She'll help me keep all these gloomy feelings at bay.

Mid October, 1969

I'll admit it—I'm not in a good way. Sitting in my chair, I stare out the parlour window and watch as the butternut leaves, clinging in vain to the stems, tumble to the ground. I swear I could sit here and watch until the branches are completely bare and the area beneath the giant tree is a carpet of gold. Autumn is near its end and winter, the dark, and dreaded season of the year lingers around the bend.

Music drifts in from my kitchen AM radio. These days, it's on most of the time, keeping the silence at bay and my mind from wandering down dark paths. It plays an old favourite song sung by Ed Ames, and for the life of me, I don't know why I love this song. The tune is wistful, the words even more so. Even when I'm in good spirits, the nostalgia of this song brings me down, and if I had any smarts about me, I'd get up off this chair right this minute and turn that blasted thing off.

But today, more than ever, the song suits my disposition.

The musical introduction concludes and Ames' smooth voice rings clear with the words 'Try to remember the kind of September. . .' I lean my head against the chair back and close my eyes as the lyrics and tune wash over me.

My throat thickens. I mouth the familiar words. I'm sure everyone, in their later years, can relate to the words. There's one line, though, that has always unsettled me. It's 'Try to remember and *if* you remember, then follow.'

And there it is. The big *if*.

Tell me. How do I go back to that time *if* I can't remember? Because, as the years slip away, so do more of my memories. It seems as I tack on one more year to my life, another one drops off the beginning. God help me; it's terrifying. I need help, but the idea of being institutionalized again is inconceivable.

I think back to the time before my hospital stay, when I was at my lowest. I thought I knew how to *follow*, how to take myself back to a place or time when life was tender. To do that, I needed to escape the life I was living. Now, as I think back on it, I was not following; I was merely escaping. I had totally given up on life. I had wanted a way out.

The memory of that day returns in perfect clarity—like a recurring bad dream. I remember dragging myself out of bed, slipping my feet into my rubber boots and trudging through the deep snow to the workshop . . .

A strange feeling settles over me. I stand, and retracing my steps, I plod to the shed, my feet heavy as they drag through the fallen leaves, as if they're ploughing through deep snow. Before I open the walk-in door, I glance around. The farm is quiet, as it was that day, although this time Charles is not in the barn. He's at the local coffee shop, visiting and gossiping with neighbours.

Inside, the shed is cool and shadowy, heady with the odours of grease, oil, and dust. I'm not out here often, only when I'm looking for Charles. I move to the workbench and glance up the wall. Yes, there they are. Charles is a man of habit, organized; the ropes hang in the same place they've always hung. They're not the same ropes, of course; there's always need of a rope on a farm. I reach up, my hand scarcely grazes the lowest loop. I scan the room. A step ladder leans against one wall. I drag it over, climb, and remove the first coil from the wall. Standing a few steps up the ladder, I stare at the rope in my hands. It's old and frayed. I'm surprised Charles has not replaced it with a better one.

I blink hard, several times, as if surfacing from a deep sleep. *What am I doing?* A tremor begins in my hands.

Tires crunch over gravel. I climb down, dash to the window and peer through the grimy glass. It's Ernest. He parks his pickup truck, and eyes on the ground, he walks toward the shop.

I gasp as my gaze falls from the window to the rope in my hand. I drop it to the floor and rush back to the ladder as Ernest's bulk fills the door.

He stops. His eyes widen when he sees me. "Oh, it's you," he says. My presence doesn't seem to deter him. He flicks a switch and the overhead lighting buzzes to life. Making a beeline to the toolbox, he pulls open a drawer. Without looking at me, he asks, "Where's Dad? When I saw the shop door hanging open, I expected to find him out here."

I lean against the ladder, hoping to conceal it with my body. "Oh, he'll be at the coffee shop." My voice is weak, anxious. I stare at the rope lying on the floor under the window, and quickly look away. "I would've thought you'd be there, too, this time of day."

Tools clunk and bang as he rummages through the drawer. "I wish I were, but I've run into a problem with the combine. Been working on it all day and then, wouldn't you know, just as I was about to finish, my five-eighths wrench broke. Thought I'd borrow Dad's until I get to town to replace it. I want to get back to harvesting the beans tomorrow, that is, if I get the combine fixed."

I clear my throat. "Sure. Help yourself." Still, my voice is reedy.

Ernest locates the wrench. He turns his gaze on me, his eyebrows raised.

I swear I can see the questions racing through his mind.

He voices the first. "What are you doing out here?"

My mind scrambles. What *am* I doing out here? I struggle for a credible excuse. There's none. I cross my arms over my chest, "Do I need a reason now to be out in the shed?"

Immediately, I regret the tone of my voice, my sarcastic reply, my deceitfulness. I clasp my hands to still the tremors. "I'm going to the house; it's time I started dinner."

I scurry through the door, across the lane and through the yard. Before I head inside, I turn and glance back at the shed. Ernest's silhouette is visible through the window. He's staring at the coil of rope gripped in his hands. I hear another vehicle and look toward the road. Charles' car turns in our lane.

I scurry through the door and race to the kitchen. From here I can keep an eye on the shop. Ernest stands in the open door of the shed, the rope hanging from his hand. Charles parks his car and follows Ernest inside the shed.

Minutes tick by. I'm standing at the kitchen sink, a potato in one shaking hand, a paring knife in the other. One lone potato lies submerged in the pot of cold water. I take a deep, calming breath. Dinner will be late if I continue peeling at this rate. I grip the potato and draw the knife toward me. The blade slips against the tough skin of the spud, slicing the tip of my thumb. I watch as a tiny ribbon of scarlet fills the shallow wound.

I turn on the tap and run my thumb under the cold water. It's not safe to be handling a knife right now—I could hurt myself.

Laughter bubbles up inside me. *Hurt myself.* Those words sound absurd, coming from a woman who let herself follow her crazy thoughts. *Good Lord, what was I thinking?* Leaning on the counter, my giggles turn to sobs.

I gulp back my tears; I would never have followed through with another suicide attempt. I could never put Charles through that again. *So why did I even go out there?*

It was that damned song.

I march over to the radio, wanting nothing more than to shatter it to smithereens. Instead, I turn the dial off. The room falls silent.

I look out the window. The men have been out there now for more than a half hour—a lifetime on my frayed nerves.

Something's brewing.

My pulse beats a rapid staccato. I imagine their conversation. It's not about the broken wrench or the combine repairs. No, Ernest would have told Charles about finding me in the shop, my defensiveness, my evasiveness, my abrupt departure. He would have showed him the ladder and the rope.

Thank goodness I had pressed Charles into making that promise years ago. And even though I would never doubt his word, I start to tremble.

The window is open, enough to allow a trickle of fresh air into the warm kitchen. I hear the shop door close. Their low voices drift through the screen and over the sill. They're tramping toward the house. Ernest's gait is rigid and determined, like his face, his mouth set in a resolute line. In contrast, Charles' head hangs, he's staring at his feet as they drag across the gravelled lane. He finally looks up. His face is cruel with restrained feelings.

I cover my mouth with my hand to silence my cry.

Chapter 23

Ernest parks his olive-green Mercury Marquis in the parking lot of the Cheltenham Public General Hospital. Ernest made this decision, so he's the one delivering me to the hospital. I doubt Charles had the stomach for it.

He retrieves my suitcase from the trunk, walks around to the passenger door, and opens it. His voice is gentle. "C'mon Mother. Let's go inside."

I stare straight ahead, ignoring him. I've done my utmost to make the half hour drive uncomfortable for him. He stands beside me for a moment before tentatively slipping his hand under my arm. "Please, Mother."

I haven't spoken a word to him, not one word, since he walked into my kitchen two days ago. Charles slowly moved to the table, pulled out a chair, and sat. Ernest told me—he didn't ask—he told me he would call the doctor and recommend I return to the hospital. I looked at Charles. His eyes were downcast, studying his clasped hands.

Ernest spoke, his voice gentle, yet firm. "Mother, I know Dad promised he would never have you committed again." I pulled my gaze from Charles back to Ernest as he continued. "But I didn't."

I pushed past Ernest and stood before Charles. I placed my hands on his shoulders. "Charles?"

He said nothing.

I shook his shoulders.

He raised his face. My heart skipped a beat—he looked like a broken man.

"No . . . please," I begged.

He slowly shook his head and his voice cracked as he said, "I'm sorry, Mary, but Ernest is right. You need help."

Ernest has always been the strong one. The one who takes charge. The one who gets things done. The one who has his way.

And Charles gave in to him.

I turned my back on them, hauled myself to the bedroom, and slammed the door.

I shrug, dislodging Ernest's hand, and step out of the vehicle. Holding my head high, I march to the front steps of the hospital, a red-brick, three-storey building. Ernest follows one step behind. At least I'm not being admitted to St. Tomas Psychiatric Hospital; Cheltenham now has a psychiatric ward of its own. My family has assured me I'll have visitors regularly—I won't be alone this time.

But, honestly, I don't care if I ever see any of them again.

The admission process is complete, not that I had much to do with it. My headstrong, take-charge son looked after it. We follow a large, stout nurse. She glides silently, well, almost silently, in her serviceable white shoes. Her thick, white-stockinged thighs hiss as they rub together beneath her starched white uniform. We wait before a bank of elevators. The door to one glides open, we step inside, and she pushes the button for second-floor west—the psychiatric ward. The elevator stops, dings, and the door opens.

We proceed down the hall and enter a room, a semi-private with two beds. A sleeping, shrivelled shell of a woman, her scraggly dark hair strewn over the pillow, occupies the one by the window.

Figures, she gets the good bed.

It's feels familiar, like I'm doing it all over again. I keep my eyes on the nurse; I can't bear to look at my son. He lays my suitcase on the mattress and snaps open the clasps, like he knows what he's expected to do. I watch the nurse's large hands rifle through my clothing and toiletries, making a complete muddle of my things. And here I thought Nurse Ryckman was bad. At least, when she searched my belongings, she had the decency to hang up my clothes and put them away. The nurse locates my razor and pockets it. She extends her hand toward me, palm up. "Your bag, please?"

I take a deep breath before passing over my handbag. She unzips and flips it over; the contents spill out. She confiscates the small glass bottle of aspirin. It disappears into her uniform with the razor.

She addresses Ernest. "I'll leave you to get her settled." When she reaches the door, she turns, and says, "Visiting hours are almost over, so don't be long."

I move to the bed and retrieve my purse. Ernest's hand covers mine as I reach for my billfold. I draw in a quick breath.

"Ma," he says.

My heart clutches; he hasn't called me Ma in years. Both he and Tom started calling me Mother shortly after my first hospital stay. It was as if I'd turned my back for only a moment and something had shifted. They'd grown into men.

"Ma, I'm sorry it had to come to—"

I pull my hand away. "Go. Just go. Please."

He stands beside me for several seconds—it seems like hours—before he leans over and places a light kiss on my forehead. "I love you," he says, his voice breaking. He turns, and walks out the door.

The days drag. My roommate's name is Claudia, although that's all I know about her. She has no desire to get to know me, nor I her. I believe we're going to get along just fine.

As promised, I have visitors every day, around one-thirty. They're punctual—I could set my watch by them. One day it's Charles, the next Ernest, or Ada, the following day Tom, or Marilyn. There was one time when Ada and Marilyn came together. They didn't say; I'm guessing they combined their obligation to visit me with a shopping excursion.

One morning, shortly after I was admitted, I heard a soft, familiar voice call my name. I opened my eyes and there was Jean, looking lovely as always, standing in the doorway. She sat on the edge of the bed beside me and reached for my hand. Tears pooled in her eyes, but she bravely blinked them away. She did everything right—of course she did—she said the right words in her expressions of sympathy and encouragement. But hard as I tried, I couldn't find any words, nor could I stop my tears. Good Lord, I hate how I can't control them, how they flow so freely. I felt wretched, having her see me this way, and I was so thankful when she finally left.

She is one brave soul, though, that woman. She shows up at least once a week, always a fresh bouquet of her signature flowers clutched in her hand. And even though I'm mostly silent, she sits on the side of my bed and talks to me. Sometimes, she brings a book, or a magazine, and reads aloud. And then, after a while, she leaves.

When my family comes, it's different. The one-sided conversations usually revolve around the capers the grandkids are up to and, if they come in twos, they talk amongst themselves rather than with me. That's fine; I have no desire to talk with them. Honestly, I'd prefer they all just stayed away.

All but Charles.

I'm not upset with him anymore—I don't think I ever really was. Initially, I was disappointed in him, but like I said before, Charles and

Ernest are not cut from the same cloth. It would take an exceptional individual, someone with great strength, to stand up to Ernest, and Charles is not that person. Nor am I. Besides, my heart aches more for him each time he comes to visit. He looks like he's aged two years in the past few weeks. He says he's eating well—he goes to Ernest and Ada's every evening for supper and spends the night there in their spare bedroom. After breakfast, he returns to our farm to do the barn chores and then heads on over to Tom and Marilyn's for lunch. It's obvious they're all doing their utmost to care for him.

So, why then does he look so dog-tired?

If I'm honest with myself, I'd have to say I'm not even angry with Ernest anymore; he did what he felt he needed to do. However, I can't see how being in this hospital will have a positive outcome. Other than the increasing number of pills they feed me and the one-sided psychiatric discussions which go nowhere—well, that could be my fault; it must be a challenge when a patient refuses to talk—nothing else is being done. But then again, I wouldn't want *anything else* being done to me like there was at that other place.

I find it exceedingly difficult to believe I will ever go home again and, as each day grinds by, I care less if I do.

Charles was here yesterday, so I suppose today's visitor will be Ernest.

I've been staring out this window for some time, watching the traffic in the street, the pedestrians on the sidewalk, everyone in such a gosh-darn hurry. A young man strides toward the front door carrying a bouquet. I push my glasses up on my nose. From this distance, it looks like pink miniature roses arranged in a ceramic baby bootie.

My elbow rests on the arm of the chair, my head propped on my hand. *How nice for him*, I think, *he's the father of a brand-new baby daughter*. My last miscarriage comes to mind, the daughter Charles and I never got to raise. A tear slinks down my cheek. I can't even be bothered to wipe it away.

An extra pill was on my tray today at lunch—I guess they're upping the ante, but I willingly swallowed it. I have no appetite. Sometimes I think about all the food that returns to the kitchen—such a waste! What do they do with it? Why don't they ask if I care to eat or not? But, no, they don't—the trays keep coming three times a day, whether a person's hungry or not. Unlike St. Tomas Hospital, there's nothing to do here—there's no dining room, no library, no lounge, no working in the laundry. There's nothing to do except sit in this damned chair and watch life happening outside the window.

I glance over at the clock on the wall. It's already two-thirty and Ernest has not showed. I wonder why he's so late. Oh well, it doesn't matter. I'm tired of waiting for him, and my eyes are heavy. I believe I'll go to bed.

Someone's shaking my shoulder. "Ma." It's Ernest's voice I hear.

My eyelids are so darn heavy. *Go away.*

"Ma." I hear another soft call. That's not Ernest's voice. It's Tom's.

I'm lying on my back. I turn my face away from him.

"Ma, please wake up." It's Ernest's voice once again. It's so tender, though, it scarcely sounds like him.

I drag one eyelid up, and through a thin slit, I notice the room is semi-dark, the only glow coming from the reading light over Claudia's bed.

Why are they both here? Together? And so late?

I drag myself into a sitting position, hunched and rigid, my legs dangling over the side of the bed. I gaze up into my sons' faces.

Their eyes are glassy, swollen and red. The bed squeaks as they cautiously sit on either side of me. Ernest tentatively wraps his arm around my shoulder.

"What is it?" My voice is feeble, frightened. My body shudders and my hands begin to shake uncontrollably. Tom reaches for them and holds them in his.

A tear spills over the rim of his eye and runs down his cheek. He turns his face away. I turn to Ernest and search his face. My son, so brave and strong, struggles for control. His face spasms. "It's Dad."

A white wave of grief crashes over me. I clutch at my breast as something like a severed muscle palpitates and quivers beneath my ribs.

Chapter 24

February, 1970

Several weeks have passed.

I'm lying, fetal, in the narrow hospital bed. Waiting.

For what? I don't know. Perhaps I'm waiting for the end, or maybe I'm waiting for the new beginning after the end. All I know is I'm waiting for something.

I've been told, many times, by the psychiatrist, my sons, and their wives that, whether I like it or not, I must deal with Charles' death.

Why? I ask.

Why must I deal with another loss?

Oh, there've been plenty of times I've met up with loss and death and, as far as I'm concerned, they're the same thing. For whether you lose a loved one through death or by any other means, they're still gone. And if you can't be with that person again, well, they may as well be dead. I thought if I lived long enough, surely I'd get used to it, that it wouldn't hurt so much. I was lying to myself.

The other day I actually listened to my psychiatrist. My problem, he said, is that, unlike most people, I lack the capability to process grief. Now that I've had time to think about it, he may be right. People have always told me, "Mary, you need to learn to let go," or "Mary, you need to move on," or "Mary, just hold on to the memories and carry on."

But, what happens when you no longer have memories? What do you hold on to then?

My thoughts on this are: Because I can't remember those I loved as a child, they're lost to me. And since I can't hold on to them, or even to the memory of them, instead I hold on to the grief.

Would you look at me now? Analyzing myself.

So, those who tell me I must deal with this loss don't seem to understand that, no, I don't have to. Charles' death is the greatest loss of my life and I would rather join him, wherever he is, than remain here without him. And if there's no heaven, no afterlife, nothing, well, that's still better than this.

I remember the shock of it, the day the two of them showed up together. My mind was already in a very fragile state when they gently broke the news to me. I heard Ernest say "He's gone." It was days afterwards—four, they said—before I came around.

And during those four days, they had laid Charles to rest. Without me. I didn't even kiss him goodbye.

Charles' last day on this earth was the seventeenth day of November. I blame myself. If I had been there by his side, he wouldn't have died.

I've taken the snippets gleaned from my sons and sewn them together, like the many quilts I've stitched over the years. My sons didn't tell me everything, mind you, but it wasn't hard to fill in the blanks. Now, I've enhanced the story so that, in my mind's eye, it's like watching it on a television screen. I clearly see every detail: Charles, alone in the morning, struggling to change the flat tire on his car and then later, cleaning out the eaves troughs on our house. He's gripping his chest as he climbs down the ladder. At the base, he sits, leans against it, and goes to sleep. Or at least that's how it looked when they found him.

If only he had asked for help.

But, no. Charles never was one to ask, and no one knew that better than I.

The nurses have dragged me from my bed, through the shower, into clothing and propped me in the chair by the window. According to them, the sheets needed washing, and so did I.

I think my visitors come less often, although I'm not sure; I've lost all concept of time. Ernest and Tom still show up a few times each week. Ada and Marilyn, well, I'm not sure when they visited last. I sleep most of the time—not so much from the sedatives—I just have no desire to be awake. I haven't seen Jean for some time, although she's been here; the bouquet is always fresh.

Voices tumble down the hall from the nurses' station. I recognize Ernest's strong tenor, the other is a child's. I hear a nurse clearly say, "Go ahead, she's ready."

And then they're standing in the doorway, hesitant. Ernest stands tall while Sam, so tiny and fearful, grasps his hand.

I raise myself and grip the arm of the chair. My legs muscles spasm as I stand; there's little strength left in them. Sam races across the room, almost knocking me off my feet. She wraps her arms around my legs, her radiant face gazing up at me. "Grandma, you're not dead."

Well now, doesn't that just beat all? "No, I'm not dead." I glare at Ernest. "What does she mean by that?"

Ernest gently kisses my cheek. "It's good to see you up, Ma. How are you?"

"Well, I'm not dead," I curtly reply as I totter over to my bed and sit on the edge. "Take the chair, Ernest." I pat the mattress. "Sammy, come sit on the bed with me. Here, let me take your coat off before you get overheated."

Ernest interrupts. "No, leave it on, Ma. We can't stay long."

I turn my head in his direction.

"I'll explain in a minute."

I pause a moment while we all get settled. "So, I'll ask once again, what did she mean by that?"

Ernest nods. "Ma, what I'm about to say is going to sound harsh, yet it needs to be said." He takes a steadying breath. "I know Dad's passing has been hard on you, especially coming when it did, and the way it did. I know how much you loved him and I can only imagine how you miss him. We've all been waiting for you to come to terms with it, move on, get well and come home. But from what I see, I'm guessing you don't want to." He pauses a moment and looks me straight in the eye. "Tell me I'm not right?"

I lower my face. "You're right," I whisper.

"That's what I thought," he replies. "But, what you need to know is Dad's passing hasn't only been hard on you—it's been hard on all of us, even the littlest. Now Sam here knows her grandpa died—she's been to the cemetery, and she understands he's not coming back." He glances toward his daughter. "Don't you Sam?"

She nods.

I look down at her face, winter pale and freckled as she watches her father speak. For the life of me, I don't understand why Ernest is saying these things with Sam right here—she shouldn't be hearing this conversation. My heart aches for her; her eyes are watery, and her pointy, little chin quivers.

"Ma, the little ones haven't seen you since you came to the hospital. It's been three months, and three months is an awful long time for kids." He pauses. "And I'll tell you, nothing short of seeing you in the flesh would convince Sam you didn't die, too."

"Ah, Sam." I lean over and draw her to me. She circles her small arms around my neck.

Ernest continues, "Anyway, children aren't usually allowed in this ward. So, I had to get through some red tape and a couple of roadblocks to get her in here. First, I had to get through Ada—she was dead set against her coming."

My eyes flash at him.

"No, it's not that she didn't want her to see you. She was afraid of what other sights she might be exposed to outside your room—you know what I mean."

I nod in understanding.

Sam's hand trails over my shoulder, up my neck and rubs my cheek. I lean in to her touch; it feels so good.

"So, I spoke with your doctor and the nurses, and they've assured me she won't see anything she shouldn't. But they only gave us fifteen minutes."

Sam draws herself from my embrace. "Grandma, do they feed you here?"

I nod. "Yes, of course they do, sweetie."

"Is the food yucky?"

"No." I laugh. The sound of it startles me—it's the first time I've laughed in over three months. "No, it's not yucky. But I wouldn't say it's good either."

"Ohhh," she says. "That's why you're so skinny. You should go home and make some good food." Her head bobs enthusiastically. "And when you do, then I can come over again, and we'll play match game, and ear soup. And we can make daisy chains and ice cream."

"We can't make daisy chains in the winter, but come summer we can."

Summer. Spring and summer *will* come again. I glance away and stare at the wall for a long minute. "Yes, I suppose you're right. I should go home and make some good food."

Ernest rises from the chair and leaves the room. "Now, where does he think he's going?" I mutter to Sam.

She shrugs her shoulders. "And when you come home," she says, giggling, "I can have a sleepover again, and maybe I can even sleep with you since Grandpa—" The words are out before she has a chance to process them. Her giggle turns to a pout, and she sucks in her bottom lip. She reminds me of myself.

I take a deep breath, fighting tears.

Ernest is back, a clipboard in his hands. He passes it to me. Attached to the board is a blank sheet of paper. I look up, puzzled; I have no idea what he expects me to do with it.

"Ma, do you want to get out of here and go home?"

Until a few moments ago, my answer would have been no. I suck in my lower lip, just like Sam had done. I look at Ernest through bleary eyes and nod.

"Okay, so this is what I want you to do." He pulls a black marker from his pocket and removes the cap. "I want you to write these words . . . "

I take the offered marker.

"Write I WILL GO HOME in big, bold capital letters and beneath that, I want you to sign your name."

Tears stream down my cheeks and my hands shake as I print those few meaningful words.

"Good." He gently takes the clip board and marker from my hands. From his pocket he pulls a small dispenser of tape and affixes the paper to the wall.

Through grateful tears, I smile. Ernest wasn't going to let me shrivel up in this bed and die if he had anything to do with it. My clever, take-charge, get-it-done son came here with a plan.

"There now. Every morning, when you open your eyes, this will be the first thing you see. And every time you read it, it'll remind you of what you're working toward."

I nod and wipe my face on my sleeve.

Sam scoots her plump little bottom over beside me. I curl my arm around her as she lays her head against my chest. Ernest's face breaks into a huge smile—the first I've seen in weeks. He sighs. "Ma, I hate to drag Sam away, but it's time we go."

I nod again.

"Sam, say goodbye to your Grandma."

I gaze at her, my sweet little reason for living, and run my hand over her blonde silk hair.

She plants a gooey kiss on my cheek. "Bye-bye, Grandma."

"Bye for now, sweetie."

Ernest kisses my forehead. He grasps Sam's hand as she slides off the bed.

I hear Sam call, "Hurry up and come home, Grandma," as they leave the room.

I remember hearing these words at a funeral some time ago, 'When we lose someone we love, we must learn, not to live without them but to live with the love they left behind.' I must learn to do this, for even though Charles is no longer here, his love still lives on. Our family is waiting for me, our farm is waiting for me, and our little home is waiting for me. There is more love to share and more golden memories to make.

I will go home.

Early Autumn, 1970

I draw the sharp knife through the sandwich and carry it, along with my cup of tea, to the table. Most days, this four-room house seems large for only one person, but today, the walls are closing in. I take a bite, and while I chew, I glance out the window. The maple trees lining the lane to the forest are coming into full colour, a splendid mixture of gold, orange, and russet.

A walk will do me good; I need to clear my head. I pack up my lunch and head out the door.

The air is saturated with the scents of autumn. Heading down the lane, I consider the past six months of my life. According to everyone, I made a remarkable recovery. I returned home with a plan, which I put into effect immediately. Other than a few of my favourite hens, I sold off the livestock. To keep peace in the family, I sharecropped my land with both my sons, each of us reaping one-third of the value of the crop.

What could go wrong with a plan like that?

Well, lots.

I enter the woodlot and tramp along the well-known trail. Created years ago by deer, their tracks are now buried by cattle hoofmarks and human footprints. I marvel how every person or creature who walks the face of this earth leaves their mark, if only for a moment. Charles has left so many on this property—the property he loved. I stop at the place we had picnicked many years ago. I imagine two young lovers entwined on a plaid wool blanket surrounded by blooming trilliums and violets. Not long after that, I realized Charles would be the only man I would ever love. What if I hadn't run away? If I had accepted his offer of marriage? Would things be different now? Perhaps not, but at least I would have had a few more years with him. I raise my hand to my heart and take a few calming breaths. Oh, what I wouldn't give for a few more years.

I move along to a huge deadfall, an ancient oak. I sit upon it and open my lunch sac, my mind revisiting the dilemma of my failed plan. A grey squirrel scampers down the trunk of a young sugar maple, his arms, and legs spread-eagled. He abruptly stops, and his head jerks up as he eyes me. Unsure of his next move, he holds his position without a single movement. He doesn't even blink.

No, my sharecropping plan didn't work, not one bit.

"What was I thinking?" My voice startles him. He scolds me and races back up the tree, out of sight within a canopy of limbs and leaves.

How could I have been so foolish? I should have known my sons wouldn't work well together. Some can, but not my two. They're both too strong-willed, stubborn, independent—that's why they each have their own farming enterprises. And, to top it off, my daughters-in-law, normally good friends, are now bickering and unhappy. My plan has done nothing but cause grief.

And am I happy living here by myself? If I were honest with myself, which, I assure you, I *now* am, my answer is, "No." Without Charles, it's simply too quiet. The radio or the television is on all the time to keep me company. And it's not only the house. The entire farm is silent. It's not the same; it's not home without Charles. There are far too many reminders of him everywhere. Most times it comforts me, but sometimes I wonder if it isn't too much. I find myself glancing up, expecting him to come through the door, and as a thought comes to mind, I've caught myself talking to him. As if it's not bad enough I talk to myself, now I'm talking to him too.

I've finished my lunch and continue my walk. I follow the cattle trails through the forest, eventually coming out the other side, and amble to the line fence. From there I walk the perimeter of our land, following the fence row to the southeast corner. The gravel pit on the Sherman farm is no longer in operation. The sunlight glints on the clear, blue water. Given time, the earth will reclaim herself—small trees and shrubs have already sprouted. I continue on along the southern and western boundaries, ending up in our farmyard. I enter the barn—Charles' domain.

I tread down the centre aisle, gazing at the empty pens and stalls. In my mind's eye, I see Charles, his head tucked into the flank of a cow, a stream of milk ping-pinging as it hits the metal pail. Barn cats line up, waiting for a shot of milk to come their way.

I stroll to the old staircase and climb to the loft. I stand there, as still as the barn itself. The loft and granary are empty now, the wide boards of the loft floor covered in a thin layer of old dusty straw. I see the wooden rungs of the ladders, which run against the upright timbers high into the peaks. The barn echoes with the sounds of yesteryears. I hear my boys' laughter as they play with Ruby, taking turns jumping off into a huge haystack, and down below, the cattle are bawling, pigs are grunting, and horses are nickering. I hear Charles' voice as he croons to them all.

I drag myself from my musings. Over the past few months, I've been reading a lot, specifically works on death and grief. I recall a quote by Elisabeth Kübler-Ross: 'The reality is that you will grieve forever. You will not 'get over' the loss of a loved one; you will learn to live with it. You will heal and you will rebuild yourself around the loss you have suffered. You will be whole again but you will never be the same. Nor should you be the same nor would you want to.'

I marveled at the wisdom in her words and they comforted me. I finally felt affirmed that I am not expected to 'get over' the loss of Charles or any of my loved ones. I will heal and I will learn to live with the grief. And it's okay that it remains with me forever.

I am learning to live with the love Charles left behind.

And I can do that anywhere. Changes need to be made, and it is up to me to make them.

Chapter 25

June, 1973

I'm seventy-one years old. I live in a tidy one-bedroom apartment in the Fenland Apartment Building. It's a pleasant spot; my balcony overlooks the community pool and green space of the park.

The changes I put into effect three years ago have worked splendidly. After much deliberation, I sharecropped my land with Ernest. Now, I know what you're thinking—how could I choose one son over the other? Oh, believe me, it was a hard decision. I prayed my choice wouldn't cause hard feelings, but I didn't have any other option other than to rent it to someone outside the family. And if I did that, both sons would be angry with me. I was relieved when Tom accepted my decision without question.

Next, I secured a tenant for the house—a nice young couple with a baby on the way. The rent isn't much, but then neither is the house. Along with my share of the crop sales and my government pension, I live comfortably and independently in my new apartment.

As I suspected, I had difficulty filling my time. You know, you can only impose on your best friend so much before you become a nuisance, and hanging out at the Seniors Centre gets old fast.

But all that changed today. I was strolling down Main Street, no specific destination and no errands to run, just simply filling in another hour of another long day. A sign, 'Volunteer Help Needed' was propped in the window of the Salvation Army Thrift store. I marched inside.

The sales lady behind the counter was reading a magazine. She peered at me over her eyeglasses. “Can I help you?”

A filmy memory flickered through my mind. I smiled. Ah, yes, it was Florence. *May I help you?* almost slipped through my lips, but I curbed myself. “Yes, I noticed the sign. Are you still looking for help?”

She raised an eyebrow. “Yes, we are. Do you have someone in mind?”

I cocked my head. “Yes.”

“Who?”

The nerve of this woman! “Me,” I huffed. “That’s the reason I walked through the door.”

“I’m sorry.” She glanced me over from head to toe. “I don’t mean to offend, but do you mind if I ask how old you are?”

Her words stunned me. “Yes, I do mind, and you are offending me. I don’t see how my age has anything to do with it. The sign says volunteer work, does it not?”

She sputtered. “Y-yes.”

I glanced around the store, giving myself a moment to think. I was so eager for a purpose in my life, I didn’t think to ask what type of labour this volunteer work entailed. My voice softened. “I apologize. I’m not making a good first impression, am I? Please let me start over. What type of work, exactly, would be required of this volunteer?”

“Sales. What I’m doing right now. Some sorting, arranging items on the racks, pricing, that sort of thing.”

And reading magazines, I added in my thoughts. “I can do that. I’ve worked in retail, and even though I’m seventy-one years old, I’ve got plenty of energy and lots of free time on my hands. If you give me a chance, you won’t be sorry.”

Those words finally caught her attention. “Retail experience?”

“Yes. Many years ago, though.”

“You’ll be on your feet a good portion of the day.”

“I understand.”

She sat and considered while I waited. Eventually I drummed my fingers on my handbag, just enough to get her attention.

Her eyes focused.

"So, am I in, or not?"

I guess I'm in—working as a sales clerk for the Salvation Army Thrift Store three days per week.

August, 1975

I'm seated, comfortably, in a corner of Ada's living room. The air is humid and hot, satiated with female voices and the sickly sweet combination of perfumes and body scents. I glance around the two conjoined living rooms, separated by a wide wood-trimmed arch. Folding chairs are placed between the comfortable sofas and loveseats; the ladies talking amongst themselves, their voice buzzing, like bees in a hive.

I consider the occasion of this day and smile to myself. My family is growing. Oh, if only Charles could be here; our two eldest grandchildren will soon be married. Eddie, no, Ed, will be the first, and then Vashti.

Ed's fiancé is Donna. When I first met her, she was so shy—I didn't expect their relationship would last. *That timid girl will never fit into Ernest's sociable, talkative family,* I thought. *My goodness, they'll eat her for breakfast and spit her out at lunch.* I was wrong. Their relationship blossomed, and before I knew it, they were engaged. Then I thought, *that poor little thing, she's going to need an ally. I will be that person.* However, I realized soon enough that, as quiet as she is, she can hold her own. She works as a waitress at the local truck stop where Ed is apprenticing for his Class A Mechanic's licence. One day, while I was working in the store, I overhead two women, friends of Ada's, talking about Donna. They were far enough away, and obviously, they misjudged my sharp hearing. In a low voice, I heard one say to the other, "I wonder what Ada thinks of her."

"What do you mean?" the other had asked.

The first cupped her hand over her mouth, but I could still hear. "Well, you've heard of her cousin so-and-so, right?"

"Oh my. He's *her* cousin?"

"Yeah. There are a few wild ones in that family, I'll tell you. Plus, she's only a waitress."

I wanted to yell, *"Shame on the both of you!"* but, just at that moment, another customer came through the door. I held my tongue. After all, I was the one eavesdropping, and we were in a public place. I felt a combination of anger and shame for Donna. I remember how it felt to be judged, how small it made me feel.

But enough of that. Today is a good day. Ada is generously throwing a bridal shower for Donna. *Good Lord, it's sweltering in here.* Not a breath of air stirs the sheer curtains in the packed double living rooms. I glance around the crowded rooms once again. Other than immediate family, I can't imagine Donna knows one of them. From across the room, I watch her. In this heat, she should be flushed, like the rest of us, but her face grows more ashen as the minutes pass. Finally, the silly games are over, the gifts opened, and the women flit about the room, socializing as they enjoy iced glasses of lemonade, tiny sandwiches, and sweets. Donna's mother follows Ada to the kitchen. I amble over and take her seat.

"You don't look well, sweetie. Are you okay?" I ask.

She nods, lifting her long brunette hair off her neck and drawing it over one shoulder. Sweat glistens on her pale face. "Yeah, it's no big deal. Just a headache."

"Ah, that's too bad. Could be the heat. Or stress. A little overwhelming, isn't it?"

Her shoulders relax. "Yeah. I've never been good with crowds, especially if I'm in the spotlight." She sighs. "Whew, it's hot in here."

"It is," I agree. "This big old house heats up like a brick oven."

She sips her lemonade and then presses the cool glass against her temple. "It is a beautiful home, though. Ed and I plan to have a farm of our own someday with a big old farmhouse and barns." She adds, "Lots of barns—I love animals. And lots of trees. I'll bet this house wouldn't be nearly as hot if it had a bit more shade around it."

"You're right. Ernest should have planted more trees years ago. I don't remember my house at the farm ever being this warm. Has Ed shown you where I used to live?"

"Yeah, he did. It's a pretty property. He was going to ask if we could rent the house from you, but then his dad offered us the house next door, on his other farm." She nibbles on a piece of shortbread and washes it down with her drink. "To tell you the truth, I'm really glad he offered. Your house is *so* small."

I chuckle. "That it is. You know, when I was younger, all I ever dreamed of was living in a big, beautiful house."

"Really?"

"Uh-huh. Actually, there was this one time when my husband, Charles, offered to sell our farm and buy another, one with a lovely brick farmhouse, just so I could have the house of my dreams. I'll point it out to you someday."

"So why didn't he buy it for you?"

"Oh, it's a long story, and I don't want to get into all that right now."

"Can you make it a short story?"

I shake my head and laugh at her impish grin. "Alright. To make a long story short, it basically boiled down to the fact I didn't need it."

She inclined her head, willing me to go on. "I don't understand. You wanted it though, right?"

"I thought I did. The thing is, a beautiful house doesn't make a happy home. My best friend always told me that, but I never listened. I guess I needed to figure it out for myself." I feel like I'm lecturing her, so I change the subject. "Ada tells me your family moved to this area a couple of years ago?"

"Yeah. We came from Essex County, although my father grew up around here and always wanted to return. What about you? Did you always live around here?"

"Oh no. I was born in England."

Her eyes fly open. "That's so cool. What brought you to Canada?"

I take a sip of my lemonade, the ice long since melted. "Oh, I don't want to talk about me; it's your day today." I spin the conversation back to her. "You're happy here?"

"Yeah, I love it. The countryside is so much prettier than Essex County. My parents' farm backs on to the river. I love forests and there's lots out our way. Lots of places to hike."

"I know the area. It is really nice." I think back on her comment about her father growing up in this area. "Now, I didn't know your father's parents well, but I knew of them. They moved away from this area a while back, if I remember correctly. Are they still alive?"

"No, they both passed some years ago. I hardly remember them."

"And your mother's?"

Donna shakes her head. "I never knew them at all. My grandfather was killed in an automobile accident when my mom was a teenager and my grandmother died when I was a baby. I guess you could say I've never really had any grandparents—none I was close to, anyway."

I sit my glass on the side table and reach for her hand. It feels small and delicate clasped in mine. "Well, you've got one now."

She smiles. Her dark brown eyes gaze into mine. And, at that moment, I gained another granddaughter.

May, 1979

It's been a long week. My feet ache, and my brain is weary; I'm not as young as I used to be. Nowadays I tire easily, I'm short of breath, my ankles are thick as stumps, I use a cane, and my hands shake. Now, wouldn't you think a person might consider it's high time they retired?

The bell above the shop door tinkles, giving me a gentle prod. My eyes focus on a young woman struggling through the door, a chunk of a baby balanced on one hip, a toddler holding tight to her free hand. It's late in the day—she'll likely be my last customer. "Good afternoon," I greet her as I pull myself up off the wooden chair. "May I help you?"

"Sure, if you don't mind." Her face is weary and her shoulders hang. She looks as if she's carrying far more than the weight of her baby.

"You've got your hands full." I walk toward her. "There's a playpen set up over there," I say, pointing. "And if your little girl likes to colour, there's a child's table and chairs."

She makes a beeline to the play area. "Thank you. This is great!"

I follow her. "I don't think we've met. Are you new in town?"

She arranges a few toys around her baby's feet in the playpen. "Yeah. Moved into the new apartment complex a few days ago."

Ah, yes. The new geared-to-income apartment complex.

Once her children settle, I introduce myself. "Welcome to Ridgeland. My name is Mary."

She nods. "Thanks. I'm Debbie."

"So, Debbie, what can I help you find?"

"Oh, I need just about everything," she replies with a sigh. "The kids really need summer clothing. Me too." Under her breath, she adds, "If I've got enough."

"Come this way." Glancing toward her children, she follows me across the store. "Here's the children's clothing. The ladies' section is over there, and the dressing rooms are at the back of the store. We've a nice selection of clothing, and if you look closely, you'll see there's many have never been worn before."

Debbie raises her eyebrows.

"Here, let me show you." I rifle through the rack of children's wear. "Here's one, for example." I hold a child's cotton print dress. "Check out the fabric. See how it's crisp and the weave of the cloth is tight?"

Hesitantly, she fingers the hem of the dress.

"But the telltale sign is the tag." I turn the collar over, exposing the manufacturer's tag. "When it's stiff, like this one, it means the piece of clothing has never been washed."

And there it is—the look I get when I talk about the brand-new-never-been-worn clothing. Usually Ada or Marilyn wear it, sometimes the older grandkids, but I didn't expect it from her, a young woman in need. Of course, her generation doesn't know what it's like to make overalls from flour sacks, turn collars, patch holes, or darn socks. They don't realize what a blessing it is to find an article of new clothing at a fraction of the original cost.

No, they don't understand.

"I'll leave you to your shopping. If you need me, I'll be right over behind the counter." I return to my chair.

I watch Debbie out of the corner of my eye as she chooses several articles of clothing for her children. In the ladies' section, she selects a t-shirt and a pair of jean shorts for herself. She mentally tallies her purchases and returns the shorts to the rack. My heart aches for this selfless young mother.

Not to rouse suspicion, I wait until she approaches the checkout. Placing her selection on the counter, I exclaim, "Oh, where is my head? There's a twenty-five per cent discount on clothing today."

She narrows her eyes. "There are no signs or mark-downs on the tags."

I choose my words carefully; I don't want to wound her pride. "No, we don't always post our sales. They can be quite random. Could be any day, any time, on anything—usually when we're overstocked and want to move some items quickly. As you can see, we're way overstocked on clothing in every department right now. I'm sorry, I should have told you when you first arrived." I lower my eyes and feign embarrassment. "I guess I'm showing my age—it's late in the day and my brain is tired. I'm sure glad I remembered, though. I'd hate to think all the other customers today benefited from the sale and you didn't."

It appears I haven't totally lost the knack of telling little white lies. Her face beams as she scurries back to the ladies' section and retrieves the shorts.

As I ring in her purchases, I notice a few of the manufacturer's tags on items she chose are stiff.

"Thanks for the excellent shopping advice, Mary," she calls, closing the door behind her.

I open my billfold and make up the difference.

Another work week is finished. My feet throb, but I'm happy, and my heart swells with gratitude for this new life of mine. Every day, especially those like today, are gifts.

It's odd. Now I no longer live at the farm, I feel Charles' presence all around me. At times, it is so strong—like a soft, warm glow shimmering around me, comforting me. Perhaps it's not his presence I feel, but his love. I have not only learned to live with the love he left behind, but whenever I can, I honour his memory by assisting those in need—like I did today with this single young mother—an act Charles would have done himself.

Today was a good day, and tomorrow will be even better. Donna has promised to join me for lunch at my apartment.

I set a pickle tray along with a plate of egg salad sandwiches on my tiny drop-leaf dining table. "So, what's Ed up to today?"

Donna sits in the comfortable, stuffed rocking chair in my living room. My apartment is open-concept, which is ideal for this small space. If I'd ever thought my home on the farm was small, this one surely has it beat. "Oh, he's at the airport, as usual."

"My goodness, that boy sure loves flying."

Donna cocks her head. "Sometimes I think he loves it more than he loves me."

"Now, that's not true," I say, shaking my head.

"I wouldn't be so sure if I was you."

The electric kettle whistles, and I unplug the cord. "If anyone had told me, years ago, that Ernest would own an airplane, I would've never believed them. And now I have a grandson who wants to be a commercial pilot. Who would've ever imagined that?"

"I would." She laughs. "I remember Ed telling me he had his glider pilot's licence when he was only fifteen years old."

"He did. He was crazy about flying—long before Ernest got into it. When Ed was a little boy, he would try to fly off the barn grade—you know, with a blanket, like kids do." I fill the teapot with water. "Is she just about finished?"

"Yep, down to the last ounce. It doesn't take this little piggy long to drain a bottle." The baby drags on the nipple until she draws air. Donna raises her to a sitting position and, placing her hand under her chin, she gently rubs her back. Within seconds, the infant burps, loud and wet. "Jeez, I hate the spit-up, though," Donna says as she catches the spew in a paper towel. She wipes the child's mouth with the receiving blanket and lays her in the carrier.

We visit while we eat. I share advice on motherhood and listen as she talks of her hopes and dreams. When her maternity leave is over, she'll return to her office job. She's saving toward a farm of their own.

I half listen while my mind drifts. Some time ago I had read a line, 'You should never judge a person's life story by the chapter you find them in.' Well, isn't that the truth? Donna's a smart, hard-working girl, who has held down a respectable office job here in town for the past three years. And what a godsend she's been to me. Never does a week go by she doesn't walk into the store for a visit, her bagged lunch in hand.

It's funny how life circles back on itself, showering you with little blessings when you least expect them. I glance down at my first-born great-grandchild, Annie. *Now, why did Donna choose that name?* She'd never heard it from my lips. It troubled me and I needed to know, so one day I finally asked. She just shrugged. "No reason," she said. "I just love the name."

Although she speaks of her childhood, I never share mine with her, and she never asks. Likely Ed or his parents have told her I don't like to talk about it. They all think I'm still ashamed of my beginnings. But the truth of the matter is, there is no tangible beginning. My earliest memories are merely fragments of a pleasant dream. My reality, the vague memories I do recall, begins when I stepped off the SS Corinthian.

Annie cries and, using her foot, Donna rocks the little carrier. My mind wanders again as she tends to her.

Donna's not unlike the other privileged young people of her generation. She's never done without, and life has been kind to her. When she and Ed were first married, I had said to her, "Now, if you ever need money, come to me. I can help; I've got a little put aside."

"Oh, don't you worry about us, Grandma. We're fine."

"Yes, I'm sure you are right now. But if times get hard, I don't want to think you're going hungry or you can't pay your bills."

"Grandma, we're fine," she reassured me.

No, they don't understand. And I hope to God they never have to.

We've moved from the table to the living room. This time I'm in the rocker, Annie nestled in my arms. She was fussing, hungry again. My goodness, this plump baby is greedy. Of course, if she kept her food down, she wouldn't need to take in so much. She has colic, but it's apparent by all her dimples, she's thriving.

"Grandma, would you mind if I left her with you while I pick up a few groceries?"

I draw in a quick breath. "Mind? Are you kidding me?"

"So you'll keep her?"

"Certainly." I pause. "But, are you sure you trust her with me? I'm not very steady on my feet anymore."

"Of course I do—you'll be fine. There are only a few things I need. I won't be long."

Glancing at the side table, I stammer, "O-okay. Her soother's right here on the table, if she wakes and is fussy. I guess there's no reason we'd have to leave this chair." I hesitate again. "Are you sure?"

"I'm sure." Donna grabs her purse. She places a light kiss on my cheek and heads for the door. "Thank you," she calls over her shoulder.

I hear the apartment door open. Suddenly, a delicate golden glow bathes the room. I gaze at Annie, her tiny head cradled in my palm. "Do you see her, Charles? Do you see our Annie?"

Donna spins around. "Sorry, Grandma. Did you say something?"

I shake my head; I thought she had left.

"I didn't hear you. What did you say?" she says, walking back to me.

I feel a blush creep up my neck. "Oh, don't mind me. I was just talking to myself."

She kneels at my feet. "But I thought I heard you say Charles."

I lower my eyes, embarrassed.

"Grandma?"

"Okay, if you really must know, I *was* talking to Charles. I wish he were here. I wish he could see this baby."

"You talk to him?"

"Sometimes I do." I don't look at her, I keep my eyes on Annie. "I suppose you think that's strange?"

She places her hand on my knee. "No, not at all. I think it's beautiful. He must have been a very special man."

My eyes grow teary. "He was." I caress Annie's forehead with a fingertip. She raises her eyebrows, tiny wrinkles furrow her brow. I finger her silken hair, brushed into a kewpie-curl on the crown of her head.

I gaze into Donna's eyes, and my voice breaks as I murmur, "Charles would have loved this child; he always wanted a little red-headed girl."

The End

Author's Notes

Thank you for reading *My Mary,* a work of fiction loosely based on the life of Mary, a Barnardo Home Child.

The immigration of 100,000 British Barnado Home Children to Canada is a fascinating, albeit sad and shameful part of history. An estimated one in every ten Canadians is a descendant of a Home Child. My husband, daughters, and grandchildren are among them.

Although Dr. Barnardo's philanthropic intentions were honourable, many of these young immigrants were little more than indentured servants. I am hopeful *My Mary* will instill in readers knowledge and empathy for these children.

Several years after Mary's passing, some of her descendants became fascinated with her mysterious past. One granddaughter began the research by acquiring Mary's Barnardo records, which included her birth details, entry photo, immigration specifics, and placement records, along with social workers' comments. She wrote Mary's foster family in England, eventually receiving a reply from Dorothy's daughter, who remembered her family receiving letters and packages from Mary. She expressed the love they had for her, and the heartbreak they felt when she was parted from them.

And so, two years ago, I began to write *My Mary*. From Tommy (91 years old) and Mary's six grandchildren, I gathered their memories and spun them into this story.

Now, on to what is fiction, and what is fact:

Fiction: Names of characters and places have been changed.

Mary did not leave Ruby to die at the back door.

Sam did not accompany her father to visit Mary in the hospital.

Mary did not write a journal, nor keep a diary; therefore, I imagined how I would have felt had I been given Mary's lot in life. Using the social workers' comments in the Barnardo reports, I envisioned the possibilities of Mary's early life. She was described as "a well-groomed, nice-looking young girl, good hard worker, thorough," and, other times as being "saucy, careless, and not truthful." Needless to say, my imagination found plenty to work with.

Fact: Mary's birth circumstances. Foster family (daisy chains, gifts of clothing/toys). Immigration. Placements. Charles' family history line. The family farm. Small four-room home. Butternut tree. A suicide attempt, by hanging, was suspected. Twice institutionalized. Charles' bright blue eyes, his loving nature, milking routine, and love of whittling. The collie dog's tricks. Ear-Soup Game. Mary's insistence on hand washing. Talking to herself. Little white lies. Cheating while playing games with grandchildren. Homemade ice cream. The brand-new-never-been-worn clothing at the Salvation Army Thrift Store.

Charles death. He passed while Mary was in hospital. She did not attend the funeral.

Ernest championed Mary's return to health by having her write the note, and attaching it to the wall.

Mary did say, "Charles would have loved this child; he always wanted a little red-headed girl."

As a young woman, I was blessed to have known Mary, if only for a few brief years. In the story, I am 'Donna,' and the Mary I knew, and loved, was a kind-hearted, generous grandmother.

If you enjoyed *My Mary*, please consider leaving a review on Amazon and Goodreads.

–Dawn Beecroft Teetzel

Mary Mae Houghton, September 1913, Barnardo Archives

About the Author

Dawn Beecroft Teetzel is a Canadian writer and poet, retired farmer and shepherd, a spinner of tales and wool. Using her descriptive writing, she reflects on her idyllic childhood, the love she has for family, and all things past. Her short stories and poetry have been printed in several magazines and anthologies.

Dawn Beecroft Teetzel resides in a small town in Southwestern Ontario with her life-mate and love, Ted.

Note from Dawn Beecroft Teetzel

Word-of-mouth is crucial for any author to succeed. If you enjoyed *My Mary*, please leave a review online—anywhere you are able. Even if it's just a sentence or two. It would make all the difference and would be very much appreciated.

Thanks!
Dawn Beecroft Teetzel

Milton Keynes UK
Ingram Content Group UK Ltd.
UKHW041820140224
437823UK00001B/43

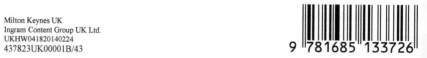

9 781685 133726